# A SONG WITH
# NO WORDS

### A NOVEL BY
### ROB RITCHIE

Ritchie, Rob, 1964-
A Song With No Words / by Rob Ritchie
ISBN 978-1-55483-462-4

Editor: George Down
Cover Photo: Tanya Grace
Design and Typography: Ardith Publishing

Published in 2019
Colpoy Editions
Box 1363 Wiarton ON
Canada N0H 2T0

Printed and bound in Canada

Other books by Rob Ritchie

*Orphans of Winter* (Seraphim Editions 2004)
*In a Company of Fiddlers* (Seraphim Editions 2011)

*For Joe*

# *Mill Run*

## *'Go West' Winter Tour*

Feb 3 - *The Station Arts Center*, St. Paul MN
Feb 5 - *The Wharf,* Duluth MN
Feb 6 - *Olaffson Theater*, Grand Rapids MN
Feb 7 - *Rainy River Community Centre*, Rainy River ON
Feb 8 - *Coleman Hall*, Winnipeg MB
Feb 9 - *Prairie Folk Concerts*, Brandon MB
Feb 11 - *Swift Current Arts Council Presents*, Swift Current SK
Feb 12 - *The Fairground Lounge*, Medicine Hat AB
Feb 14 - *Foothills Arts Society*, Calgary AB
Feb 15 - *Ramblers Concert Hall*, Calgary AB
Feb 17 - *Northern Lights Concerts*, Edmonton AB
Feb 19 - *The Roxy*, Prince George BC
Feb 20 - *Cariboo Centre for the Arts*, Quesnel BC
Feb 21 - *Williams Lake Folk Club*, Williams Lake BC
Feb 24 - *Mountainfolk*, Squamish BC
Feb 26 - *Island Roots Concert Series*, Nanaimo BC,
Feb 27 - *Cabin Fever Concerts*, Salt Spring Island BC
Feb 28 - *The Victoria Folk Club*, Victoria BC
Mar 2 - *The Reginald Theatre*, Vancouver BC

www.millrun.org/shows

~

The highway tumbled out to the south beyond the car's hood, glistening in the late-day sunlight. On the far side of the valley, it narrowed then disappeared over the upcoming brow before re-emerging on the far hillside, dark and grey and shadowed. This was the first of the series of valleys, still a few kilometres north of the spot he had selected.

Part of him wanted to pull to the shoulder. Another part, to continue on into the city as he had feigned he would. Still another – the now panicking part – just wanted to end it right there. Just wanted to let the car drift into the steady ribbon of oncoming traffic. Let the hell that had invaded his life crash up against some other unsuspecting soul. End someone else's chance for amends and conclusion and closure, and all those other words that secretly rely on the illusion of unlimited time. Like an endless roadway through valleys and meadows and forests.

But that was not an option.

It would happen as he had planned. He would wait for the

next valley, just up the far slope where the road took its sharp left and where, in the absence of direct sunlight, his running lights would hit the bright yellow sign warning drivers of the severity of the curve.

He dried his palms on the thighs of his pant legs, one then the other. Refastened his fingers to the wheel and blew towards the windshield as he fixed his gaze on the crest of the hill. One more down and up and he would be there. Once there he would, in spite of his resolve, begin to scream. With a crescendo of horror, he would empty his lungs. He would leave no ounce of hell behind. Then he would slam his foot down on the accelerator, ignoring the bend ahead.

~

## THE FIRST VERSE

*Of course traditional folk music should never take too much pain to isolate her organic components verse from verse, stanza from stanza ...*

**Chetwynd C. Lovett**
*The Orthodoxy of Folk Song*

# ONE

*As part of the ongoing "**In My Own Words**" series, **Roots Cellar Magazine** invited members of the former Canadian folk band **Mill Run** to reflect on the successes and failures of their band. In this instalment guitar player and tour manager **Myles Thomas** focuses his thoughts on the reasons for the group's retirement from active touring.*

When I was first asked to write for this series, I was intrigued. There was something appealing about being able to give a true account in my own words. No wasted type on the over-and-over-again parade of questions that used to bog down so many an article.

*So tell me, Myles, when was Mill Run first formed?*
*How did you come up with the name of your band?*
*How would you classify Mill Run's music?*

That said, please know that I have accepted the request to

write this piece fully understanding that what is hoped, is not so much a celebration of a band's legacy, but more, an account of its fall. A band-member's-eye view of what went wrong. My insider's take on that lingering question which may well be the last damn thing of interest about this band before our inevitable fade-out ... the answer to the question, *what the hell happened?*

Well, to this I want to say – be careful what you wish for. Because while I take no pleasure in what might come across as speaking ill of a man's misfortune, I will sugar-coat nothing. There's no point. Not when Mill Run has absolutely nothing left to salvage, promote or preserve. Not when the only other options are either some piece of fluff (born out of those years of experience with benign interviews) or else ... well, just being forgotten.

So let me begin with a brief history of the band.

"Millrun" was founded in 1985 by Dan LaForge and Christopher Lucan. The two had met the year before supply-teaching for the Toronto School Board and had quickly struck up a friendship based on their second careers as weekend musicians working in and around the city. This, despite the fact their styles were not the least bit similar. Chris had been a regular on the local trad music scene for quite a few years, leading song circles and open mics at any number of the pubs up and down Bloor and Danforth. Dan, on the other hand, had plied his trade with a succession of rock and metal bands, the most successful being his stint as lead singer for the Led Zeppelin tribute act *Kashmir* that had been fairly popular in Toronto, and out along the bar circuits of Eastern and Northern Ontario. And yet, so the story goes, there had been one fateful day they were both filling in for music classes at the same high school when they began jamming a few songs and everything just clicked. Instant alchemy.

For Dan, it was nothing short of an epiphany. He was completely blown away by everything Chris trotted out ... Stan Rogers, James Keelaghan, Dougie MacLean. He had never come across music like that before; songs with strong narrative lyrics that still had all the muscle he was used to. Within six months he had abandoned his stacks of pulsating Marshall Amps (not to mention the impressively stacked patrons who pulsated in front of them) and had transformed himself into a zealous convert of all things acoustic. For his part, Chris just loved Dan's energy. The way he could attack a folksong like *Northwest Passage* or *Frobisher Bay* with a rock-star mentality. And it was that delivery that soon started turning heads at the open mics and song-circles that Chris dragged Dan out to every weekend. Two or three notes, Chris used to tell me ... that's all Dan needed, and he had the room.

By the fall of '85, they were gigging together exclusively, doing all of Chris's regular haunts, churning out these energetic covers of Gordon Lightfoot and Ian Tyson, not to mention older traditions ... souped-up versions of fiddle tunes that Chris had been raised on back in the Ottawa Valley. Jigs and reels. French Canadian paddle songs. But as polished as they had become entertaining a pub, or winning over the crowd at some corporate event, it wasn't until Chris tried his hand at writing his own songs that the seeds of "Millrun" – so named, for those who don't know, after the restaurant where they played their very first gig – were truly and firmly planted.

◆ ◆ ◆

I became Millrun's bass player – along with a fair bit of secondary guitar and some mandolin – in the summer of 1991. That said, I should mention my association with Chris and Dan began a couple of years earlier as the studio engineer at Campbellford Sound where they recorded their second CD, *Back to the Mill*. Chris had particularly liked a number of my rough mixes for that album, and more importantly had heard me laying down some guitar and vocal tracks on a few other projects that were being done at the studio around the same time. So when the time came for their third CD, the call went out for my input on some harmonies and some ideas for second guitar parts to thicken up the sound a bit.

I came on board officially following the release of that album, *All Good Things Come In Threes*, and immediately was charged, as it was put to me that very first band meeting, with the task of applying the same measure of professionalism that Chris had witnessed from me at the recording studio, to the operations of the band as a whole.

It was the chance I had been looking for and I was licking my chops. Because what was needed from me was the very same combination of skills I had been honing in the music industry for the better part of two decades. I had started out as an apprentice at Mountain West Sound in Hamilton right out of college and very quickly learned my way around a console desk. I had also demonstrated sufficient musical chops to fill in on guitar and bass, anytime a particular session was light on players (or, as was more often the case, on budget). That demonstrated versatility, in turn, garnered me a steady flow of freelance work. Soon I was contracted out on tours – sometimes doing concert sound, other times on stage myself ... every genre imaginable: punk bands, country and western bands, Christian rock bands, reggae bands ... you name it. I even had a stint promoting a couple of local acts on the side – actually managed to get a small record deal for one of them. And all of that in and around freelance run-outs to the studio back up in Campbellford. All fascinating and interesting work involving – for the most part – fascinating and interesting people.

But here's the thing. None of it – not one of those groups or recording projects or tours –*ever* came anywhere close to getting me fired up like the opportunity to join Millrun did. Not even remotely. With Dan's voice, and Chris's creativity, I finally had something with sky's-the-limit potential. Something I could grab onto and take somewhere. What I *didn't* immediately appreciate was how many hats I would end up wearing to accomplish just that.

From the outset Chris had admitted that organizational skills were neither his nor Dan's forte. And yes, I guess I had seen some evidence of that working with them on the recording ... misplaced chord charts ... arriving late for sessions because *someone* had to pull over and jot down a song idea he had on the way to the studio. Little things like that. But once I arrived full-time? Well let's just say Chris's assessment demonstrated a true gift for understatement. Incomplete contracts, unfiled tax statements, unpaid bills, unreturned calls on the answering machine for gig inquiries. Suffice it to say, in very short order, in addition to learning and advising on guitar, and harmony arrangements, I would also soon oversee all of the technical, promotional and administrative duties for the band, and in so doing, see if Mill Run – in one of my first official tasks, I changed the name to a two-word moniker for the purposes of graphic aesthetics – could climb its way *to that next level*, as Chris had put it to me.

It was a long road, but this, I'm still quite proud to say, I did.

A week after its completion, I made sure every radio programmer of every radio format in or even remotely close to our sound had a copy of *All Good Thing Come In Threes*. Same with print media contacts and reviewers. Next came a complete overhaul of the band press kit, updated with proper 8 x 10 glossies, ear-candy quotes about Dan's voice, and Chris's writing, a steady stream of favourable press clippings that had begun filtering back to my newly-constructed home office almost as soon as the CD dropped.

Then it was on to booking gigs where I was determined to cast our aim further afield than the well-respected but by now predictable Ontario venues where Mill Run had been showing up like clockwork for the last few years ... the Beaches Folk Club and Ottomans in Toronto; the Rainbow Room down in London ... Calloway's in Kingston. We began showcasing our repertoire for Arts Councils and Folk Conferences all across Canada, then began tackling their counterparts in the US, gladhanding every music festival artistic director and booking agent along the way. In less than a year I had secured the band's first American tour, three weeks in New York, Pennsylvania and New England, followed closely by stints through Michigan, Wisconsin and Illinois. These would be the beachheads I would build on, year after year, until soon we were up to over 100 shows annually, each performance garnering more reaction and audience buzz than the last. Our schedule started catching the eye of the industry proper – those intrigued by our dedication to such a busy calendar. Our whereabouts were now being listed in the trade papers; as well as the mainstream press of any city we visited. We were getting regular air play on the CBC in Canada ... NPR south of the border.

And then, in the spring of 1996, after five years at the helm, and another CD – *Snowbound Headlights* – the bar was raised again. First, we were invited to sign on with Northern Harvest Records out of Toronto. Then shortly after that the band hit the UK for the first time and discovered a folk scene that was tailor-made for what we were selling: club after club after club with this vibrant appetite for older musical styles, but also a yearning for something rejuvenating. With our combination of traditional instrumentation and original songs we couldn't miss. Add to that the fact there was something of a folk revival happening over there at the time. Teenagers and twenty-somethings *discovering* the genre for the first time, heading for the concert halls and clubs at an unprecedented rate. Soon we were the choice for the entire gamut of the scene. I mean everybody from the most diehard English floor singer, still honking out 200-year-old ballads, to the new wave of folkies, dusting off their parents' Lindisfarne and Fairport Convention LPs. Then add to *that,* the appeal from the band's slightly exotic rough-around-the-edges look ... Dan's long flowing hair, Chris's lumberjack beard ... and, well, by our third tour we were selling out every booking I could find, emptying boxes of merchandise as fast as we could get them shipped over.

Upon returning home, we were scheduled to record our fifth album, *Distant Shores*; this time with a sizeable advance from the record company, a move from the cramped confines of good old Campbellford Sound to downtown Toronto and Metro Soundworks, complete with its 48-track digital studio, and the addition of a co-producer to help me get the most out of Chris and Dan's takes.

Life should have been good.

In all honesty, I think the seeds of our demise could have

taken root as far back as those three torturous weeks locked away in that studio. It was so much bigger than either Chris or Dan had ever seen before. And with the endless photos of top-shelf acts adorning the walls, not to mention the seen-it-all looks from the assistant engineers and staff shuffling about, there was definitely an intimidation factor at work. It was also the first recording project either of them had ever undertaken with any real pressure of a time line. Metro rented out at about $275 per hour – another $100 when using the outboard gear – so you could make the case that this is where the first signs of stress actually began for Chris.

My co-producer was a man named Bill Worth, well-known in the Toronto scene and certainly a nice set of extra ears for me to bounce ideas off of. Bill's theory was that since Mill Run had made its name as this energetic touring band, we should try to get the "live" experience into the flavour of the recording as well. Guard against a careful, contrived sound, he said. That meant recording all the instrumentation together off the floor and then, only if really needed – Bill would soon learn just how often this was – we'd go back and punch in corrections and over-dubs on any individual parts that required improvement. Now that may sound like an economical approach, but it also meant a lot of pre-production on my part, experimenting with different microphones and sound levels, not to mention the different configurations of band members spaced out and around the studio floor, all in the interest of getting the best natural sound. So into this complicated sea of cables and cords, compressors and acoustic baffling comes Chris the folkie, completely unfamiliar with any experience beyond the tiny analogue set-up we had shared back in Campbellford, where finances had always been low enough that a much more laid-back trial-and-error process had been the order of the day.

Not that Chris ever came out and actually admitted any of this was getting to him. Such was not the Christopher Lucan Way. No, our good bandmate much preferred to greet an obstacle with a rotation of excuses dressed up and disguised by his considerable talents of impressively philosophical and flowery speech. And I say *rotation*, because one carefully crafted bit of rationalization never seemed to suffice. Monday's problems would inevitably be greeted on Tuesday morning with a freshly-squeezed brand-new excuse. And if *that* new excuse happened to contradict the previous day's ... well strangely that somehow didn't seem to matter. And this was not just my take on Chris. Dan had long since made me aware of the phenomenon, even going so far as to name it the *Lucan Shuffle* (though never to Chris's face – such is not the Mill Run way).

A case in point was sometime around our fourth morning of recording ... so this is after three days of aborted takes on just about all of the fiddle parts; parts, I should add that Chris had written himself *and* had been playing flawlessly not a week before. I can still see Bill slapping the STOP button on the recorder over and over again, whipping off the headphones, and squeezing his eyes closed trying to muster up as much diplomacy as humanly possible before reaching for the talk-back mic. *OK, not bad ... just a bit sharp on that first phrase.* And when he could no longer manage to summon the effort for even that much encouragement, he would call for a break, grab his coat and a smoke and head for the door. (*Distant Shores* had a significant budget for cigarettes.)

So on day four, during one of those breaks, I head into the studio lounge and find Chris hunched over the coffee maker, stirring his usual four or five teaspoons of sugar into his mug. He won't even look up at me. Just mumbles something about how it's just not happening for him and he isn't feeling it today.

Kind of like yesterday and the day before, I try to point out but I don't get an answer right away because clearly, Chris the Shuffler is busy choreographing a worthy reply. So I ask him if he worked on his parts overnight and he claims he did. But I'm not convinced, so I press him, asking if he went over the specific riffs we're now trying to get down.

"It's not the songs, Myles," he says, and proceeds to tell me that I don't understand how he approaches his craft. Tells me how his fingers need regular doses of familiar muscle memory from time to time before he can move on to current material. (May I have this dance?) How they have been acting up of late so he decided to go back and pull out some old fiddle music he used to play to get recalibrated.

"So let me get this straight," I say. "You're telling me that instead of going over the songs we were scheduled to record here this morning in a studio that is costing us $1500 a day ... you spent the night practising a bunch of fiddle tunes you already know how to play?"

He tells me I just need to trust him. Tells me he figured out a long time ago that the only way he can *assimilate* himself into a *comfortable space* with a new song *is* to first play something where that level of comfort already exists. So that way, the same *sense of relaxation* can be *translated* into playing the newer, less-familiar material. And when I point out that the so-called less-familiar material he's talking about is actually music he has written *himself*, he says it doesn't matter. Explains that it's this trick he needs to do to get in tune with his playing ... no matter what he's playing. "To get the music over to the left side of my brain," he tells me.

"A trick?" I ask him.

"That's right," he says.

"On your own brain."

And he snaps. "Look, I'm just telling you what works for me, OK?" And he grabs his fiddle and headphones and makes a beeline down the hall for the studio.

And I so desperately want to call after him. "But if you're trying to trick *your own* brain, aren't you already in on it?"

But I don't ... (Such is not the Mill Run way.)


Bill phoned me that night to tell me that he and Northern Harvest had come up with a solution. He gave me the number of a session player named Ian Station: keyboards and whistles. Assured me Ian was very easy to work with, a quick study and low maintenance, and that if we were willing to switch out some of the fiddle parts, he could help us get through a lot of the bed tracks far more economically, and salvage the two weeks they had budgeted for recording the CD.

Now with the benefit of hindsight, I know Ian was a great addition. But at the time ... well I had to pull off some fairly delicate manoeuvres to get Chris to buy into the idea. I had to be pretty careful not to phrase Bill's proposal in any way that might be construed as replacing or marginalizing Chris's contributions. So I made sure to frame the discussion as a matter of bringing in some extra instrumentation merely to add a bit of sheen to the existing musical arrangements. And I have to say, the approach worked pretty well. I mean in those last years as a four-piece, far from being a threat, Chris never treated Ian like anything less than a long-lost friend. A little brother even. I mean, of the four of us, you could make a case that, by the end, Chris and Ian were the closest-knit of anyone in the band.

As for Chris and me?

Well to be fair, my role must have been difficult for him. On the one hand, Chris the songwriter truly wanted me getting his music out there and heard by as many people as possible. But on the other hand, Chris the musician would have been far happier back in The Painted Shamrock on the Danforth for a Sunday afternoon sing-around. Charming and intimate, no doubt. But not the type of lucrative gig that he had mandated me to pursue when he took me on. And I don't know for certain, but maybe because I was that person who had been successful landing all those gigs, *and* the recording deals, *and* the radio play *and* the promotional appearances I was actually pulling him apart ... Chris the songwriter versus Chris the musician. Maybe that's where the resentment came from.

But when I say resentment, I should be clear that it was never anything direct (such is not ... well, you get the picture). It was just hints of dissatisfaction now and again; sometimes in the form of prolonged periods of deliberate silence, sometimes episodes of being difficult just for difficulty's sake. In the first months, even years, following the release of *Distant Shores*, these were still only occasional occurrences.

It really wasn't until we headed out west on that final tour that things really took a downward turn.

Case in point. A radio interview the two of us did in Winnipeg on that last trip. CKTZ, the afternoon drive-time show on the number one station in the city. Not an easy spot for a folk band to get in on.

It started off like any other interview, the typical drive-time voice lobbing the typical "I've actually never heard of you but just spent the last four minutes scanning your press kit" sort of questions that you'd expect from commercial radio. How did we all meet? What's the significance of the band's name? But then he sees that our tour schedule includes a lot of US dates, even though the caption on the website's title page describes us as *Intensely Canadian Roots Music*. So he's curious about what kind of response we receive from audiences south of the border. And I answer that we really don't see that much difference. That the venues we play in the USA seem to attract people who, at least for the most part are sufficiently open-minded to enjoy music from abroad. So he asks if he should be picturing folk festival crowds full of flower power and ponchos and headbands? And I play along with it and reply that is certainly one component of the audience, at least at some of our shows, when Chris just cuts me right off. "No," he says. "It would actually be completely inaccurate to characterize our shows that way." Word for word, that's what he says, and then goes on a bit of a rant that if someone came to our show expecting some sort of Woodstock experience they'd be extremely disappointed. And furthermore ... whatever success Mill Run has gained in the States hinges on nothing more than how well the band has tapped into the common experiences of everyday folk regardless of which side of that border they call home.

All of which, I am quite certain, was a far deeper and more earnest response than CKTZ drive-time programming generally looked for. So dutifully I try to weigh in, explaining that Mill Run shows offered a bit of something for just about everyone, from our takes on old voyageur paddling tunes, to a song about running contraband whisky across the Great Lakes, to a ballad about life on the prairies during the Depression. And here comes Chris again, jumping in to belabour his last point a bit longer, snapping that whether somebody in the audience puts on a suit and heads into an office building every morning, or whether she's done up in tie-dye, as apparently I contended, doesn't really matter, does it?

So the host tries changing it up and picks out *The Monument,* off the *Just a Stage We're Going Through* CD, as the sample play and asks us to set up the song. I jump in as fast as I can, before Chris has any chance to come across any more belligerently than he already has. I explain that it's one of our most successful songs to date; a love song from a wounded soldier's point of view. How it was inspired by a visit Chris made to some of the World War One battle sites in northern France some twenty years earlier. How it was a place he had found simultaneously reverent and disturbing, with all the remnants of trenches and charred earth fanning out around this huge beautiful sculpture ... how he had said it was like the ghosts of all these poor soldiers were still right there waiting for someone to discover their stories. And let me be clear, I wasn't trying to steal any thunder. I made sure to praise the virtues of my bandmate's songwriting, pointing out how a song like *The Monument* merely typified what Chris had said earlier about audience appeal. That it was a poignant portrayal of a soldier's vulnerability that put the audience right there in the trenches, feeling the pain of a dying man singing to a fiancée he knows he will never see again. A song, I conclude, that, as our other band member Dan LaForge liked to say, puts the flaws in the call for war, rather than in the heroes who had to answer that call.

And I can tell I have saved it. Just in the way the host is back with us, nodding, asking Chris again whether that specifically non-glorifying approach really hits the ears of Canadians and Americans the same way.

I swear, it's like we've wakened him from a nap. He looks up and around the room, mumbling and grumbling like he's not really sure how he got there. "What? ... um, I'm not sure," he says.

Now the guy was a pro, but I can tell, by now he's getting

pretty pissed off. *So anything else to add before we give a listen? Maybe something specific about the trip that inspired the song in the first place?* And in what can only be described as riveting radio, Chris leans into the microphone and shakes his head, no.

I don't remember too much after that. I'm pretty sure I was still trying to jump in with something that might salvage the efforts it took to secure the time slot, but it was all to no avail. The only lasting image I really have is the DJ shaking his head with this slight amateur-hour sneer, as he read out the details of our show that night at Coleman Hall. It was a look very much like the one that had flashed across Bill Worth's face on so many occasions. Usually just before he called for a smoke break.

The timing always struck me as strange. Prior to that day, the tour had actually started out pretty smoothly. All three shows were well-attended in Minnesota, then we were back into Northern Ontario for a fill-in gig in the small town of Rainy River. Not a show you'd plan a tour around by any means, but still a very advantageous eleventh-hour booking that fell into our lap just a couple of weeks before we hit the road; a fundraiser for something or other in the town arena. And while cinder-block auditoriums had long ceased to be my preference for acoustics, a mid-week gig for four and half grand directly en route to our next show just made too much business sense to pass up.

It was the last time I remember seeing Chris *on*. The last time, you could say, that Chris the songwriter and Chris the musician ever played together on stage, bouncing around from start to finish. I remember him holding court for what seemed like a good two-thirds of the audience that had lingered afterwards to shake his hand, get a hug or an autograph ... or both. And then, just one night later in Coleman Hall – a venue that I had been jumping through hoops to get a booking in for years, I might add – out of nowhere, all bets were off.

It started with the set list. I had marked down what I thought was our strongest material for the night, leading with *The Schooner From Shelburne*. It was fast-paced, rollicking ... always won over new audiences. From there we would segue right into a couple of Chris's favourites from the early albums: *Dance Away Mary* and *Hitch Me to Your Plough*, then follow that with one of our most popular ballads, *Winter Lullabye*. But an hour before show time, while the rest of us are getting ready in the dressing room, Chris walks in, notebook in hand, and announces that it's time to go in a totally different direction and *reawaken the set list* with some old jigs and reels that Mill Run hadn't played since back in the pub days.

"Just to guard against going stale," he says, and starts scratching out the song titles.

I ask him as politely as possible exactly what the living hell he's talking about.

"Instincts, Myles," he says. "It's what I rely on ... instincts."

"And your instincts are telling you we've grown stale?"

"If we're not proactive, we very well could."

So I start in, demanding to know what led him to this strange and unexpected epiphany. Whether it was the standing ovations at the end of our last four shows. The double encores? The three boxes of CDs we sold back in Rainy River?

He tells me I just have to trust him. But sadly, after his per-

formance at the radio station, and with such a high profile gig
ahead of us, I am not in the trusting mood. So I draw my line
in the sand. And I say *my* line because even though Dan and
Ian were standing right there listening to the same preposterous
song and dance I was, true to form they remained silent (the
only bit of solidarity coming in the occasional nod from Dan).
So, once again, I, Myles Thomas – band manager, booking
agent, bookkeeper, negotiator of whims, massager of egos,
catcher's mitt for all topics too uncomfortable for other band
members – was left to explain to Chris that after wooing a concert venue like Coleman Hall for the better part of a decade,
sending CD after CD, press kit after press kit, enticing them
with the material that we had nurtured for the better part of fifteen years ... and after having them finally accept us as worthy
of an appearance, then promoting us rigorously as a band full
of ingenious and masterful songwriting, it would be nothing
short of complete disaster to walk out on stage and launch into
a bunch of fiddle tunes that anyone could hear at any fall fair
from here to fucking Nova Scotia.

"No, we need to do this," he says by way of a reply and pulls
out a pen and drops the set list onto his lap, all the while trying
to look very deep in thought. But I had to call him out.

"We need to do this, or *you* need to do this?" I say in a loud-
enough voice that instantly reminds Ian he has something to
check back out on stage. Meanwhile Dan has this sudden pre-
occupation with his shoelaces.

Chris just shakes his head, and stares at the page in front of
him. So I start pacing the floor, saying that – at best – we can
maybe ... *maybe* change a few things up if he's not comfortable
with his playing on a couple of the songs on the list."

"Goddamn it, Myles, it's not about that!" And he gets up
and stumbles around the room. Almost falls, actually. "Christ!

Never mind. Do whatever the hell *you* want," he says and fires the pen across the floor, pushing Dan aside to get to the door, leaving the two of us standing there staring at each other wondering what in Christ's name just happened.

We ended up opening with *Barn Dance Romance* instead, thinking that a song from the first album with so many miles of performance under its belt would be a suitable compromise if the man's confidence was suffering a bit. But the thing is, it didn't matter. His playing was all over the map. He began his first fiddle intro in the wrong key, then stopped, and restarted only to slip up on the turnaround into the first verse, making for an unintended modulation before Dan had even sung a note. The next song was no better. In the introduction Chris spent an inordinate amount of time, for some reason, talking about learning to play the fiddle from his grandfather (even though the song was about a shipbuilder). Sadly, since it had been featured on the radio that afternoon, and since it had been the song that had finally nailed down the booking with Coleman Hall's artistic director in the first place, I had no choice but to leave *The Monument* in the set, even though I knew, of all the material, it could be the most problematic. My fears proved well-founded. Chris jumped his solo entry by a bar, playing right over the end of Dan's vocal line, then realizing his mistake, stopped abruptly, leaving empty air where he should have started playing in the first place. By then the song was lost; this epic ballad that should have left the hall gasping, reduced to nothing more than an exercise to get to the finish, though not before one more mother of all miscues. The arrangement is supposed to leave Dan singing the last line of the chorus all on his own, with the guitar and fiddle and piano fading away ...

> *... 'til the cold and the pain are gone*
> *'til there's warmth once again in the dawn,*
> *'til you hold what's left of my soul in the glow of the prairie sun*

It's this fantastic bit of songwriting – *his own* fantastic bit of songwriting – but it was foiled by the fiddle bow droning on the low E string as Chris – for some reason – began tuning for the next number. The visual was bad enough. But sonically? Suffice it to say ... *The Monument* is in E flat.

The next night in Brandon, I attempted to remedy the situation by shrinking the playlist a bit more, cutting out a number of more complex pieces in favour of older, less challenging material. But if anything, his playing was worse, as it was in Swift Current two days later, and Medicine Hat the day after that. It was as if each show was not only failing in its own right, but also serving to reset the bar lower and lower, playing out of time, out of tune, forgetting his parts ... *especially* forgetting his parts.

By the time we hit Calgary for a couple of sold-out shows, he had taken to laying out chord charts on the floor. Honestly. There were strips of cardboard duct-taped flat to the stage in a wide semi-circle around his mic stand for quick reference to those songs giving him the most trouble. A few nights later in Edmonton, those charts had grown to include virtually the whole evening's repertoire. But despite the fact he was now literally spending the whole show with his head down, and his eyes glued to these big block letters, his contribution was still nothing more than a steady succession of slurred phrases, weak backing vocals and stepped-on lyrics. By Quesnel, BC – a smaller, comfortable community-hall gig that should have been just what the doctor ordered – things had gotten so bad he actually pulled out a folding chair from back stage and sat down for the whole second set, deferring all song introductions and stage banter to Dan and myself. And that wasn't all. Beginning with the shows back in Alberta, Chris had steadily been reducing his time spent meeting and chatting with fans at the end of the night. He started ignoring specific requests from theatre staff to come out and have promotional pictures taken, or posters and CDs signed – the very enterprises the man had always enjoyed most about touring. By the time we reached the coast he was ducking out of venues and heading for his motel room as soon as the last song was done.

Needless to say I didn't sleep well that tour. A lot of time was spent lying in the dark, wondering if this was all just some new and amplified version of the Lucan Shuffle, or if I was actually witnessing a musician's anxieties get the best of him. And if it was the latter, the question was why. What had changed? Was I the reason? Was this the boiling point of a long simmering friction over the way I had been running the band's business? Had it been gnawing at him over the years, festering inside and pissing him off more and more until it was bound to explode into something like the fiasco that was our final tour?

I tried confiding in Ian at one point. I took him aside after the Williams Lake show and asked him how Chris had seemed lately … in their motel room, during meals … out on the road. (For the sake of those holding onto some romantic image of Mill Run, all stuffed into a VW van or some modified RV, rolling down the highway from gig to gig, all for one and one for all … I should mention that we never actually travelled together. Not all together anyway. When I joined, Dan and I would drive to gigs in his car and Chris would head out separately ... at first by himself, then with Ian once he came on board.)

My piano player wasn't all that enlightening. He would only admit that Chris had been sleeping a lot, then wanting to put in long hours behind the wheel.

And so the deterioration of Christopher Lucan continued ... Squamish, Nanaimo, Salt Spring Island, Victoria ... right up to the very last note of our very last frighteningly forgettable show at the Reginald Theatre in Vancouver. It was a gig that I had at one time looked forward to with as much hope and excitement as Coleman Hall, but by then – with my expectations so thoroughly beaten down – it was something I just wanted to get over with. As soon as the half-hearted smattering of applause faded away, I marched back into the dressing room to find Chris already hauling off his stage shirt in favour of flannel pyjamas. I asked him to wait a moment so I could address the fact that the tour had been an unmitigated disaster, and that I thought a band meeting was needed as soon as possible.

True to form, Chris's response could not have been predicted.

"Myles is right, we need to all sit down," he pipes up. "The sooner, the better." Then with more energy than any of us had seen out of him in two weeks, he pulls a road map out of his duffle bag and advises us to all get a good day's drive in tomorrow, then rendezvous in a town he has already circled, at a motel that he has already booked us into, for our first night's stop on the way home.

It's funny, but I actually had to go back and consult a map to remember the name of that town. Even then, I confess I'm not

one hundred percent certain. That's the consequence of performing so many shows year after year. The image of one
town tends to blend into another. So I am only reasonably sure
it was Keremeos, British Columbia and that the motel we pulled
into was called something like Spirit Shadows Inn. That foggy
bit of geography aside, however, the rest of evening will always
be crystal clear.

Dan and I were the first to arrive and immediately we set out
to deal with our anticipation each in our own way. I went and
checked in so I could settle into the tasks of fidgeting, pacing,
absent-mindedly flipping through every available TV channel
and back again (all of a half-dozen or so), downing a gallon of
motel-room instant coffee. Dan, on the other hand ... well in
true Dan fashion, our lead singer decided it was the perfect
time to go for a stroll. To each his own. Especially since
neither approach, at the end of the day, would prove to prepare
us even remotely for the mother of all *Lucan Shuffles* that was
about to take place.

A few hours later Chris knocked on our door and marched in
with Ian in tow. He had a stack of coil-ring notebooks with
him stuffed with reams of additional loose papers which he
immediately began pulling out and spreading across the nearest
bed. At that point I still had no idea what it was all about, but
after the last three weeks, I was in no mood to do anything but
take charge, saying how the first order of business was to go
over some of the problems we've had been having onstage re-
cently.

Chris cuts me right off. "Myles ... please. We all know
what the problem has been," he says. "It's me ... me, and me
alone." Then he tells us that because he is to blame, he has two
things to put forward. And for a few brief moments I am actually hopeful, thinking maybe the man has finally awakened to

the reality of the situation and still cares enough to want to do something about it. Especially when he proceeds to apologize and tell us that he has been quite concerned with how badly his playing has been suffering, and that he's ready to begin to take steps to rectify it.

But then ... (Maestro, if you will) ... out came the first hand-out. Four stanzas of lyrics ... as of yet untitled ...

"This one came to me right before the Williams Lake show," he tells us. Says that it's just one of many new songs in the works. That for the past few weeks he has been *inundated* ... just *inundated* with musical and lyrical ideas, to a greater depth than he could ever remember before. Tells us that for the first time in a long time – *maybe ever* – he feels *connected* to a *positive and precise creative direction.* I remember his exact words. Tells us that it's as if a long-dormant portion of his brain has been reborn. That it has sprouted from beneath the constant forces of touring and performing, and having to be *so on,* so much of the time ... again, his words ... which in a perfect world was understandable I suppose, although it did overlook the fact that to be a fiscally viable band Mill Run had to tour all the time. And it was my job to make sure we were exactly that and more.

"But that's the thing," he said. "My creativity just doesn't respond to that motivation any more. Clearly the past couple of weeks proved as much, didn't it?"

And this would be the moment I lost it.

"You sure about that?" I fired back. "You sure you haven't just gone out of your way to make sure this all happened?"

"What's that supposed to mean?"

And so I told him.

"Sabotage, Chris. I'm talking about sabotage." I reminded him how he outright refused to play half our repertoire for the bulk of the tour. That he refused to work on the parts that were giving him trouble. Refused to interact with the audiences … to meet with people after the shows … sign CDs. "You don't want to tour so much? Fine. We can talk about that as a group. But to dream up some theory about how it's the tours I book that have caused you to play so badly is absolute horseshit!"

But he refused to get into it. Just shook his head and calmly told me I'm dead wrong. Told me that he's just trying to *understand* and *explain his situation* as honestly as he can, because in the end, he still *needs us all* to truly *and fully* explore the deluge of creativity that has been revealed to him. That lately he has become *distracted* as an artist. And sadly Mill Run, *in its present form,* has become the source of that distraction.

"So we need a new direction," he announced, as if everything was just one second away from sunshine and sparkles. "We need to chase these new creative impulses to their full extent; no matter where that takes us musically. And we need to do it immediately. Back in studio as soon as we get back home." (And here I should explain that by studio he did not mean back to Metro Soundworks. No, it turned out Chris had already gone ahead and booked us in for two weeks back in the cramped confines of Campbellford Sound as soon as we returned home.)

I'm not sure how long I was silent, but I know it was quite a while. Probably whatever time it took to consider the possibility that he was actually just joking … that he was just having us on a bit before we settled into a proper meeting … then, of course, the subsequent seconds required to realize this was not the case. Unfortunately, when I finally did manage a reply, the best I could do in the moment was sarcasm.

"So what is this new direction then? You see Mill Run throwing some reggae into their concerts? Some techno-dance tracks maybe? A few banks of synthesizers for Ian?"

He sighed and rolled his eyes. "My point is we need to broaden our scope," he said. "Become a bit more, to more people."

For the love of Christ, did the man even pay any attention to his own press? Did he not remember the glowing *Globe and Mail* review for *Distant Shores*? How Chris Lucan *can take a particular tale and weave those particulars into a yarn for the Human Condition as a whole?* Men and women, young and old, the rich and the poor, recent immigrants or sixth-generation Canadians, farmers and welders, bankers and lawyers ...!

But he claimed that it's exactly that kind of flattery that had been co-opting him into a safe song-writing niche for far too long – at which point I'm just marching around the room, stammering and swearing. "You can't be serious. You can't be f**king serious!"

Somewhere around then I recall Ian cutting in with, "Chris, maybe you should move on to the second thing you wanted to cover tonight."

And if I hadn't already been so flustered, I'd like to think I would have picked up on something cryptic in the suggestion ... something beyond the usual paralyzing discomfort that greeted our piano player any time a difference of opinion of any size broke out.

So Chris moved on. Told us it's important we strike while the iron is hot, because he thinks these new songs will prove to be the most rewarding material we ever do ... maybe even *the pinnacle* of Mill Run's whole body of work, which I confess spiked my bullshit meter and pinned it in the red. I grabbed the notebook from his hand, slammed it down across a night table and just started screaming, PINNACLE? PINNACLE? over and over. But Ian grabbed me by the arm and urged me to let him go on.

Only then did I take note that Chris's tone had changed some-where in the midst of our arguing. For the first time I could ever recall, there was doubt on his face. Doubt and worry. It was as if, all of a sudden, he was no longer completely buying his crap either.

"Look, guys I'm not getting any younger," he said. "And I'm really sorry for the timing of this, but it's something I just want to get done before ..." But he couldn't finish the thought. Would in fact, *never* finish that thought. "Christ, this is harder than I imagined," he mumbled and the next thing we know we're all silently listening to his footsteps trail out into the parking lot from our room. I look back at Ian and ask if he was really saying what I thought he was saying. Ian leaned over and handed me one of the loose sheets of paper Chris left behind.

"I swear, Myles, he only told me earlier today," he said.

There was so very little to it really, for such a monumental note. Barely enough to even warrant a list in the first place. Unless, that is, it was being written by someone who worried he might not be able to remember even a few details in the days to come. (But I'm getting ahead of myself.)

The note read as follows:

#1 – Discuss plans to record new body of songs

#2 – Inform band of decision to retire immediately after-wards

One week later, armed with chord charts and lyric sheets, he marched into the studio (half an hour late) and, without so much as a hello, launched into a reaffirmation of his *vision* be-hind the recording project at hand. He told us he could see precisely how he wanted the session to go; the order he wanted the songs to be on the CD; the order he wanted them to be recorded. He said he wanted a more organic recording experience to shine through, and was hoping for as quick a process as possible; that after a couple of run-throughs of the material, we could start laying down the instrumental takes – even keep the rough-guide vocal tracks if they weren't too pitchy. "I need the music to breathe without too much manipulation," he said, the comment obviously intended for my ears. It was a line drawn up front to let me know he was at the helm now and he wasn't going to – as he put it later in the day, when I thought one of his fiddle takes was getting ahead of the beat – "lose the soul of the music by scrubbing and cleaning the tracks to an unrealistic polish". (Forgive me, Chris, for trying to keep us all on the same beat of the same bar.)

As for the fruits of these hasty labours? Well, I think the CD Quick Pick review in *Toronto Vibe Magazine* was probably the most brutally accurate.

**Swan Songs** *Mill Run (Northern Harvest Records)*
*With what is now rumoured to be the final release of these cross-Canada balladeers, we can close the books and say a final farewell to this band. Those of you who, like myself, have had your fill of the tired-white-men-in-ponytails variety of folk music, may want to add a "don't let the door hit you on the way out". And for those of you out there in the world of folk music who still like their acoustic fix in this particular form, upon listening to this package of poorly written and poorly recorded songs, you may want to reconsider or, at the very least, perhaps redirect your attention towards the Valdy's and James Keelaghan's of the genre. As for this band's last kick at the can? Well, if this was all that was left in the tank ... as I*

*said ... see ya.*

So why did we go along with him?

I would love to state it was a mutual decision on behalf of the rest of us to grant an ailing musician his last creative request. But that really wasn't the case. We didn't learn definitively that Chris was suffering from the early stages of Alzheimer's until well on after that. The truth is, at that point, I was merely done with the battle. If it was a hurry he wanted, it was a hurry he would get. And having been divested of any real personal involvement in the project, I adopted a role somewhere between a disinterested studio musician and meek and well-beaten dog, intentionally making a point to offer absolutely no resistance to any of Chris's suggestions or directions for the duration of those ten days of recording hell. (The only exception being my insistence that my name be left off all liner note credits for the engineering and production of the end product.)

In Dan's case, I think it was more a matter of being in the throes of grief. I think as long as he gamely slogged his way through all those vocal tracks, he could still cling to the last remnants of what he and Chris had started so many years ago. But I'm not really certain about this. Dan and I have gotten together now and again in the last few years, but somehow we've never really discussed the end days very much. (Not the Mill Run Reunion way.)

One thing I do know. Once I learned about the health issues Chris had been going through, it was next to impossible to replay just about any memory of the last tour without wondering to what degree his illness played a role in its failure. In one sense it seems obvious that it was front and centre, but at the risk of sounding insensitive, the truth is, there were always el- ements of erratic behaviour in Chris long beforehand. If anything about the man had ever been predictable, it was his un-predictability. So often he could come off like the sort who had no trouble abandoning reality whenever it suited him. Witness his five-year sojourn into the world of holistic health. (Not that I'm saying it's a field without its place in the world – but I'm sorry, sometimes a headache right before showtime is better treated with a double-blind-tested anti-inflammatory than rubbing the stem of some root vegetable across your temples.) Or his forays into the world of conspiracy theories. The Single Wheel Folk Club in Madison, Wisconsin was run by a man named Ernie Bruin – a man acutely skilled in leading the logically-challenged down paths of intrigue like a rabbit out in front of a greyhound. We must have played that club three or four times after 9/11. And on each occasion Chris could be found hanging on the man's every word for two hours before and after the show, then regurgitating it all to us and anyone else who would listen for weeks after that. (An inside job; a government plot to instigate a reason for military action in the Middle East; a staged event that presumably sacrificed four jet plane-loads of its own population to achieve the goal. Sadly though, while they were always delivered – much like my band-mate's own theoretical footwork–- with no shortage of conviction, poor Ernie could never offer up any firmer proof than his inevitable ... *because you're not gonna tell me a bunch of religious freaks are gonna take down a country as big as mine with a set of box cutters!*)

So how much was illness and how much was just Chris-being-Chris? Who knows? All I can say is this: Knowing that, at least to some degree, there was a medical condition creeping into play, I am satisfied that – in the end – we did the right thing closing shop. Sure, we could have continued as a three-piece. The phone calls from the record company and the emails

and cards from our fan clubs had certainly begged that we try.
And certainly when the opportunity for one final Mill Run concert did come up, that opportunity did have us seriously entertaining the idea. But in hindsight I have to admit there were
too many impediments. First there was the aforementioned fa-
tigue factor. If I was too tired to fight with Chris and his
creative surges, I was too tired to refocus my energies into selling a pared-down version of our band, and certainly too tired
to recast Chris's spot in the group, no matter how much an up-
grade it might be performance-wise. But even more problematic
than that was the Catch-22 situation that this disaster of a
recording had caused. Because the truth is, the travesty that
would be our last CD – that favour which we, against all better
judgement, had granted to our outgoing bandmate – had sealed
the fate of the band far more completely than Chris's decision
to retire ever could have. And just in case you think this is too
harsh an assessment, I will remind you of another one of our
wonderful zero-out-of-five pans; this one from our former
stomping grounds in England, included here in full for your
consideration.

*Is it a sign of arrogance when a group so completely shifts
the focus of their material that audiences have no choice but to
feel alienated? Before one deems the question too vague or
arbitrary, one might perhaps first check in with the thousands
of fans of one of Canada's pre-eminent folk bands following
the release of Mill Run's* Swan Song *CD last week. And if not
arrogance, does not the utter failure of this CD put into question
the laud and esteem that reviewers like myself had heaped upon
them for previous works? Truly I would like to think not. I
would like to think that the mess that greeted my ears when I
plopped this disc into my stereo was not the result of a band*

*who had actually merely 'lucked out', as it were, with their beautiful music and lyrics for the past fifteen years and five CDs. Yet this latest work is so ghastly, so undeserving to be set alongside their previous recordings, it is enough to give me a great deal of pause. To those who like art that leaves the listener asking questions, perhaps there is a bit of something here for you. Unfortunately, I fear that question will only be 'What were these lads thinking?'*

*Chetwynd Lovett*
**The Yorkshire Folk Review**

He wasn't wrong. None of the reviews were. The songs were, if you'll pardon my bluntness, utter garbage. And to be clear, I'm not harping on this to amplify the downfall of a great songwriter, but in fact to do just the opposite. To keep silent and pretend there was the slightest merit in a CD so painfully below the standards that the Chris Lucan I used to know would have ever settled for ... well, it only serves to discredit all the truly ingenious music the man penned beforehand, doesn't it?

Take the opening track, *Night Storm*. Chris had presented it to us as *an Orwellian-folk tune that used climatic instead of anthropomorphic imagery to illuminate the inequalities inherent within capitalism and mercantile economics.* I swear to God, that's what was on the notes he brought to the motel room. All I can say is if you can glean any of that from the lyrics he came up with, you're a smarter man than I am. The same with that most curious of songs he insisted on calling *An Instrumental*, even though – obviously – it wasn't. Those are just two examples. In truth I could make just as strong a case against any of the other tracks that ended up on that last album.

What I don't have any sense of is how Chris himself felt about the negative reaction to the recording. Whether he thought it had still been worth it. Whether he cared at all. The fact of the matter is that once the final mixing and mastering had wrapped up, and once the song order and liner notes had been finalized, I never laid eyes on the man again. As far as I know neither did Ian or Dan. True to his word he just took off, leaving the rest of us wondering if that was all.

We, along with the record company, sent emails, left phone messages to see if he wanted some sort of a more formal send-off ... something more celebratory ... maybe one final night in one of his favourite folk clubs, or something at one of the old pubs on the Danforth where it all began. There was no response, which I have to say, in hindsight, I now get. It would have been a pretty conflicting proposition; caught between the possibility of doing one more shit-kicking concert, and the probability that he was probably already too debilitated to risk stepping back on stage.

But then came that eleventh-hour invitation. A spot at the Vimy Memorial Anniversary over in France. National exposure. Part of a live-show broadcast back home to the whole country. It was an opportunity that was simply too big not to trump all our own difficulties. So we began the process of re-arranging Chris's vocals to fit Ian's range; started converting the song's violin passages into piano solos and some guitar work; asked the record company for help to rework the press kit and website to reflect the band's de facto change in personnel. And for a brief few weeks, it was like the cloud that had followed us around was actually lifting. (And yes, for a few days, we even started entertaining the notion of a Mill Run life without the great Christopher Lucan.)

My cellphone rang, I swear, less than an hour before I was to leave for the airport.

"Myles. It's Chris. I need to come with you."

My expletive-laced reply focussed on the man's utter gall, as I pointed out how much effort we had spent over the past ten weeks trying to contact him and discuss the nuts and bolts of his pending retirement; how our inability to reach him had made planning the future of our own lives a near-impossible task … and how just when we thought we had turned a corner on our own, suddenly here he is, *shuffling* back to complicate matters once more.

And just like the good old days, he wasn't the least bit interested in anything I had to say, telling me instead about how he had already phoned Ian and asked him to swing up to his apartment and get his fiddle so it could be checked in together with all the other instruments. Because he was still a few hours north of Toronto, and was driving like hell to try to get down there and grab the first available flight over … either London and rent a car down to Calais … or to Paris and go up. Before I could argue any further, or get any other details out of him … even swear at him a little more … he was, as you, the reader, undoubtedly know – gone. Quite literally … gone.

As I stated at the outset, it's clear what was hoped for when I was asked to write this article, but I'm afraid this is as far as I go. Maybe Dan will choose to offer something more in his segment; I don't know. The truth is I am no more ready to speculate on anything more than I was twenty-five minutes after Chris hung up on me that April afternoon when news reached us about the crash. And if that reads as unsatisfying or unresolved ... well, all I can say is welcome to the Lucan Shuffle Dance Club.

Now you see him ... now you don't.

**Myles Thomas**

~

*Dear Bronwyn,*

*As you may or may not know, a few weeks ago I left Mill Run. Had I more time, I would share in far more detail the events that led up to that decision. But right now time is of the essence. And because my today doesn't know what my tomorrow may bring, I'm afraid I must stick to some necessities with this letter. So, in the absence of fully disclosing my reasons for retirement, let me instead state that there will be explanations that simply aren't true, no matter how often you hear of them or how widely you see them written in the future. In fact, when it comes to explaining myself in this matter, it may well appear as if even I myself haven't stuck to any one consistent rationale. But if so, please know I had no say or choice in the matter.*

*It is a difficult state to be in – confronted by the realization that you are no longer in control. That in fact you may not have been for quite some time. (Rest assured, I have researched my fate quite well.) The point is, given my situation, moving forward I would urge you to take any and all quotes or citations attributed to me with a well-earned oceanful of salt, or – as is your right given my shortcomings as a father – as complete and utter fiction ...*

~

# Two

*Ladies and Gentlemen ... they're on their way to the West Coast, but we've got them tonight! Put your hands together and give a great big Rainy River welcome to MILL RUN!*

What was it about that show? What was there, in the course of events, that made that particular night, and not some other moment, a point of no return? It was, after all, nothing but a small mid-week add-on gig; a town fundraiser for the town's minor hockey program booked but one week before; put on in the makeshift environs of the town arena's banquet hall, complete with orange stacking chairs lined from wall to wall, framed by decorations of draped and twisted red and white crepe paper, all laid out before a temporary plywood stage, the carpeted surface of which was still being glued down even as the band arrived for afternoon set-up.

Certainly there had been nothing in the performance itself. Even Myles, for all his post-tour analysis of what went wrong, had to admit that, for such a last-minute addition to the schedule, the Rainy River concert had been an unqualified success. The locals had clapped and whooped their way through two full sets and three enthusiastic encores. Good and brisk business as usual.

Nor had there been anything telling following the show. (Unless one could find something cryptic in the way the Ladies' Auxiliary had presented the band with a large slab cake, the frosting of which had been done up with the piped-out likenesses of each member.) The merchandise table had buzzed with the flow of pleasing commerce: three entire cartons of CDs sold. Everyone had settled into their well-delineated post-show roles. Myles – steadfast keeper of books and paperwork – was sitting down in the arena manager's office to go over the breakdown in pay, giving cursory responses to the town's mayor and his humble apologies for not drawing even more folks in.

*I know you boys are used to bigger crowds than this. We were just so damn lucky to have got ya up here ... and when one of the businesses jumped in to underwrite the whole thing ... well it was a no-brainer for us.*

Dan, for his part, was holding court in front of the stage – the hub for the usual wheel of middle-aged women circled around him, spellbound by his smooth gentle-eyed smile and the croon of his words, delivered with the same clear-blue resonance with which he had just sung.

*No ... thank You so much for coming ... a picture with you and your mother? No problem. We can do that ...*

And then there was Chris. Having jumped down from the height of the concert stage to equalize his interactions, he straddled one of the vacated stacking chairs, eye-to-eye with everybody who wished to share a word. From Ian's usual slightly distant vantage – relatively undisturbed by the crowd – this was the band's foundation. Not that he didn't appreciate the nuts and bolts drive of Myles or the obvious appeal of Dan's stage persona and how those contributions had over the years, combined to create a whole that was far beyond the sum of its parts. Nor how he himself – a sideman really – had been a beneficiary, having come on board the good ship *Mill Run* only after those contributions had fully matured. When rarely a show passed without thunderous approval by night's end; without at least two encores; without all of this tangible evidence that each and every performance only furthered a successful process set in motion long before he joined the band. But after a few tours worth of parsing out Mill Run's individual personalities, he had long since concluded that beyond business acumen, and a silky voice, at the heart of it all was the everyman-attraction to Chris's songwriting that propelled the group ever-forward. And furthermore, all of that mutual visiting-of-equals after each and every show was the very fuel that charged his creative motor. The way he would lend a disarming ear to anyone sufficiently inspired to come forth to thank him and pay tribute to one of the evening's particular songs that had struck a personal chord. The way he would patiently wait while they worked up the nerve to describe some important detail about themselves ... their own lives. The way he would pointedly ask an elderly fan about his beloved town's history ... or a shy child if she played an instrument ... if she would like to try to bow his fiddle.

That night in Rainy River had been no different; a lengthy chat with a large amiable man looking rather ill-fitted in his suit jacket. The owner of a hunting lodge up on the east shore of Lake of the Woods, he had told Chris by way of introduction.

"I imagine that's a business that does pretty well up in these parts?" Chris had replied with a smile and a handshake.

"Well, we make do ... Can house a couple of dozen or more in the main lodge, plus a few more at the hunt and fish camps out on Big Island. Mostly folks from the States ... Chicago,

Detroit … as far as Texas even."

"Really?"

"Well you're not gonna pay the mortgage advertising to folks in Winnipeg and Thunder Bay when they can walk out their back door and practically get the same experience for free. Would have loved to have put you boys up for the night instead of here in town, but I understand you have to hit the road bright and early tomorrow..."

The night before it had been a retired postmaster who fancied himself a spare-time poet and would be 'tickled crimson' if he could send Chris a few of his verses. The night before that, a beekeeper from Duluth would have been happy to show off his swarms if the band had time to stop by the farm on the way out of town the next morning.

With just a question or comment, the man could connect with people so quickly and effortlessly, honouring them by his interest in the simplest details of their lives. Asking not just for asking's sake. That was the key. That was the difference Ian had discovered personally on his very first tour with the band, a road trip that had also happened to be a swing through northwestern Ontario with shows in Atikokan and Fort Frances before three weeks of gigs on the Canadian prairies. And while that first journey didn't include a stop in Rainy River, it did lead them right through the town and across the top of Minnesota before spitting them out in the woodlands of southeastern Manitoba forty miles or so down the road.

It was a route that had begun two and a half days earlier, back in the rolling farmland of southern Ontario; a route that had afforded plenty of time for Ian to get to know his new employer. To settle in and listen to his voice. To note the free-form manner of his thinking, his speaking ... his story-telling.

To note as well, the *way* he spoke – the slight inflections, the little bit of a down-east hard *r* whenever he got on a roll with some tale.

From subsequent travels with the subsequent sharing of life stories he would learn that it was a result of Chris spending the summers of his formative years with his Mom's side of the family on Cape Breton. That mixed with whatever linguistic sensibilities he had internalized from his hometown of Bancroft, Ontario. It required a bit of a bracing of the jaw, Ian determined – unnatural for him, but for Chris the result was most engaging. A style that lent a certain homespun wisdom to the man's often challengingly esoteric convictions, so even when he soared ahead to survey notions and ideas from what would be uncharted skies for most, he could fly back to firm and familiar ground to express those notions in such beautiful everyday style. When he wrote a song about the early settlers, even the most knowledgeable on pioneering assumed this songwriter must have solid first-hand experience with milking cows and mending fences. And any songs with a maritime theme left lifelong fishermen convinced that Chris, or someone close to him, must have been born at sea. His lyrics, simply put, bred reality with poetry. Allowed him into peoples' hearts and let them trust he understood their particular way of life. How they worked, and earned and lived and built things. And all this simple-life heroism from a man who, left to his own devices, seemed more likely to pull out a book on speculative metaphysics, or cosmology.

"What can I say," he said one night over a post-show pint. "Dad was a philosophy prof who commuted down to Kingston every week. I imagine I'm a hopeless mix of being influenced by and rebelling against all that that entails."

Perhaps, but if so, from where Ian sat, it looked completely genuine. He once changed a flat tire on the side of a New Brunswick highway while debating whether the works of George Orwell had value as dystopian literature for the youth of the day. And one morning outside a motel in Iowa ... well, nothing suggests a discussion of medieval Spanish mysticism like drying out your spark plugs over a bathroom light bulb. And there was the often-recounted conversation, occasioned in one instance along a highway rest area somewhere east of Quebec City when Chris had stopped one afternoon to repair his violin with a tailpiece fashioned out of bent cutlery ...

"Have we ever had a discussion about Reinhardt Flath?" he blurted out of the blue, vice grips in hand as he twisted the tines of a fork.

"The philosopher who did all that research on LSD?"

"Not on ... *with*. And he wasn't a philosopher, he was a psychoanalyst, so his research was on the alternative states of reality that LSD could facilitate, not the LSD itself."

"So you told me last time. Backstage at the Oak Center, remember? Myles thought you were nuts, by the way."

"Was it because I got into the bit about dinosaur genitalia?"

"How's that?"

"Well actually, it wasn't so much their genitalia as their erogenous zone. You see Flath had been conducting experiments on his subjects with LSD, trying to regress them as far back as possible to explore people's capacity to break free of the bonds of their own temporal lives. See, he had this theory that biological organisms were hard-wired with a genetic memory, and he thought if he could find the right means, he could take them way, way back."

"Way, way back where?"

"Not where, my friend ... when. Transpersonal psychotherapy he called it. See Flath had long been testing regression experiences in which people were describing recollections of their own birth, their journey through the birth canal, even their own conception, but then this quantum leap occurred and he started having subjects recounting events that predated their own lives with incredible accuracy. Predated their own epoch in fact. The most dramatic was this woman that he regressed right back to, well, for lack of a better description, her life as a dinosaur ... and specifically the strange pleasurable warmth that she felt in her neck when she was about to mate. And sure enough when Dr Flath consulted with experts in the field of palaeontology, he was told there were a number of species that they believed had their erogenous zones in their necks. And just for the record, I am fully aware of the look you're giving me."

"Well, I mean, come on..."

"Yeah, I know, Flath's always been a bit of a stumbling block. I mean on the one hand it's all just so brilliantly out there. The idea that this woman allegedly bypassed the entire history of mankind, hell the entire history of mammalia, so she could hang out with these hundred-million-year-old reverberations that were echoing deep down inside her ... or, on the other hand–"

"Bullshit?"

He shrugged and then nodded. "Complete and utter," he said, pulling out a fresh fiddle string. "But don't tell Myles I said that. You'd spoil the fun."

~

Once back inside the Canadian border, the first community of any measurable size north of the 49th parallel was the village of Sprague, just off Manitoba's Highway 12. And though the sign announcing the village had advertised both food and lodging, upon investigation Chris and Ian found only a small tavern, that was by every indication well past its prime in terms of both lustre and popularity.

"We'd be the only thing in town," the bartender informed them with a put-upon sigh. "Got a room upstairs with a bed and a cot. Forty bucks."

Having come all the way from the top of Lake Superior that morning, the two had accepted the terms and settled down in the smoky ambiance of the bar's heavily-varnished walls, generously adorned with racks of antlers and well-polished fish. There, amidst suspicious sidelong glances, the two tucked into the first of four bottles of Labatt's Blue, and a bag each of salt and vinegar chips, which, as it turned out, was the only thing in town in terms of a menu.

"So what do you think of touring life so far," Chris asked in a voice slightly louder than Ian would have preferred. "You think it's something you might go for?"

The comment caught the piano player a bit by surprise. *Something he might go for?* He had signed on with the understanding he would be a full-time member in good standing. Yes there had been a few things that had given him pause; the article in *Folk Roads* magazine, for example, labelling the addition of a piano player as *an experiment*, describing his role with such phrases as *adding a bit of decoration* or *just a little extra sheen*. But he had written those off merely as record-company spin, aimed at appeasing whatever portion of Mill Run's long-standing fan-base might not take kindly to change. And yet a comment like that begged the question, how invested should he be? He had, after all, answered their offer of employment far more out of restlessness than conviction, having spent the better part of the last ten years dispassionately paying his bills by teaching private lessons to children who would rather be anywhere else in the universe than hunched over a piano, struggling through stop-and-start attempts at scale after scale; hands jerking up and down over the keys like some dull can opener from their grandmother's cutlery drawer. It was the same for his so-called career as a performer ... cocktail piano bar gigs, wedding receptions, the odd birthday party ... incidental droning at best, for the cacophony of conversation that those events engendered, delivered with only negligible measurements of energy on his part. Yes, he had been trying some other things of late. Writing mostly, but nothing of note. A few short stories in a couple of obscure literary journals that remunerated in nothing beyond a free subscription.

"Oh don't get me wrong," Chris continued. "What you bring to the band is great. I just remember that you said most of your playing has been in and around Toronto, so I wasn't sure how you'd find the travel."

"All good, so far," Ian replied with a nod and a swig. "But you're right. I haven't been out too much ... not like this, anyway." He leaned back in the chair, trying to relax against the spindles as he watched one of the men at the bar, a rather elderly and inebriated sort, pull out a plate of false teeth for inspection.

"The beauty of this job," Chris said with the first of what would be many beer toasts that evening, "well, one of the beauties anyway... is places and occasions like this." His eyes scanned the room taking it in, as Ian would come to recognize was usually the case, with more detail than most anyone else would ever leave time for. As if an extra sense was at work promising that within his immediate surroundings lay some gem of an observation just waiting to be discovered. Sure enough ...

"Look at that, look at that!" Chris hissed, leaning in and giggling like a kid getting his very first dirty joke, pointing with his eyes over to a sign magic-markered in bold red lettering and taped to the cash register. NO MORE CREDIT TO BILL MacNALLY. "That's just awesome. Makes you wonder how long the guy milked his tab before they had to resort to public incrimination! Oh shit ... and over there!" He blurted out, this time definitely too loudly. "Those hooks ... are those fencing staples?" He camouflaged a nod towards the wall behind the bar with a swig of his beer.

Ian offered a shrug in place of confessing he actually had no clue what either a fencing staple was or what it looked like. Not that it mattered. Chris's reaction was all that mattered. It was more than just laughter, more than merely making fun of the place. It was a kind of joy ... happiness, even.

"My God, they are! They're actually using staples to hang those mugs. That's brilliant. Oh and there too ... for coat hangers," Chris said, and pulled a coil notebook from his coat pocket to jot down some reflections on the scene.

"No ... what I wanted to find out," he continued presently, returning pad to parka, "was whether you were finding the road, well ... like I first did, I guess." He shifted his chair, angling it sideways from the table so he could better stretch his legs. "See, for me to be out on the road this much ... I had to develop a penchant for a lifestyle of reductionism. If that means anything to you."

Ian shrugged again. "Simplicity?"

"Close. But not *just* simplicity. It had to be more active than that ... more verb than noun, you could say. It's like I had to discover this yearning I never knew I had. Discover it and let it become a way of being. It's a strange thing in a way. I mean after any given show, night after night, people will come up and ask me ... well *tell* me in many instances ... how hard it must be to travel so much and be away from home. And I'll smile and nod and tell them how perceptive they are for understanding that. But it's not the case. The truth is I'm probably most *at home* when I'm out on tour. And that's because I'm reductionist by nature. I like the fact that out here, life gets so clearly delineated. It shrinks down to these clearly defined tasks. Today for example. All that was asked of us was to get further down the road. Drive west. That's all. That was the day's only goal. So the fact that we're now sitting here in a tavern in ... where are we again?"

"Sprague, Manitoba."

"The fact that we're here in beautiful Sprague, Manitoba means the day has been an unqualified success. And it will be the same tomorrow on a concert night. Set up. Sound check. Do the show. In fact, on stage is where it's most acute. I love it. I love the fact I get to pare myself down to one single song ... even one moment inside that song ... a specific musical phrase or lyric ... trying to deliver it just right."

His hands were cupped in front of him, forming a snowball of imagined music, his torso for a moment compelled to leave its comfortable slouch and lean over the table. "It's that single-mindedness ... the luxury of it. That's what makes creativity work."

"But hang on ... wait a minute," Ian held up a hand. "I was under the impression that Chris Lucan was this totally prolific songwriting force constantly juggling dozens of inspirations on a daily basis. Eyes wide open for the next idea wherever it might be.

"You mean like the *Chris sees songs from a long way off* line? Yeah, we've put a lot of mileage on that one, haven't we?"

"But it's true, right? I mean you're here spouting a theory in front of me, but I'm also watching you glance around at this place. Probably thinking about making some more notes. Wondering if the credit sign could work its way into a song ... or whether there's a story to tell about those mug hooks."

Chris shrugged. "Actually the song ideas tend to find me ... I don't go searching as much as you might think."

"But still, an idea can hit any time – correct?"

"True."

"So what happens when you're absolutely bowled over by something while you're on stage in the middle of a show, or driving through a blizzard or ... I don't know ... getting a root canal for that matter?"

Chris leaned in and took a long sip then returned to his straight-leg stretch, "I would say that moments like those are a reminder of how fortunate I am to be as much of a reductionist as I am."

"Because ..."

"Because it's true. The real world is full of multiple layers of simultaneous roles that people need to figure out how to juggle. Parent ... spouse ... wage-earner. I mean even within the confines of this band there's singer ... songwriter ... driver ... personality."

"Sure, but you – wait ... personality?"

"Absolutely. It's not something usually thought of as a role in life, but yes ... one's personality is definitely something that is honed and shaped and worked on over time. Something put on far more like a sweater, than worn like skin, if you know what I mean."

"What makes you say that?"

Chris folded his arms, sent his eyes up to the ceiling. "What makes me say that? ... Well ... because I believe these so-called roles actually run far deeper than merely our chosen vocations. *The very nature of the self is manifold with an endless possibility of archetypes.* That was one of my dad's philosopher quotes ... can't remember who. It means we all have within us the blueprint of potential saint, or murderer, of villain or hero ... lover or recluse ... sorry, remind me how I got onto this?"

Ian played at the label on his beer bottle. "I think you were trying to answer what happens when you suddenly get a song idea in the middle of a show."

"I was?"

The piano player nodded, emptying the remainder of his opening drink.

"Well ... in that case I guess you could say that losing my train of thought probably just demonstrated the limitations of reductionism."

"Sure ... and if you could just reduce *that* a little?"

"I generally fuck something up."

"Fair enough."

"But ..." his finger jabbed triumphantly towards the ceiling, "I still maintain it is a worthy goal, so ... here, see if this makes things any clearer." He paused to redistribute his weight once more, leaning even further back in his chair, his fingers braided across his chest. "Lately I've been rereading this one particular writer, this guy named Martin Buber. Ever heard of him? He was a Jewish rabbi and a philosopher with a real mystical approach to things. Probably the only writer I could ever really stomach way back in my university days when I still had aspirations to follow in my dad's footsteps."

"Really?"

"Short-lived phase. See, what I gravitated towards and what classical philosophy offered turned out to be two radically divergent paths. Even during those early survey courses, they would take some philosophical issue; something like perception versus reality; or the nature of good and evil. They'd always start off with some reasonable precept but then inevitably proceed to expound the living shit right out of it to some subatomic degree. Qualifying every notion. Forever honing a previous worked-out thesis with another."

"Thesis, antithesis, synthesis?"

"Hegel ... good for you. But here's the thing. At some point it becomes an endless battle. Qualifying, mitigating, chopping up and amending each and every idea in the vain attempt to come up with a philosophy that covers every imaginable contingency of life–"

"–when all you really wanted to do was reduce those concepts to their abstract?"

"I wouldn't say abstract. I'd say *essence*. So you could sit with an idea and get a sense of its *entirety*. Now ... my ex-wife has a completely different take. She used to say that if God was in the details, then surely I must be an atheist. In fact a few years back, after all the custody and settlement issues were in the rear-view mirror and we could be at least slightly civil to one another, she suggested that this was probably the biggest irrevocable problem with our marriage. Which frankly was pretty surprising to hear since I had been working under the assumption it was the affair I had with a waitress at O'Malley's pub back in '92. Anyway, according to her, I and all true poets, she said ... which was nice of her, given all we'd been through ... we use language to push aside the specifics and include as much emotion and human experience as possible. Whereas she, on the other hand, being a lawyer–"

"Your ex is a lawyer?"

"Came in handy for her," Chris sighed. "Me, not so much. Anyway, she maintained the law needed language to do the exact opposite. Whether it was a brief or a discovery paper or a statute itself. The job was to find language that sharpened the intent of something right down to only the finest of applications, and mitigate out all possible misuses and misinterpretations."

"Like your classical philosophers?"

"And to think we met in Aristotle 101," he replied with another toast and handful of chips while Ian took a turn scanning the room.

There was a large man by the bar in a very animated conversation with the barkeeper, about the tab, the piano player thought at first – but on further scrutiny it appeared to be over something they were watching on a small television mounted on the wall behind them. "So what was it about this Buber guy that struck you?" he asked, his eyes still trained on the argument at the till.

Chris straightened up, raised a palm as if he were about to take an oath. "'*The attitude of man is twofold in accordance with the two basic words he can speak.*' I can still recite the first page I ever read of him. '*The words are not single words, but word pairs. One basic word is the pair I-You. The other word is the word pair I-It.*' Still remember where I was in the old campus library too. Because he nailed it. He had reduced all of life into these beautiful little succinct couplets."

"OK, I guess ... but–"

"What does he mean?"

Ian nodded.

"Well I'd say he's offering up the belief that you and I and all mankind have this two-fold capacity for our relationships. It can either be the arms-length I-it, where we objectify all the people and places and objects with which we come in contact, or it can be Buber's I-You ... or I-Thou, as it was actually translated, in which case *the other* is given as much respect as the *I* would give himself or herself ... which goes for any relationship they have by the way, be it with other people, or places, or things."

"Sorry. Things?"

"Think Mother Earth. Think the environment. Think man's relationship with nature; or commerce or art. Things like that. And of course, since Buber was a rabbi, think God. The essay went on for about sixty pages spelling it all out, but for me that was just the gravy. The meat of it was already there in those few initial opening lines."

"So do you think he was right?"

"I think he was a poet. And I think his poetry gifted me with a valuable insight for relating to my world. But ... that was back over thirty years ago now, so by no means has he been my one and only guide. I've often been taken with Carlos Castaneda's books, especially those dealing with altered states of reality and dream-analysis."

"You reduce your dreams too?" Ian chipped in, squinting to make out the details of the TV screen.

"Then there's the theologies of Eckhart and Tillich. The economics of Levitt. Friends one and all, just like Mr. Buber was that afternoon in my college stacks. Showing a slow poor sod like me just how beautiful and holistic things could be. Even so-called mundane things."

He pulled a pair of sunglasses from his coat pocket, opened one arm and raised it professorially to his mouth. "I believe it was Kierkegaard who said to truly experience the Divine, you had to first be completely grounded in the everyday world around you."

"Like a Manitoba bar with fencing staples for mug hooks?" the piano player asked, his attention still drawn to the raised voices at the bar. It was curling, he decided. They were arguing about curling.

"You know what?" Chris said, grabbing his next bottle and raising it in salute. "You and I are going to get along just fine."

~

The room they surmised, once they finally staggered up to it, had at one point been a utility closet, judging not just by its size, but by the close air and absence of a window. The bed and the cot were both short and narrow, their only saving grace strangely enough being the severe concave sag each possessed down the middle from top to bottom – instrumental, it would turn out, in keeping the men from hitting the floor during the night, once sleep finally found them. Until then there was their very own vintage Electrohome eight-inch black-and-white TV. Void of any cable box or satellite, and unequipped with any sort of antenna, it produced no reception save for a rather snowy image on but one channel, and even then, only with the aid of a coat hanger twisted onto the back of the console and aimed towards the hallway. And yet, just as the six bottles of beer (each) from earlier in the evening would be remembered in years to come as thirst-quenching perfection – and just as those bags of chips would be recounted as the most savoury snack a weary traveller could have possibly hoped for … so too the rerun from CBC's Winnipeg Comedy Festival would be recollected and re-shared between the two time and again as possibly the funniest, most clever sampling of stand-up monologues either had ever taken in. The Irish comic with her hysterical bit about her husband watching her breast-feed their newborn. The young fellow who ranted about how his computer tries too hard to please him with predictive text – its engines anticipating each and every little thing he tried to type, with the eagerness of a border collie in a field full of sheep.

*... I put in B-A-... and up pops BABIES? BAMBI? BARBIE DOLLS? ... I punch in T-I- ... and up comes TIME BOMBS, TILLEY HATS, TITTIES ... WHAT DO YOU WANT TO TYPE NOW SPIKE, HUH? WHAT DO YOU WANT TO TYPE ... Damn it, let me finish my word!!!! ... WORD? WORD? YOU MEAN WORDPLAY, HOW ABOUT WORD GAMES? HOW ABOUT WORDSWORTH???*

"Oh God, that's so spot on," Chris spat out through tears of laughter, pulling himself up from the cot. "Hey Ian, that's exactly what happened to me with the band email the other day. Remember? I tried to send you those chord charts and the computer sent it to that woman in Pennsylvania on our fan list? I didn't even notice how close the addresses were. Shit, that's priceless."

It was dank, it was musty and it was cramped. Exactly the kind of place that a poet or artist or dreamer would drive away from with an indelible image formed and framed in his memory. And because of that, on each and every subsequent trip west, Chris and Ian contrived to time their travel such that they found themselves pulling into the Sprague Hotel just as nightfall approached. Every trip west, that is, save for that final tour when a last-minute booking in Rainy River, not more than ninety minutes back down the highway had precluded the tradition, downgrading it to a mere mid-morning coffee the following day in an otherwise empty bar.

~

For a brief moment – for the last time really – things were OK. With the bright winter sun beaming across the bar counter, through the steam climbing up out of their Styrofoam cups of instant coffee, Chris was himself, seemingly recovered from the state he had been in back in their motel room earlier that morning when Ian had awakened to find the man decked out in his parka and toque, kneeling over his notebook on the bed, rocking to and fro unresponsively.

Perhaps the familiar surroundings of the tavern had served to calm him. Or perhaps it was a function of that particular stage of the journey itself; that invigorating transition when the road finally delivers you from the constraints of woodland scenery, where it flattens out the undulations, levels the outcrops of rock and thins the tree stands until suddenly, not too long after the turnoff for Sprague, Manitoba in fact, you pick up straight-line speed. Soon you are launched from three days of forests, inland lakes and Canadian Shield, out onto an open sea of prairie with sky and cloud-line draped all the way down to the bottom of your windshield. Instinctively you stretch your limbs and you breathe a little bit deeper. Or perhaps it was simply the morning ... a brand new sun on all that vast landscape.

Chris started in on a conservation he had had the night before. "From the guy telling me all about his fishing lodge," he said, and proceeded to detail a rollicking tale from the gold rush days in the Red Lake District of northwestern Ontario. Something about a hidden stash of treasure possibly still tucked away up there in the forest somewhere.

"I actually read up on it a few years back to see if there was a song to be had. Even worked on a few verses with Dan and Myles."

He spun quickly around on his stool, interrupting himself to inspect the walls, the empty tables and the bar, the view out the front windows, the bar again. As if he were almost a little desperate to make sure everything was how he had remembered it.

"Looks a bit in different in the light of day," Ian offered, but received no reply. "But at least we don't have to climb into those bloody cots this time around. Or get that TV going again."

"The TV," Chris murmured, turning abruptly to re-acknowledge his bandmate. "We watched that comedy show the first time we were here."

"Titties and Tilley Hats!" Ian replied, believing the prompt – as it had on every other occasion – would be the catalyst for a thorough reconstruction of that first evening, complete with the requisite embellishments about the stares from the locals, their levels of toxicity – and, of course, a recitation of the comedian's monologue that for Chris had always been the capper.

But such was not the case this time. His friend's words instead simply trailed into nothing more than a steady dribble of barely audible whispers. "That's right ... that's right," he mumbled over and over, and then after three or four false starts for his coat pocket – each time stopping to mumble a little more – he pulled out his pad to finish his thoughts silently with pen and paper.

## THE SECOND VERSE

*With the professionalization of folk clubs and singers, and with the expansion of what is acceptable instrumentation for the genre, more and more a second stanza is structured to musically enhance and reinforce the story being told via counter-melodies from accordion, fiddle, penny whistle, even – though certainly not my preference – from a piano (folk being the music of the masses after all, and not the salon).*

**Chetwynd C. Lovett**
*The Orthodoxy of Folk Song*

# ONE

*In the second of two **Mill Run** instalments of our "**In My Own Words**" series, vocalist **Dan LaForge** offers some snapshot insights into the lasting effects of the band for both himself and his fans.*

Where to begin?

In one sense – it's completely obvious. Recorded, documented. A matter of public record in several newspapers the very next day. Case closed and no need for further comment.

But then again, if Myles was right in his excerpt; if what is being asked is my take on the *seeds* of our collective demise ... I will attempt some thoughts, scattered and emotional though they may be. Attempt even though much of my darkness wonders what possible yardage could be gained.

Myles's article focused on out west. The final tour. The meeting in the motel. I would like to start there as well, but with a different tack. Start with some context. Hopefully to put a bit more of the joy back in the picture. The joy that was our band. Because truth is light. And if nothing else, I need to make sure that my words don't dim the musical alchemy that was Mill Run.

Keremeos BC, Fruit Stand Capital of Canada, was how the sign on the side of the highway read. And I remember I was thinking it was nice, but not particularly relevant for a day in March.

We had arrived early enough that I had time to stretch my legs and stroll the town. I came across a small municipal park down the road, dotted with a half-dozen kids getting in a few last minutes' play before daylight slipped away. There was this historical plaque just outside the gate. Something about the sun and the mountains, if memory serves. Some First Nations' legend about the shadows forming images on the rock face when the sun began to set. The specifics now elude me, but I do remember thinking Chris could do something with that. Remember thinking it had the makings of a calling card far more interesting than the fruit stand angle.

I know I stood there for quite some time, facing those mountains ... letting the sounds of the children, and the traffic and the wind all play on me ... for a moment at least, letting go of the highway of concerns Myles had been hashing and rehashing in the car for the last five hours ...

◆◆◆

Walks had always been my instinct on the road ... Keremeos, British Columbia;  Ashland, Wisconsin;  Cockermouth, England.  Wherever.  I often deliberately struck out on my own to take in whatever place the end of a day presented.  Give it its due.  Even on show nights, as soon as sound check was over, you could find me sneaking out the door, for a look-around. It's something I got from Chris way back when.  But unlike him, I always left time at the end to come back and take in the concert hall itself.  Take in every nook and cranny.  Every interesting imperfection.  Every crack in the plaster.  Every creak in the floor.

No ... on second thought as I write this, it sounds like Chris as well.

There was a beautiful Zen that permeated there.  Every single time.  Long before the house opened. Long before those hyper-charged moments immediately before taking the stage.  When there was nothing but silence draped all over the hall.  That's why I always finished my strolls right there ... picking a seat in the middle rows to take in all the trappings that this beautiful life had afforded me.  The careful braiding of microphone and PA chords, the impressive red-dot lighting decorating each member's effects board and pedals.

It was the visual contrasts that excited my eye most.  The chrome of a mic stand, the polish on Chris's fiddle popping so crisply against a neutral black curtain.  The coloured gels of the stage lights playing across the keys on Ian's piano.  This was our office.  Decorated for business.  This is where we worked.

Would Myles rather I rhyme off a laundry list of more tangible rewards to justify Mill Run's success? ... *His* list?  Over fifteen hundred shows played?  Main stages at some of the biggest festivals on either side of the border ... Winnipeg to Philadelphia, Ottawa to Newport? Sold-out tours in the UK year after year? Thousands of CDs sold?

Impressive sounds that miss the point. Because the essence of Mill Run's success was nothing more than what we left out on the stage night after night. The faces hanging on our every note. The rush.

Having said this, please don't think I define Mill Run in terms of the attention we garnered.

It is true that being on stage is, in no small way, addictive. And it's also *very* true there was a time in my life when I was completely guilty of such addiction. But thanks to Christopher Lucan I learned, before it was too late, that as a roadmap for your music career, it was a one-way street. A dead end even.

Mill Run was different. Mill Run saved me. Mill Run was a symbiotic connection of band-to-audience and audience-to-band that previously I never knew existed, complete with all those indelible moments that can never be taken away ... never be denied, no matter how *forgotten* Myles might worry Mill Run may one day become. The energy of a room when we'd open a concert. All three of us going airborne to land on the first downbeat. The visceral feel of singing Chris's songs, the way his music could fill up my lungs and soul. The way the last notes of a ballad could spin out of me while the band cycled through a chord progression. The end-of-the-night feeling of sweat dripping off my forehead, from my shoulders and arms, my happily-soaked sleeves. And the crowds. Jumping to their feet to help us finish off the final notes of a show well-played. A show well-heard ...

But sadly, I am digressing, aren't I? Stalling even.

Myles had always presumed to place me in his camp when it came to Chris. Were there problems on stage? Absolutely. Did that last western tour go poorly by our standards? I cannot disagree. And yes, like Myles, I was concerned about the growing frequency of Chris's struggles. Him tuning over top of a song ending. Stepping in front of me during an introduction. But unlike Myles I resisted the urge to compile them. Make them into some sort of case file. (Though Myles would no doubt argue *I* was merely choosing to avoid an uncomfortable issue. A character flaw for him to add to whatever file he had stored up on me? Maybe.)

The truth is I had known Chris far longer. *He* and *I* founded the band, not Myles. More importantly, and something I'm not sure Myles can truly claim, we were, at least in the beginning, as much friends as we were bandmates. And those symbiotic connections I described earlier? None of them would have been possible if this weren't the case. Not if we weren't first and foremost in sync with one another on stage. Our connection with audiences was a by-product of our own joy for playing music together. An extrapolation.

And that, in turn, became the perpetual energy for Chris's writing. On any given day, the performance of his story-songs occasioning more anecdotes from those for whom we had just played. A trucker's account of his life on the road. A housewife's description of a long-lost first love. A concert promoter. A janitor in a theatre. A waitress in a restaurant the morning after the show. Everyone completely worth his time. Everyone a possible seed in the cultivation of art from life.

I think this actually drove Myles a little bit crazy. I think it all seemed a bit too arbitrary. The way Chris accepted each successive conversation – seemingly without criticism or analysis – with no less enthusiasm than the last. But it was a problematic take, as well. Because if everyone else in the procession of encounters that was Chris's life, actually gained his favour by nothing more than indiscriminate happenstance, then somewhere back at the start of that same parade would have been Myles himself. He and all his fresh, new ideas on how to promote and sell Mill Run ... back when Chris was *suddenly inspired* to take *him* on.

The official Mill Run bio stated that Chris and I first met supply teaching in a Toronto high school. This is true. However we quite likely crossed paths much earlier than that, in the summer after I graduated from high school. I had decided to cut a summer job short at a bookbinding plant so I could jump in my uncle's beat-up VW Bug and see Canada. The grand adventure ended four days later in northern Ontario with the transmission shot and no means to afford a replacement. The best I could do was a tow into the town of White River where I hung around for a few days camping in the municipal park, trying to negotiate a price with a local mechanic to sell the car for parts and grab a ticket for the next bus south.

As it turned out, Chris had been working for the MNR that summer planting trees just to the north. Had my visit happened to fall on a weekend – I couldn't recall for certain if that was the case – we may well have passed on the street, a full twenty years before we finally did introduce ourselves to one another.

(It seems the planters would hitch rides down into town on Saturdays to catch a movie and a meal, or, at the very least, catch sight of a female under the age of twenty-five. As Chris said, "We knew we'd been in the bush too long when the 250-pound camp cook started looking good.")

I've always quite liked the fact we had a prehistory of shared proximity. As if my calling was already in place. Hibernating. Letting me meander through my twenties and early thirties, dabbling in this and that until I was ready to hear it ... carpenter, roofer, what-have-you by day; bar bands by night. The decision to go back to school. To finish my BA. Get my teaching cer-tificate. Why else would I have picked up the phone that Friday morning and agreed to a half-day of supply work in a school all the way across the city? The morning after a gig all the way out in Kitchener the night before. Ninth grade instrumental music no less.

Pass the aspirin.

He was just finishing up a senior class. This bearded scrawny little folkie surrounded by an array of mandolins and banjos and fiddles he had brought in to show the students. Completely full of life. Completely engaged. When I introduced myself, he was instantaneously interested in what I had to say. And when I gave him a rundown of the bands I had been in, his eyes grew wide and he got up and all but danced around the classroom. He told me he was pretty certain he had seen me singing down at one of the Harbourfront clubs the previous summer. My reply must have included a skeptical look, because without any further prompting he wagged his finger and told me how even a hick fiddler from the Ottawa Valley needs a hit of The Stones and Aerosmith every now and again.

Two hastily jammed songs later, he dropped his fiddle from his chin and pranced around again ...

"You know what?" he said. "Singing like yours may just be exactly what music like mine has been crying out for."

It was that simple. Mill Run was born.

Chris had always been scattered. Unpredictable. Even back at the start of things, changing his tune back and forth. Suddenly redirecting his energies away from one idea and towards another ... the *Lucan Shuffle*, as Myles liked to call it.

But I likened it more to an absent-minded professor head-space. Something that just came with the territory. When I think of all those many occasions I watched the man's Muse take hold of him ... saw what a demanding sort she could be ... leaving him time and again in a daze by the compulsion to get a sudden musical thought on paper. Here-and-now be damned. Quite literally I could find him stumbling into closets. Walking into doors. Even coming offstage at the end of a set, totally somewhere else. But man, the results! The results were nothing short of genius. True artistic genius.

The problem for Myles was while he could market that genius, all day and all night, in the end he just could never wholly trust it. Couldn't get that Chris's bouts of confusion were the price to pay for the creative engine behind Mill Run's popularity in the first place. Couldn't trust that most of his foibles, if just left to be, would work themselves out on their own.

◆◆◆

Myles Thomas played the part of a folkie just like the rest of us … big blond-haired ponytail, wire-rimmed glasses, fluent on every stringed instrument known to man. But make no mistake. Myles Thomas is first and foremost a businessman. And an awesome one at that. All those shows and tours. All of the accolades of reviewers and critics he chased down year after year.

If only he had been there from the outset. Experienced the initial spark from which the flame of creativity had ensued. Been there to feel that same sense of *destiny* Chris and I held for the band. Another *if only*.

Because without that certainty, the music *business* is a desperate place. It's a place where you might just lie awake at night trying to connect the dots between the most recent spree of glitches and its impact on future bookings … especially if a *clammed* fiddle solo in Winnipeg one night was followed by a missed vocal entry in Brandon the next, followed by the strange introduction of chord charts on stage in Medicine Hat after that. Because while *destiny* sleeps soundly, business plays it all back, over and over again, correlating it with the less-than-sold-out theatres in Prince George and Quesnel. While destiny dreams, business tosses and turns, fretting that if a band isn't growing, it surely must be shrinking. Fretting how all those successive concert halls on the prairies, the Rockies, on the west coast were always half-empty … never half-full.

It occurs to me that, as the newspaper people like to say, I have buried the lead.

Chris had been ill. That was the report we eventually received from the family – by way of Ian. Not surprising I guess. Ian had firmly replaced me in the *friend* category almost as soon as he joined the band. But while I have worked through any residual feelings of jealousy, it does lead me back to the matter of these *seeds*. Those, and the lead I fear I have tried to smother. Not just here, but, in effect, every day since Chris's death. Buried and subverted.

Because when it comes to talk of *seeds* ... never mind the news of his diagnosis ... the pending Alzheimer's. What I have trouble speaking of, is the fact that when his end came Chris was all alone. Completely and utterly alone.

And as irrational as a therapist can try to make that observation sound – on my bad days ... my worst days – this *fact* will always haunt me. Because I was complicit in its making ... many, many years before.

Therapy is a funny thing. For months you can get nowhere near identifying sources of guilt and pain. Unwilling, unprepared to bear its weight until the foundational work required to get there is complete. For me, it was learning to leave the edit button off. Leaving it off for any and all parts of my life I was not proud of. It meant acknowledging my own failures. As a husband, a father ... all in the pursuit of my music.

(It also occurs to me that neither Myles nor myself have mentioned anything about our spouses or families at all up until this point. It would seem we come by buried leads honestly.)

Anna and I had been together virtually from our first day of teachers' college. When she walked into class and sat down in front of me, that long flowing hair over those tanned shoulders and down the back of her chair ... I was gone. Later that afternoon, with a little prompting on my part, she agreed to sit down with me and over a coffee and a pack of cigarettes we introduced ourselves to each other's lives.

We were married the week after we graduated. Skye was born the following year. Autumn came two years after that.

But my wife suffered by me. Those years I played the double life, ignorantly believing she was sheltered and unaffected by my exploits. The affairs and one-night stands. The hotel rooms above any given tavern's week's worth of gigs, the women who listened to my take on *Stairway to Heaven* and were only too willing to make the climb themselves. (Don't screw the messenger. Maybe that's the moral of the story for any bar band worth their salt.)

She knew. She had always known. And in silence, day after day, year after year, prayed and waited for me to change.

Mill Run was the answer to those prayers. I changed. Came

clean with my shortcomings and, thanks solely to her capacity to forgive, came out the other side a new and improved version of myself. Spit-washed and scrubbed for inspection.

Another thing about therapy. It's led by those whose bullshit meters are really quite extraordinarily calibrated. And my therapist could never resist hooking up the needle to my backstory. Leaning on specific wording I used, challenging my necessity to describe past indiscretions – as she claimed I did time and again – as something predestined, even bordering on pathological.

"Are you competitive by nature?" she interrupted me once, and the question left me at a loss, since I couldn't ever remember coming across that way. She said she asked because she couldn't help noticing how I liked to portray myself in extremes. How I had been exceptionally blessed, (Mill Run) ... or exceptionally selfish (infidelity). So either I was ultra-competitive ... either I had to be the best at things – successes and failures alike – or else I used terms like *destined* and *pathological* as a crutch. Subconsciously distancing myself from responsibility.

The revelation sent me down quite a path of land mine questions. Was it wrong to credit Mill Run for helping to save my marriage? (I don't think Anna would say so.) By giving the band so much due, was it inevitable that I would suffer when it came time to mourn its passing? Would my grief seek out some portion of personal blame for its demise? Personal blame that on some subconscious level was conveniently beyond my control? (By describing Chris being so much one way when Myles was so much the other.)

Some of this seems so obvious now. It's true, Mill Run did

help put a stop to my wandering ways. It let me love the stage in a far more *unadulterated* manner that was in a sense (as I have tried to illuminate) *higher*, based on connection instead of conquest. Connection, I should note that my therapist was also kind enough to remind me (especially on days when the gloom would start to overtake me), that I helped create as a founding member of the band.

Sometimes she would have me go through it all, remembering the good times with specific stories and anecdotes, to remind myself of the totality of what it was I was grieving. How I had loved my twofold life; loved the performing, and touring and travelling ... loved driving Chris's beautiful songs across the land; because I now *also* loved the retreat back to my own little bungalow ... back to my Anna and the girls ... back to those who having kissed and hugged me full of best wishes before embarking on my tours, would stir ever so slightly in their beds when I would slip in the door to kiss their sleeping cheeks. Whisper Dad was home. The back and forth. The ebb and flow ... the balance.

So why is this testimony so relevant? And why is it still not completely worked out? As it turns out, those two questions are rather intertwined.

In the early days of Mill Run Chris had always been the official driver. He said the rhythm of the road soothed him and kept him occupied. Let him go over new material. Drum out some beat in his head onto the steering wheel or mouth over a

line for a would-be song. The arrangement worked fine ...
until our popularity broadened. Until the bookings started sending us further and further afield. Then, every once in a while,
one of those troublesome rhythms or stubborn lyrics would be
strong enough to veer the car uncomfortably close to a guardrail,
or retaining wall, or oncoming traffic.

The first few instances I gave him the benefit of the doubt. I
have no defence for it. Nothing beyond citing the character
trait Myles used on me in his article; that I would do anything
– (or *not* do anything?) – to avoid a confrontation with anybody,
especially my best friend. (A theory my therapist pointed out
may have merit, since I never bothered to confront Myles about
this take on me.)

Yes, it was denial. I know that now. Denial aided by good
fortune ... the bear on the road in the Muskokas, the transport
truck east of Kingston, the many sudden swerves for exit ramps
and unexpected U-turns, never resulting in anything more than
blaring car horns and near-misses. But even the most steadfast
fence-sitter has his limits.

I can thank the Lunenburg Folk Festival back in '89 for re-
vealing mine.

It had been such a great weekend otherwise. We were over
the moon. We had been given the last set on their Saturday-
night main stage. There must have been a thousand strong,
cheering and clapping and imploring us back for two more encores. A seminal night. The night we decided we just *had* to
take our music to the next level. Head back to Ontario and put
the finishing touches on our next CD, then officially abandon
our fledgling teaching careers and go out on the road full time.

(The very same night Chris got the idea to bring Myles on board as a third member of the band.)

We were only a mile or two from our B&B, out along the shore road leading back towards Mahone Bay. Lots of curves and bends. It was pitch black, save for some intermittent patches of pretty thick fog. Enough for plenty of cause and effect right there, if I hadn't known any better. But I *did*. I knew it was the excitement, exploding into a myriad of chaotic thoughts and ideas … immediate and plentiful, dancing right in front of him like a movie playing on the windshield. Spurred on, perhaps by the little old man from the Annapolis Valley. The story he had shared right after our set about his ancestors leaving the New World via the docks of Liverpool … visions of the crowded creaking cargo hold of some merchant ship. Or it could have been the conversation with the Celtic harpist backstage, telling us how we just had to get over to England and Scotland with those songs of ours … images of tucking away in some shepherd's croft overlooking the sea, writing his next batch of material. Or maybe he was in the violin maker's workshop; the one from Halifax who had come running for the car just as we were pulling out of the parking lot. Handed us her card and said how honoured she'd be if Chris ever had the chance to play one of his songs on an instrument she had made. Or maybe he was still back with the gentleman from the front row who had purchased six copies of both our CDs – one for each child – all grown now and living abroad ... a tear in his eye, as he told us how we were the best thing he'd ever heard at the festival and he'd been coming for 21 years.

Whoever the culprit, the fact was by the time Chris's attention returned to the steering wheel, it was too late. The bumper had already clipped the guardrail. Sent us spinning back across the road, over an embankment and headlong into the trunk of an evergreen.

The station wagon was totalled. So was my guitar ... and his fiddle. Chris had cuts on his arms and a six-stitch gash on his forehead from the broken glass. I came away with bruises on both knees, two black eyes and a pretty good case of whiplash.

First thing the next day, we had the vehicle's remains towed to a wrecker. Then I walked (limped) Chris around town to deal with the fallout ... insurance, accident reports, arranging a ride to the car rental agency in Halifax. Once that was all looked after, I took my friend to the local pub, bought him a sturdy pint of dark ale and came down from my fencepost with a vengeance.

I began by expressing just how much I loved what we were doing, telling him how his music had truly made a new and better person of me, how thankful I was to be able to voice his songs. Then I informed him I would give all of it up in a heart-beat – (me who can't find solace now that it is actually gone!) – if he ever risked my life with his driving antics again. That the great future we saw for ourselves could never come to pass if we were both found dead in a ditch on the way to a gig.

To his credit, Chris called up no excuses. Just responded with nods and a litany of apologies (though at one point he did try to tack on to my pronouncement, by making a toast to Mill Run's success, past, present and future). I allowed him this, but only after one last stipulation. The one Anna had presented to me, also in the form of an ultimatum, earlier that morning when I had phoned to tell her about the incident. Again to his credit, it was something Chris agreed to on the spot and, as it turned out, would never even once try to undermine until the day he died. Put simply, from that point on in our touring career, we would always, without exception, travel in separate vehicles.

It was my scream, he would tell me much later, on one of the few occasions we revisited the episode together. (Apparently I scream when I hit a tree.) I asked him if I was swearing or cursing him, almost ready to apologize for whatever affront I may have hurled out in the heat of the moment. He shook his head no and stared into space. "No, I'd have come up with some sort of excuse, if it'd been that," he said. "It was just a scream."

And how is any of *this* little testimonial at all relevant?

Fast-forward to that fateful day. We were set to leave for France. Reunite for one more performance ... at the Vimy Memorial no less.

I was halfway down the block when Myles called me. Screaming that Chris wants to come along. Screaming about the logistical nightmares if that happens. He isn't on the work permit. He couldn't be identified as a band member at customs. If he takes a later flight where do we all rendezvous? What about lodging? What about rehearsing? What about all the problems he had up on stage? Did we want to risk that? "The *Lucan Shuffle* all over again! ... the mother-fuckin' goddamn *Lucan Shuffle*!" But all I heard were those first sweet words. Chris was on his way. My friend was back. It was the new dawn I had been praying for and the sun was beating down on my windshield brighter and warmer than it had for longer than I could remember. I was off to meet up with my bandmates. A*ll* of my bandmates. I was euphoric. Already in the air.

We had just nicely checked all of our luggage and all the instruments through security when my cell rang again. An OPP constable from the Dufferin County Detachment greeted me on the line. He had been directed from Chris's ex-wife, who had advised the officer to get in touch with me and the band.

It would only be much later, sometime during the weeks that followed when we were together ... in the middle of playing the what-if game that grieving people play ... Myles would tell me more about that last conversation with Chris. How Chris had balked at having one of us swing up and pick him up. How insistent he had been about coming down on his own. That he had mentioned explicitly something about not wanting to break some *promise*.

How can't it haunt me? Him honouring our agreement to the letter of the law ... racing towards the airport all by himself... racing to catch up with us. No doubt, his mind too already in the clouds.

The officer told me they get a lot of accidents in the Hockley Valley. With so many steep hills and sharp curves. That's where it happened, he told me. In the middle of a double-bend on the north end of the road. He must have been going too fast, the constable surmised ... or been *distracted*. The vehicle had exploded on impact. And while the officer didn't dare put it quite so indelicately – from the description of the accident scene ... considering *the lack of remains* – so had Chris.

Since then it's been a process. Of talking and time. Of trying to get on with things, as best I can. But often I feel at odds with the task. Yes, I've gotten back into some music. Some session work here and there, and a couple of songs for a Canadian folk compilation. And as long as I don't demand that those projects compete with Mill Run; as long as I am at peace with the fact they will, at best, be mere shadows of that experience ... really, it's OK, though these words I write are still wounds. Older? Yes. Manageable? Some days. But wounds nonetheless.

Unlike Mill Run you see, I am yet a work in progress.

**Dan LaForge**

~

*It's the damnedest thing, Bronwyn. The power of Alzheimer's seems to be its insidiousness. The only real conclusive evidence comes when it's too late. In fact complete confirmation really only happens post-mortem, when the clinical sorts get to carve you open and poke around the offending areas of your brain. Otherwise it's a bit of a nebulous diagnosis. What one medical expert sees as an early stage of brain deterioration, another might still attribute to undiagnosed head trauma ... a bad concussion maybe; or even just a form of dementia in cases involving more elderly folk.*

*It attacks at the synapses, I'm told, where the neurotransmitters usually fire away and let you think and feel and sense things freely. It starts with a buildup of plaque between the brain cells. After a time they'll start to choke off the nerves and once those start dying, these clusters of proteins called tangles come in for the kill. Soon, quite literally your brain starts to shrink and shrivel up.*

*I have been putting myself around the second or maybe third stage of the disease – the experts list seven in all. I've been reading it's kind of a cruel phase of the disease, when there's still more than enough grey matter to fully comprehend the deterioration that will follow. This will be in keeping with some of the symptoms that I've let slip out for the past few months, starting with my last tour. Forgetting the words to songs, mixing up the order of a set list. Things like that ...*

~

# Two

Their last conversation of any real substance was somewhere south of Parry Sound, Ontario, driving through a light but constant rain.

"Can you remind me how much I've told you about my personal life?" Chris asked. It seemed an odd question, after five days virtually of silent travel. "Like the letter Bronwyn's mother sent me last summer?" he continued. "Did I ever tell you about that?"

Ian shook his head. "What was it about?" he asked gently, his carefulness a function of that same uncomfortable quiet that had built up over the past few time zones. Peripherally he noted what appeared to be a couple of false starts – attempted replies defaulting to a quick sigh and a swallow, then a pause to regroup and let the road drone below them for a few miles until finally some words broke through. "You know what?" he said. "It just struck me I haven't asked you how you are doing."

"That's OK," Ian answered, his curiosity risking a slightly longer glance over.

"Like I did coming home from the Maritimes last year, remember? I was asking you what it was like growing up as an adopted kid–"

"Fostered," Ian corrected.

"... and whether you'd ever go searching for your birth mother."

Ian nodded out the passenger window. Of course he remembered. How could he forget? Not the *fact* of it. That was nothing new. Completely common knowledge amongst friends and associates. But Chris had managed to dig to the heart of it, hadn't he? The never-too-far-away, middle-of-the-night part. The emptiness-of-non-lineage part. The having-no-one's-smile-or-hair-or-speaking-voice part. The Chris part.

"You told me you'd never want your search to inflict any sense of guilt on your birth-mom. That you weren't fuelled by a need to right a major wrong, which would be perfectly understandable, by the way. No, you said you'd only want to make contact to answer some questions."

"It'd be nice to have an address to send a picture or letter," Ian shrugged, eyes out on the passing line of trees. "But who knows? Maybe having me was the most courageous thing my birth mother ever did. Maybe everyone else around her was screaming for an abortion. Maybe it was all she could do to carry me to term." Ian let a few miles pass before adding, "And really, I have no right to think of myself as abandoned. Not with the foster parents I lucked out with."

Save for the deep baritone hum of the engine and the muffled beat of the windshield wipers, the quiet returned for several minutes until Chris came back to his original topic.

"The reason for the letter was that Bronny'd been seeing a therapist for over a year. When my ex found out she wanted to make sure I knew I was responsible."

"You?"

Chris tapped his fingers absently on the dash and sighed. "I found the timing really interesting. See, the letter was waiting for me in the mail right after that same east coast trip ... right on the heels of listening to you tell me how you don't consider what your birth mother did to be abandonment. I mean I know I didn't make nearly the time for Bronwyn that I should have. Especially once the divorce got messy. Her mother made sure she had sole custody ... moving up to Montreal. Then with all the touring ..." His voice trailed away again for a moment until he caught himself, cleared his throat and sat up taller in the seat. "And now she's all grown up ... finished a Masters in journalism and she's been working for a magazine over in England for, geez, how long now?"

"Wait – she's in the UK?"

Chris nodded. "Last few years anyway."

"And you never tried to–"

"Oh our relationship ended long before that. She did come over once when we were just getting started over there. Didn't like it though. We were setting up and playing and moving every night. Not much fun for a fourteen-year-old, which I guess is how I still picture her ... this skinny waif of a kid, tiny for her age, with these long blonde pigtails and a squeaky little voice. Suffice it to say my daughter has a far different take on what constitutes abandonment. And it's not like she doesn't have an argument. I mean how hard did I really try to make her part of my life? A letter at Christmas, birthday presents. An appearance at graduation. Really ... how hard?"

He rubbed on the back of his neck and grimaced, tilted his head from side to side. "Ah shit – new topic, please. Tell me how your writing's coming along."

As a rule Ian was eager to do just that ... ever since the first time Chris broached the subject, asking the piano player's thoughts about writing literature, about his *process*, how he shuffled and balanced his creative ideas ... asking as a fellow writer. An equal.

"Well I have been doing a lot of thinking about some of the things we talked about a while back."

"Remind me?"

"We were down in the States somewhere. Pennsylvania maybe? Remember, we got kicking around ideas about the importance of a good setting for a story. I was telling you how I'd love to write something that sends the plot right across the country. Use contrasting geographical settings almost like different characters."

"No doubt a function of all of this," Chris said, tapping the dashboard once more.

"Yeah, that's what you said then too." Ian grinned, stretching his arms back behind his head.

"So if that's the case, let me ask you this," Chris continued a mile or so on, his thumb and forefinger creeping up to work on his whiskers. "When it comes to you sitting down and writing quote-unquote fiction ... how comfortable are you borrowing things from your own experiences?"

Ian squinted out towards the bumper of a pickup in front of them. "I'm OK with it, I think," he said.

"Yeah?"

"Well at some level it's inevitable, right? You have to write what you know and what do people know better than their own experiences? I did read an essay in one of the literary journals a year or so back about the ethics of doing just that. *Borrowing for the imaginary*, was the way they put it. The article came down firmly on my side, by the way. It compared a well-written novel to the swatches that make up a quilt. Each patch an experience unto itself, but then all sewn together for even greater effect. If you're a creative quilter, as it were, there's no reason to believe some of those patches shouldn't be from your own world around you."

Silent mulling returned for the next half hour or more; through a stop to refuel, a joint visit to the urinals, a refill of coffee mugs and a change of drivers, until once again without warning, Chris, now comfortably slumped in a fully-reclined passenger seat, bolted straight upright. With both a volume and conviction that were completely at odds with his preceding inactivity, he all but shouted. "Oh my God!"

Ian grabbed onto the steering wheel with both hands. "What's wrong?" he stammered.

"Each one an experience unto itself, but sewn together for a greater effect ... it's like there's always a story inside another story!"

"Yeah ... sorry, where're you going?"

Chris leaned back in the seat, folded his arms and closed his eyes. "A story inside a story," he repeated seemingly for his own benefit. But then, flashing the rarest of grins over to his friend, he said, "And since you're allowed to borrow what you write, you could do a book about a guy ... who once wrote a book ... about another guy who had been an orphan ... and who for some reason had the urge to drive clear across the country chatting with his older and much wiser friend."

"Not much borrow there," Ian chuckled.

"No, but seriously ... this is good stuff. But remind me how we got here?"

In the days immediately after Chris's death Ian would have difficulty forgiving his careless reply.

"You were telling about your ex-wife's letter," he said, and just like that, with the rain fittingly now turning to a splattering wet spring snowfall, Chris fell mute, staring out into traffic, once again fidgety, and uncomfortable. In the remaining hour it took to get to Ian's front door, that veil of isolation would stay fully stretched; with no subsequent apology or comment on the piano player's part able to fold it back.

It was a grey conclusion to touring life. But as Ian would come to consider in the hours of blackness which followed news of the car crash, perhaps it had been an inevitable shade. Perhaps, given the suddenness of the man's decision to retire, he needed to recede from the current version of himself. And perhaps this was something he had needed to do with every change in his life. After all, as close a friend as Ian had become, it was a role in the band that had not originated with him. That claim belonged to Dan and no doubt their rapport had once been just as intriguing and fulfilling as his and Chris's. But no doubt as well, there had to have been some sort of withdrawal. Perhaps this was just Chris's way ... his flow and ebb. With his once-best friend Dan. With his ex-wife. His daughter. Maybe it had simply been Ian's turn.

The final words of the journey came in the driveway as Ian was hauling out the keyboard case and luggage from the back-seat. They were noteworthy only by their contrast to the hundreds of other erudite salutations and warm embraces the two had shared at the end of all the other times out on the road.

"OK then ... I'll be in touch."

~

*... I'm sorry, Bronny. I know there is so much more I desperately need to explain. But for now please know that if everything turns out as I have arranged – God willing – I will have the opportunity to write you another, more useful account of all of this.*

*Even in the event you are reading this after my death – assuming you have even found it at all – this is still my promise; if I can get out from under the duress that plagues me, if I can find the luxury of just a little more scrap of time to manage my thoughts, I will leave you another letter.*

*But for now, please take the best care of yourself and know that I love you.*

*~Dad*

~

# THREE

Given the circumstances of the day, it would have been better had Ian not still been so preoccupied with that last conversation in the car. Certainly he would have come across more prepared – more lucid even – when it came time for his turn to speak in memory of his fallen friend. Myles and Dan had both waxed eloquent so effectively about the life and legacy of their band-mate, quoting many a poignant verse from many a Christopher Lucan song in the process, until not a dry eye remained amongst the throng of mourners who had gathered from far and wide. From Virginia and Pennsylvania; from BC to Nova Scotia; the American Midwest; even a few appearances from the UK and Ireland; they had all pilgrimaged to the modest confines of Bancroft, Ontario's St. Paul's United Church, their collective numbers overflowing from the pews to line the walls, sides and back of the sanctuary, overflowing down the creaky stair-well, into the vestibule, out the front entrance and onto the lawn.

And there, before the vastness of the gathered crowd, stepped Ian Station, who, being so much more comfortable with life from the back of a stage, could manage nothing more than random, disjointed thoughts that were hopefully written off as the weight of grief catching up with the young musician. The result of death's finality taking effect and hitting the one who had driven all those thousands of miles with the deceased – the bandmate and friend who had spent all that time in the very same car that had, just a few short days before, careened from a hillside road and exploded into a ball of flame.

Inexplicably even to himself, he began by recounting Chris's interest in the career of Reinhardt Flath and his work using regression techniques to study the possibility of a shared genetic memory living in the sub-consciousness of human beings. And though he did manage to refrain from any references to prehistoric genitalia, or indeed to the strong prevalence of hallucinogens in Dr. Flath's scientific method, he was nevertheless aware of how his words – unlike those of his preceding bandmates – echoed so nervously up into the rafters.

"So why do I bring this up?" he heard himself continue. "Well ... I guess ... I guess because that was Chris ... not that he was a psycho ... a psychoanalyst, I mean ... just that he was someone who sought out deeper possibilities. But even more ... more than that I guess, I mention this idea of genetic memory because in a way, from the first time I met Chris, it was as if we had previously connected somewhere, somehow ... and maybe you have all felt a bit like that too."

It was unclear to anyone in attendance whether the piano player had intended to say anything more, as a rising inability to form any further meaningful syllables had infiltrated his mouth, resulting in several moments of nothing more than silent swaying, until presently the presiding pastor, along with Dan and Myles, thought it best to intervene. Together, with gentle pats on the back, and nods of acceptance, they ushered Ian

100 — A Song With No Words

away from the pulpit and back down toward his seat in the front pew. Halfway down the steps, however, he was unable to abide the spectacle any longer. He bolted past his assigned seat, down the aisle and out of the sanctuary, through the maze of crowded shoulders and torsos listening from the stairwell ... likewise those pressed into the confines of the front hall ... past all those congregated on the steps down to the front door ...

So yes, most certainly upon any degree of reflection, Ian Station would have been far better off had he not been so pre-occupied by the details of his last conversation out on the road with Chris. But then again, the memory of that exchange would not have been foremost on his mind had it not been for the two emails he read just before leaving for the church.

The first was a reread actually, the note Chris himself had sent just four days earlier – (good Lord had it only been four days?) – informing Ian that he had decided to come with them to France after all. It had been brief. Specific in its request to have his friend drive up to the house and fetch his fiddle – the key was in its usual spot, on the top ledge of the far window on the veranda – then check the instrument in at the airport with all the band's other luggage. But as unwise as it may have been to revisit such a bitter reminder right before Chris's service, it was the other email – the one Ian didn't even notice until he was heading out his motel room door fumbling over long-for-gotten details of a Windsor knot – that had the piano player sprinting down the sidewalk charged with a sudden urge to be absolutely anywhere else in the world than St. Paul's United Church in Bancroft, Ontario.

It was an email that had been forwarded by one Marjorie Gruber, owner and proprietress of The Innes Street Bakery in Ridgway, Pennsylvania.

*Dear Mr. Station,*

*First, let me offer my deepest condolences. Chris was truly a gifted artist who will be missed greatly. Now I'm sorry about the timing of this, given your loss, but this email showed up on my computer by mistake again. I thought we had this email address business straightened away, but when I saw that it actually came from the Mill Run address, I figured one of your bandmates was trying to get a hold of you. And please don't be concerned about privacy. I would not dream of opening up someone else's mail. Once again, my heartfelt sympathies from me and all your fans here in Pennsylvania. – Marjorie Gruber.*

The note had also been sent the same day Chris died. Curiously, it concerned the only other affected soul who, despite having a rather essential connection to the deceased, had also decided, as Ian had with his sprint from the church, that it was better to be elsewhere that day.

*\*\*\*\*Forwarding\*\*\*\**

*Dear Ian. Two things.*
*First, please know I haven't forgotten our last chat. About the story inside a story. I pray you will do likewise.*

*Second – and more important – although I have endeavoured to sort out all my affairs, I need to say this to you, since you were my last travelling partner. Please be very careful in the days to come. Your life may well be in danger. Yours and Bronwyn's too. Please watch out for her.*

# THE CHORUS

*More traditionally known as the refrain, the chorus is, of course, the repeated mantra of the folk song. For the would-be writer, this necessitates the maturity to break from advancing a song's story line, and instead delve into the emotion that the tale is endeavouring to invoke.*

**Chetwynd C. Lovett**
*The Orthodoxy of Folk Song*

# ONE

He was face down, spread-eagled. Strewn across the men's room floor and writhing from the impact of the first wave of kicks and punches to the ribcage, the small of his back, the stomach. Anywhere that wouldn't leave visible bruises, one of them explained between shots.

"We're gonna need you doin' your thing, aren't we?"

Another fist, this one up under the musician's shoulder blade.

"What do you want?" Chris managed through a mouthful of gathering spit. He could feel the breath of the man kneeling over him.

"What do we want? We want you, obviously," he said. "Think of us as northern businessmen ... and you are our bitch. Right, Nick?"

The second man raked his bootlaces across Chris's torso as he stepped to rinse his knuckles in the sink.

Vainly Chris tried to crawl, if for no other reason than to offset the shock in his groin, the jagged pain in his midsection. The second man allowed a moment's reprieve while he washed, then, shaking the water from his hands, sighed and grabbed

Chris by the hood of his parka, throwing him up onto the vanity and holding him there so the first could speak directly.

~

It had been a completely innocuous morning. Perhaps had he not been already hunched in his booth over his usual early morning coffee and plate of eggs, buried deep in the muck of would-be stanzas and possible chord progressions, he might have picked up some sort of warning. Might have noticed the lifeless monotone of the voice addressing him. (*"You boys did a fine job last night. Treat for the whole town."*) The blankness in the man's eyes; the cold stiff accompanying handshake. (They had spoken after the show. What was his name? ... Roy?) Perhaps he also would have seen the other two who had followed the man into the otherwise empty Rainy River Café. Noted their proximity to the man complimenting him. Noted the black leather coats, the skull-hugging toques, the sunglasses that stayed on even inside the diner. The broad shoulders and thick necks ... noted any of these details before the first – the one closest to Roy – shoved the lodge owner onto the opposite bench and along with his partner slid in after to pin the man against the wall.

"Put your papers away," he had instructed calmly while the second man reached over to close the songwriter's coil note-book. "And best leave your plate. You won't want anything more in your stomach."

He stepped back out in the aisle and gestured towards the men's room. Chris looked from the one man to the other, but caught nothing more than his own confused expression reflecting off their glasses.

"I'm so sorry," Roy half-whispered, for which he earned a

lightning-quick elbow into the side of his rib cage. There was an implosion of pain as he doubled over, his eyes drawn closed. His mouth quivering.

The second man rose to join the first.

"Come with us, Mr. Lucan."

~

The room was spinning. He was going to be sick. Or maybe pass out. When his head fell slumped over the man's fist, he was shoved again up against the bathroom mirror and held with the faucet digging into his spine, so the first man could lean in even closer.

"I'm afraid business hasn't been good," he began. "These small border crossings up here used to be so good. Not much traffic ... the Reserve close by ... lots of places to hide anything you need to hide. But then that new chief gets himself elected ... doesn't know a good thing when he sees it. Gets a fuckin' hard-on to *crack down* on things. Soon he's chirping to everybody about stuff that's none of *his* goddamn business."

He took his hand, placed it flat against the musician's chest and pressed, letting the taps embed themselves further. "But these aren't things you gotta worry about. All you gotta worry about is doing exactly what we tell you. 'Cause it turns out you're the answer to our fucking prayers, isn't he, Nick? I mean we didn't know what the fuck we were gonna do. Then one day right out of the blue I see old Roy in town talkin' to his neighbours about how much he liked your fuckin' little bullshit band. How they were always playing your CDs at the lodge and in the car. How they used to drive all the way down to Duluth or even back over to the Lakehead just to catch a show. And, well, Nick here should apologize, 'cause when I told him about it, all he could say was, 'Who the fuck cares?' But then he got it, didn't you, Nick? Who better to cross a border without any suspicion than a bunch of fuckin' old fart folksingers ... comin' and goin', playin' their little songs. I even checked your website ... shit, all them concerts in all them church halls and community centres ... why you're the salt of the mother-fucking earth, aren't ya? A fucking dream come true. 'What's the purpose of your visit to our country, Mr. Lucan? ... what's that? ... you're going to sing some songs about the pioneers down in the park? Well, come the fuck right in!'"

Through the wall of agony came a glimmer of the situation at hand and slowly the songwriter's eyes rose to meet the man's grin.

"Ah somebody's a smart little bitch, isn't he? You're gettin' the picture now, aren't ya? That's right. It was all a set-up. Roy out there sold you out. Picked up the phone and called the mayor with this great idea for a fundraiser. Why that arena roof isn't gonna fix itself, is it, Mr. Mayor? The mayor gets a hold of the rec director, and she puts in a call to your band. And just like that you've got yourself a last-minute *gig*. And we got ourselves a brand new sissy boy."

He wanted to say something. Wanted to, for some reason, retaliate by telling them he had already figured this out. As if it were important. As if the timing of it actually meant some-thing. But then the next wave of pain came shooting down his backbone, and once again the nauseating rotation of the room. Floor over ceiling over floor again.

"Now ..." the man in front continued, "Nick here was plan-ning on taking you into that stall there and fucking the shit right out of that scrawny little ass of yours, but I talked him out of it. So all he's gonna do is hit you one more time. Maybe two. Then we're gonna go wait for you with Roy back out at the table. So I need you to get yourself cleaned up then come on out so we can chat a bit more."

He pulled the musician out of the sink and onto his feet and held him so his partner could deliver one final shot into the musician's solar plexus. Chris collapsed, panting for unavailable air until the room, for a moment at least, went mercifully black.

~

*He's climbing into the car, passenger side. Ian's on the phone with the others. "Hey Chris, Myles says he just got a call for one more show for the western tour. Rainy River ... up in Northern Ontario."*

*"You know what this means ... Sprague here we come," Chris declares as they pull out on the freeway, wondering aloud whether the tavern will have done enough business since their last visit to afford actual coat hangers.*

*Instantly they're back in the stairwell with its narrow dank walls and musty smell ... the crack of light seeping from under the door at the top of the steps ... the sound of a TV blaring at full volume in the room beyond. He follows the barkeeper up the steps and asks how much it'll be for a night's stay.*

*"I* say B-A- ... and up pops BABIES," *the barkeeper replies.* "BAMBI? BARBIE DOLLS? *I* punch in T-I- ... and up comes TIME BOMBS, TILLEY HATS, TITTIES!"

*Chris laughs out loud, calls down the stairs behind him. "Remember that bit, Ian? Ian?"*

*But Ian is gone. So too the stairway and the tavern. He's back in his car, driving through thick banks of fog. Only when he squints does he make out the winding, narrowing gravel road ahead. The air is different. Cooler and moist. And there's a taste to it. A saltiness.*

*"Sea air," he hears a voice he immediately recognizes as Dan's ... Dan's voice telling him it's sea air. But what else is he saying? He sounds angry. No, not angry ... scared. Dan is scared. Very scared ... and he's screaming. He's screaming to look out ... "LOOK OUT!" But for what? There's nothing but darkness and fog ...*

~

Chris came to with the sound of the washroom door slamming open against a garbage can. Two large hands slid under his armpits launching him upright, and with his legs bicycling limply in the air, he was carried back out into the restaurant. This time it was him sharing space in the booth – crammed between Nick and the man seemingly in charge, all three of them opposite Roy the lodge owner, who, despite having his side of the table all to himself, still cowered up against the far wall.

"Any questions, Mr. Lucan?"

Chris slumped in his seat and hugged his ribs.

"Ah come on now, you're a smart guy," the man in charge said, putting a tree-trunk arm around the musician. "You're asking yourself, 'How the shit do I get out of this mess?' Right?"

From the other side of the table Roy's voice once again tried to mumble something. *Let him go ... let him out* maybe. Once again he was silenced, this time by a swift kick to the shins from under the table.

"Sorry. You can't," the man in charge continued. "That's just the way it is. For you. For me. Ole Roy over here ... but hey, I don't expect you to just take my word for it. Hell, when you get right down to it, I wouldn't even expect Nick's fists here to convince you." He shifted closer and tightened his grip around Chris's shoulder. "I mean we gotta watch ourselves when it comes to our bitches, don't we? Gotta look after them. 'Cause if we happen to go a little too far ... you know, beat you up a bit too much ... well, soon you're getting one of those *what-do-I-have-to-lose* ideas. Maybe start to figure if you're going down anyway, you may as well go down playin' the hero. But that's never gonna happen. And I'd love to stick around to see the look on your face when you find out *why* that's never gonna happen. But Nick and I got another meeting with one of our *assets*, so we're gonna leave it to our buddy Roy here."

He got up from the table, pulled a plain manila envelope from an inside pocket and tossed it into the lodge owner's lap. Then he leaned back over the table. "But once he's done that ... here's what you *are* gonna do. There's a drugstore just over the border in Baudette. Very soon, I predict, you're gonna need some pain relief from our little visit here today. But you're gonna wait 'til you get to that store before you pick any up, 'cause, there's gonna be somebody waiting there. All you do is follow his instructions. That's it."

The man straightened up, re-buttoned his jacket, turned and headed for the exit without another word. With one solid push, Nick sent Chris sprawling into the aisle; then stood and stooped to pick him up and fire him back onto the bench before he too disappeared out the restaurant door.

~

The silence between them was lengthy. Like Chris, Roy's arms were wrapped tightly around his midsection as if he were in fact on the outside of the window, fighting to fend off the cold. Still slouched back against the bulkhead, Chris opened his mouth wide, trying to deepen his breaths against stabbing shards of pain.

It was too much. For such a few short minutes, too much – far too much – to take in. To make any kind of sense of.

He had been actually targeted? Picked out at large? Plucked from his own world to be a pawn in some other? Save for the smothering weight of his injuries, it hardly seemed possible. Like an avalanche in the dead of summer ... never seen ... never heard of ... and yet, unbelievably, there. His eyes grew wide. He grabbed at his temples. Slow, low *Oh my Gods* moaned from his lips over and over again. He began to writhe involuntarily, feet kicking out in desperation, rapid-fire jabs landing only against air. The lodge owner looked on ... watched, nodding faintly, as the man in front of him pushed, then banged on the edge of the table with both hands, as if that piece of furniture itself, bolted to the floor, was somehow the cause of his sudden hell. Finally, as if recognizing some particular threshold to the panic, he reached over to subdue a flailing arm. "You're going to want to do something," he said.

Chris pulled back, clutching again at his chest.

"Go to the police, or just jump in your car. Take off and pretend none of this is happening."

But no, he was mistaken. Because in that instant, what Chris actually wanted, was to reach over and borrow from all of the brutality he had received in the men's room. *Inflict it forward.* On this man who couldn't even look up at him. Couldn't meet his eyes. Could only sit staring at the table with shrugs and pointless advice, twisting handfuls of sugar packets between his fingers.

"But don't do it. These bastards, they'll find you and make everything that much worse. Everything you ever cared about ... everything ..." The rest of the sentence fell away in pieces ... into a series of deep breaths before he could continue.

"They're from the States," he mumbled. "The chattier one anyway. I think he said Chicago once. Don't know about the other one."

There was another prolonged pause owing to either Roy's inability or unwillingness to offer anything more unsolicited, at least not until another dozen or so sugar packets had met their demise. "And it's not just them," he managed finally. "Others come in on the float plane. Some of 'em from down in Toronto. Other guys ... the really big ones ... the ones that even scare the shit out of those two ... they have accents from somewhere else altogether. I mean they talk about New York and Brooklyn, but sounds to me like they're Russian, or something ..."

"Who? Who are you talking about?" Chris finally asked through a wince.

Roy shrugged and sighed. "Mob ... organized crime. Hard to say for sure. It's not like they come with name tags." Another sigh. "Rest assured, whatever name and business they register under when they book a holiday at good ole Roy Turgeon's Hunt and Fish Camp is all just a front."

"And what about you?"

Roy leaned back against the window and stared out at the street. "For the past six months, they've used my lodge to get things in and out of the country."

"Things? What things? You mean drugs?"

"Drugs ... yeah. Some. But mostly people."

"People?"

"Women, Mr. Lucan. Girls." He chewed a moment on his lip, wiped away a tear that had dripped down and pooled on his cheek. For the first time Chris regained enough composure to consider the beleaguered tone of the man's confession. How it came across as much rooted in contempt as it did in fear. As much anger as pain. Another time and place he would have answered the urge to explore the observation. Reached for his note book and started recording it. Framing it. Drawing from it some sort of poetic order.

"So just to be clear here ..." he said instead. "These guys have been forcing you to help them."

Roy nodded.

"Including luring me up here with a concert?"

"It's not like I had a goddamn choice," the lodge owner snapped back, then immediately retreated again. Further this time. Like he was trying to climb the wall. Trying to pass right through the window, to be – counter to his previous advice on fleeing – absolutely anywhere else in space and time. "I'm sorry," he said again. "I really and truly am so sorry."

"You're sorry. That's fantastic. So tell me ... what was so dire you had to ruin some complete stranger's life? I mean, to what do I owe the pleasure? You owe these guys for a deal on some construction materials? Did they buy off a building inspector for you or something?"

"No ... no ... you don't get it," he muttered, the palms of his hands now up on the glass.

"Then make me *get it*, for Christ's sake," Chris spat, lunging despite his injuries to grab and pull the man back in front of him. "What the hell have you done?"

Roy's body fell defencelessly onto his elbows. His face stiffened and grimaced, as if expecting to be struck; like prey chased to exhaustion. His eyes finally rose to answer Chris with a gaze he hoped the songwriter might read without any need for further explanation. Slowly the musician's grip slackened and Roy reached across the table for the envelope that had been left for them.

"This is actually for you," he whispered.

Inside was a stack of a dozen photos. The first showed a somewhat trendy city street, bustling yet comfortable with very much a neighbourhood feel. There was a bakery next to a bookstore, which was next to a butcher shop maybe, or small grocer's market. Each business looked like a small and friendly family-run enterprise. From the licence plate of a passing car in the foreground – not to mention the dull worn stone of the storefronts themselves – Chris surmised he was looking at somewhere in England.

The next shot would not only confirm this, but would actually pinpoint the location with specific accuracy. For despite it being almost identical to the first, on quick inspection he realized the unfamiliar scene actually held for him a connection. That it was, in fact, a place he had from time to time – during reflective moments – hoped to visit one day. To make amends. Set things right. The realization had come from the one and only detail that had changed from the first photo; the unmistakeable form of a slender woman wearing jeans and a leather jacket and looking so unbelievably grown-up. She was facing the door beside the bookshop and appeared to be locking up. But her head was swung around, as if she had just heard someone call out her name. *She lives by a book shop ... that's perfect,* he thought for one blissful microsecond before the instant was replaced by renewed and amplified panic.

Feverishly he began rifling through the rest of the shots.

She's on the street almost peering into the camera, but not quite. She's in a dimly lit pub; in profile chatting with a friend. She's jogging across another street, dodging traffic; the same leather jacket, but this time worn over more businesslike attire ... a work case slung over her shoulder.

Then, her silhouette, through a window. She's at a counter maybe. In her kitchen perhaps. He shuffled faster ... there's a closer shot ... dancing in a club with friends. His hands began to shake ... she's in a park, lounging on a blanket reading a newspaper. Walking down the street, this time in a golden-tan trench coat, hands in pockets, unaware of the camera just a few feet behind her. Then one looking into her apartment from a neighbouring window. She's only half dressed ... wrapped in a towel. He desperately wanted to stop but the second-last in the pile, again in a bar, is a close-up ... it's crowded ... but she appears to be smiling *for* the shot ... deliberately posing. Then the last. No longer through the filter of a window. No longer at any distance at all ... taken from inside her apartment itself. He was going to throw up. The pain was back in full force. Unbearable. She's in her bed, fast asleep. A bare breast and shoulder tucked around a pillow. The hand of whoever is taking the shot is lingering in front of the lens to share the scene. Taped to the back of the last photo is a piece of paper. On it a very brief message.

*You will do everything we ask.*

~

Seconds later he was fumbling for quarters at the pay phone by the door, then fumbling through his pockets for his wallet, chastising himself for not knowing his own daughter's phone number off by heart. Finally he came upon it. On the back of the business card for his fiddle-string supplier in Toronto.

*You've reached Bronwyn Lucan ... I'm unable to come to the phone right now but if you leave your name and number, I will return your call just as soon as possible. For magazine inquiries please call the* London by the Month *offices on 3510-*

*4000. Cheers.*

Back at the table Roy took in the musician's reactions. He felt a restless tingle in his own limbs as he watched the man begin to convulse. Felt his own throat also catch, when he heard the panting sobs from the lobby crest into a steady wail ... the receiver hung up, only to be grabbed again and slammed over and over and over against its cradle. Watched as Chris raced out the door, and down the street, into the cold grey sun.

# Two

*Day two of the Westgate Folk Festival in North Yorkshire. The band's first appearance there. They slip in a side door of the host pub's function room so as not to disturb the workshop already in progress. Theirs is next, billed as a 'Get to know the new band from Canada'.*

*Everyone's in a bit of a euphoric fog. The mainstage show had run quite late the previous night and was followed by lots of photos, hugs and handshakes from a good many of the thousand or so who had been singing and stomping and urging them on.*

*They try tiptoeing down the far wall of the auditorium, but it's no use. Dan is immediately recognized. Quietly he attempts to fulfill a number of requests to sign festival paraphernalia from nearby patrons; programs, admission badges, T-shirts. Myles slides by him, off in search of the 'compere', the emcee of the afternoon's event, so he can finalize details for their set ... three DIs, or else instrument mics, but at least one direct line for the keyboard, and vocal mics for all involved. Myles too is the recipient of smiles and waves from those in attendance the night before, but limits his responses to a nod here and there.*

*Chris taps Ian and points to a couple of empty chairs in a nearby row. From there, they settle in to consider the offerings of the man currently on stage. 'Explaining Folk Song Composition with Chetwynd C. Lovett' they read from a festival program over the shoulder of a woman in the seat ahead. And indeed the lone man sitting on a stacking chair on stage, leaning over his guitar, appears to be doing just that, soberly discussing his craft in front of a gathering of forty or so serious and studious attendees. He has seen Mill Run's entrance from the corner of his eye, noted with just the slightest flash of irritation the resulting bit of restless stirring in the crowd. Chris squirms down in his seat, takes out his pen and coil notebook. With a squint, he directs his gaze intently back up at Mr. Lovett. Figures it's the least he can do ...*

*"The mistake I see most young songwriters making today is their insistence on going to a bloody minor chord. Completely overused. A crutch."*

*He strums an A minor on his guitar, strums it again, then scans the faces in front of him for epiphanies. None are apparent. Chris feels Ian lean over onto his arm to inquire whether Mr. Chetwynd C. Lovett is indeed 'for real'. Chris nods in agreement though he is unsure what he has just answered. The piano player leans in once more to point out that tone clusters and jazz notwithstanding, 'Buddy here' has just banned half of his available chords.*

*"I mean it's just so obvious, isn't it" Lovett continues, to which someone in the front row charitably suggests perhaps his point would be better made with an example ... the offending chord heard in the context of an otherwise worthy progression.*

*"Wanker," someone hisses from the row behind.*

*Chris turns to face a large man ... bald, with arms folded over a considerable midsection, face scowling out overtop of a lengthy whitened beard. "Chet there fancies himself quite the expert," he explains in a voice just loud enough to make the Canadians slightly uncomfortable. "Only too willing to tell anybody who'll listen how his shite is the bloody Second Coming of the folk revival."*

*Ian leans back. "So does he ever actually sing anything?"*

*"Oh you don't want that, mate," is the reply. "That man there has been up and down this country stickin' a finger in his ear, makin' dogs cry for the last fifteen year."*

*All three fall silent as they try to make heads or tails of Chetwynd C. Lovett's response to the first-row request. He goes on at length about some issue with 'context' in modern attempts at traditional songwriting, then something about the trouble, again, 'young songwriters' have with this concept (all the while gently strumming the offensive A minor over and over).*

*The large man sighs and rises, leaning against the chair in front of him to push himself up. "Not sure I'm seeing what this emperor's wearing, if you catch my drift," he says, again a little too conspicuously for comfort. "I'm off for a pint, lads. Be back for your sesh though. Caught you last night ... bloody brilliant, that."*

~

Had it been any other day of his life leading up to that moment, the return from such a clearly-defined dreamscape would have surely been the opportunity for a wealth of self-exploration. (A full and robust delving, for example, into what might have possibly occasioned his dreaming of past memories.) But as it was, Chris awoke with only panic-sponsored longings for un-consciousness, and the ever-swelling understanding that his life, as he knew it, was quite possibly over. Fear and danger and coercion would all but surely continue, if not get worse. The stop at the pharmacy had made him completely certain of this.

"Don't turn around. I'm putting a package in your coat."

Despite his having scanned the store, the voice had still man-aged to approach unseen and startle him from behind. "Don't open it. Don't even look at it. First piss stop over the border, leave your coat in the car. Leave your car unlocked. Someone will be following to pick it up."

He felt the weight of the something land in the bottom of his pocket. Small, he judged from a quick glance down. Maybe the size of a paperback.

"And then I'm done?" the songwriter managed hoarsely after a few seconds of indecision as he stared into the shelf of painkillers. He felt a hand grab onto the back of his collar. In-stinctively he winced.

"Mr. Lucan, really," the voice whispered softly. "Do you re-ally think we would go to all that trouble finding your daughter for just one little delivery?"

Chris could not help the shudder down his spine.

"Ah don't worry. I do have some good news. It turns out ole Roy and his wife Polly needed some time off from the lodge. Turns out they have the motorhome all gassed up and they're heading west to take in a whole bunch of shows by this little folk band called Mill Run. Roy just loves Mill Run, you know. Polly's a big fan too. So big, she'll probably want to check in with you from time to time."

~

He would have to change the sets up. That was a given. Despite his assailants' crude attempts to steer their beatings – so what if they had left his hands and face alone – there was no way he could draw enough breath through his ribs to reach any of the high harmonies for the newer material. Likewise bowing some of the faster fiddle solos, especially given what Myles had been scheduling lately ...

What could he do? If he dared share his fate with the others, how long would it be before the threats against his own daughter would grow to include them as well ... and their families.

An image of Dan's daughters playing on their front lawn flashed across his thoughts to haunt him ... Autumn on a bike with training wheels, Skye making a fresh batch of mud pies. He could not let that happen, he vowed – even as his eyelids, once again, began to fall. No. He would need excuses. Vague but firm excuses, done in character ...

It was the only way he could see ...

~

*"OK, here's the deal," Myles whispers as he lands on the vacated chair. "I talked to the sound guy and we'll have to be on mics for the instruments. There's a bit of back-line for the keys. They only have limited gear in here, 'cause they want more of a Q and A session than a concert set ..." He nods toward the stage. "Or whatever this guy thinks he's doing."*

*"Well, he's doing a workshop in the proper sense, actually."*

*"And putting the room to sleep in the process. – 'Don't go to the minor chord'?? – What the hell is that about?"*

*"I don't know ... I think I see his point."*

*Myles sighs and laughs at the floor. He's irritated, but only slightly ... still too buoyed by their standing-room-only performance from the night before. "Really? You're going to be that guy today, Chris?"*

*"What guy?"*

*"The guy who needs to be contrary for contrary's sake. I swear, if I had sat down here and said hey Chris, I just heard this fantastic guy, Mr. ... whoever-he-is up there sharing the most enlightened insights about songwriting, you would have insisted he was a full of shit."*

*Chris shrugs.*

*"In any event, he wraps in about five, so we should get tuned up. We've been charged by the sound man to wake these poor people up."*

*They watch Myles head for the stage, busy himself with his guitar, then the strap, then an extra set of strings. "You do enjoy pulling his chain, don't you?" Ian asks, rising to head for the stage as well.*

*Chris shrugs again. "Maybe," he says. "But if you went and told him, apparently I'd have to deny it."*

~

He bolted straight upright, his bruises catching against the shoulder strap of his seatbelt. "SHIT."

"Shit indeed," Ian replied, amused by the sight of his friend stumbling back into the here-and-now, eyes rolling around semi-focused, glancing this way and that – out the side window, down the road ahead ... then to the back windshield.

"Where are we?"

"About fifteen minutes further down the road than the last time you woke up and asked me."

Chris swallowed and rubbed his knees hard with the palms of both hands, then lowered his seat to a more reclined angle, drawing his boots up on the dashboard; all as casually as possible, trying desperately not to divulge any discomfort in the manoeuvres. From there he could keep an eye on the passenger-side mirror ... and on the black pickup truck that emerged moments later on the horizon behind them, gaining speed until it settled in at a distance of a hundred yards or so.

Chris took a deep but silent breath, then let it out slowly through a crack in his lips. "When you see a place," he said.

"Sprague's just up the road."

"Good, I could use a pee."

# THREE

"50484."

*–Bronwyn?*

"Dad?"

*–Hey I hope it's not a bad time, but I need to talk to you about something pretty serious–*

"Dad, if this is about money shit with Mom, I told her, and now I'm telling you, I'm not getting in the middle–"

*–No, Bronny, that's not–*

"Because it's not fair, got it?"

*–Listen to me ... it's not that–*

"No matter how hard you or she tries to justify calling me–"

*–Honey, please.*

"Honey?? You're gonna pull that crap? Really?

*–I'm sorry, I should have kept in touch, I know. But Myles keeps us so busy–*

"Myles keeps you busy. Right, Dad. Whatever ... look I can't talk now."

*–But I need to tell you–*

"Send me an email."

*–Bronwyn, wait!*

"Seriously Dad, I'm late for work."

# FOUR

It was the following Friday night. An hour before curtain for their show in Swift Current, Saskatchewan. The door crashed open and Myles exploded into the dressing room marching to the clothes rack on the far wall to give his gig shirt a brush and a tug.

"We've got a few minutes before they open the hall," he announced. "We should run over the solo in *Barn Dance* a few times. I want to get it back in rotation, so we should try to get you locked back into the groove ..." Then spun on his heel and strode back out the door.

Chris let out a long but shallow sigh. It grabbed too hard if he dared inhaling any deeper, twisting pain burrowing through him like an auger. He slumped to the side over the arm of the chair he had been clutching onto just before Myles had come in, gearing up for the inevitable spasms along his spine when he reached down to put on his shoes.

"... and we should check the harmonies at the end of *The Monument* too," came his bandmate's voice from out in the hallway. "They went a bit sour last night."

He thrust the cuff of his sleeve between his teeth and chewed. Wiped away the sweat already collecting on his forehead and above his lip and came up with a Plan B for the shoes, hooking them up onto his lap with the aid of his fiddle bow, tying the laces loose enough that when he returned them to the floor, he might slide his feet in without bending over. Once that was accomplished, he reached in his pocket for one more muscle relaxant – his fourth of the day – fully realizing whatever benefit they supplied in keeping him upright would be sacrificed when it came to technique and a clear head. With one more silent grimace and his breath held tight, he again gripped the arms of the chair and grunted himself to the standing position. He told himself that, once underway, it was only an hour to intermission ... an hour until the next opportunity to rest for a few minutes at least.

Winnipeg had been a nightmare. He could barely remember the radio interview. Just the vague notion that had entered his mind when he walked into the studio to keep everything completely benign. Offer up nothing that the world at large (especially the vengeful and violent part of it he now assumed was watching his every move) could take issue with. No us-versus-them, Canada-versus-US talk. Not out of his mouth. Not if he was going to be sneaking illegal packages across the border. And if that plan got in the way of a smooth-talking publicity opportunity for Myles, well so be it. All the better even, since he had already decided that alienation from the band was the best tack.

No doubt the show that night had helped on that score. Christ, there was no way he could have got through the set Myles had drawn up. Not with the constant pressure digging in under his left shoulder blade, snaking its way up through his neck and his jaw to throb arrhythmically behind his eyes. *The Schooner From Shelburne* and then *Dance Away Mary*? Right out of the gate? He was going to be lucky just to keep the damn instrument up under his chin that long. So he had hit upon the idea of starting with some of the old tunes. He knew them with his eyes closed. If need be he could even drop the instrument down to rest in the crook of his arm and it would still be right in the spirit of the song.

But that had only looked after his physical liabilities. There was still the psychological damage of his assailants' promise to expect repeat visits ... more of what had already been inflicted. Because more than the bodily harm itself, it was that distraction that had left the musician so absent from his craft up on the revered Coleman Hall stage, when a mere three bars into the opening song, his eye had fallen on Roy, about a dozen rows back, slumped with his arms crossed and eyes averted, next to a taller heavier-set woman clapping along enthusiastically. He had lingered around in the lobby after the show meeting and greeting audience members, but neither the lodge owner nor his wife stepped forward to have a word.

It was the same the following evening in Brandon, a much more intimate concert held in the banquet room of a local hotel with the band squeezed onto an undersized riser in front of a hundred or so tightly-packed enthusiasts. There they were once more, this time front and centre. Again, Chris made a point of loitering about at the end of the night. A photo with a family from Dauphin, another with a woman who had driven all the way up from Minot in North Dakota. (*Sorry I couldn't get my husband out of his easy chair,* she had claimed, though not with any undue concern.) A dozen or so autograph seekers, (*Can you put, 'To my friend in music and make it out to Lorraine?'*) But again, by that point Roy and his wife were nowhere to be found.

Then came Swift Current.

He heard her address him from behind just as he was making his way down the hall to join the band.

"If you're planning on getting a bite to eat after the show, it sure would be swell to join you. Our treat, Roy and me." There was a cheerfulness in her voice, very much compatible with the image he remembered – clapping and whooping along to his songs for the past two nights – however completely at odds with the stone-cold expression that met him once he turned around. "We're at a motel up on the North Service Road, but we'll be next door at the Tim Horton's," she said and turned to walk away. "I hear they do a fucking great soup."

~

Claiming a need for fresh air, Chris left Ian lying prone across his bed surfing the channels of their hotel room's satellite package. Once out the lobby door he scanned the rows of businesses dutifully lit and aligned for late-night Trans Canada traffic. Motels, fast foods, outlet stores, gas stations ... more motels. In a mere dozen strides he spotted the coffee shop up the road, but after a mere dozen more – if even that – he came to an abrupt halt, all the pain of the past three days suddenly surging through the entire length of his body, the voices of those who had inflicted it bouncing around his head.

He was frozen. Caught in the purgatory between fight and flight, with the dreadful realization that those impulses were actually just idealized polarities; unattainable and impossible goals for the flesh-and-bone decisions with which he was now burdened. He could no more scurry back into the warm confines of his room and check out whatever TV program Ian had found, than he could launch himself forward, striding headlong into whatever God-forsaken fate awaited him one block away. For the moment it was a battle of inertias. Rooted to the spot and completely still, save for the gentle buffeting of the gathering prairie wind, until ... ever so gradually .... like the come-and-go of the cramping in his ribs and stomach ... he felt panic's tide begin to ebb, its clench momentarily slacken ... so once again he could move.

He chose a circuitous route. He wasn't sure why. Some vague veneer of security in not being seen before he had to be seen, perhaps. It was a wide and careful arc in the general direction of the coffee shop. Through the parking lot at their own hotel, around behind the empty but clearly-lit lot of the Canadian Tire, then similarly the BP station. He made sure to circumnavigate the entirety of its property, out well beyond the long diagonal line of transport trucks idling away sleepily. Over a gravel road that seemed to come up out of nowhere, but actually – upon second inspection – fed off of the service road, running down a slight hill out of town and onto the pitch-black prairie. He crossed it and found just enough peripheral light from the city to make out the terrain ahead. A small field of dead grass coated in a crust of snow, strong enough to hold his weight only in some places. It made for a slower pace, but was a small price to pay for the shadows it afforded. Shadows he could keep, he calculated, almost all the way to the side door of the Tim Horton's itself.

He paused. Glanced back at the route already taken. Took a few steps forward ... paused once more to fight the urge to give up on the night and simply retrace his steps back to the hotel. But then came the image of his daughter, asleep in her flat, peacefully unaware of the intrusion closing in on her. The

threat to *her* safety and *her* future, a mere arm's length away.
And so he went on.

~

The first sirens met his ears just moments later, as he was
reaching for the coffee shop door. They came from behind
him, from the east. With lights flashing and tires spitting ice,
several squad cars fishtailed onto the service road with barely
a break in speed, their whirling red and blue lights painting the
sky, illuminating the ground he had just covered, which included
another overflow parking area not more than a hundred feet
beyond where he had trudged. How could he have missed it?
Right there – open and vacant save for the ghostly outline of a
small sedan with its grill aimed towards the side of a motorhome
and the silhouette of a man – a man Chris instantly recognized
not from the beam of the car's dim grey running lights, but
from the pleading voice and defeated posture. Presently he
made out two large figures holding the man up. Then he saw a
third pacing faster and faster in front until suddenly, without
warning, the third figure reached inside his coat, pointed and
fired. The victim slumped and slid down the panelling of the
motorhome as all three men bolted. The shooter leaped into
the waiting car and spun off into the night. The two others
raced around the RV, sprinting back across the road to disappear
into the sea of tractor-trailers in the service centre parking lot.

Chris back-pedalled blindly until his heels hit a patch of ice
and he fell to the pavement. But before the police cars had all
fully skidded to a stop he was up, scrambling back into the
shadows, westward again, around the far side of the Tim Horton's ... distancing himself from the strobing lights of law enforcement, the chaotic sound of the radio static interrupted by

calls that shots were fired ... that there was *a man down*. Away from the businesslike urgency of the paramedics who would follow, searching diligently and pragmatically for any sign of life in the body of one Roy Turgeon, and then – when none was to be found – would arrange his frame into a long slender bag and whisk it off past a steadily growing ribbon of bystanders ... curious motel guests, coffee drinkers, diner staff, truck drivers, all now clinging to the periphery of the crime scene like human tape.

Chris struggled for breath as he half ran, half lurched as far away as he could – the image of the lodge owner's limp body sagging to the ground and the sight of a wide swath of blood smearing down the wall of the motorhome urging him on. Had he actually seen that? Or was his imagination toying with him, inferring plausible graphic detail ... panic upon panic. He crossed the highway to return to his hotel by the opposite service road, even detoured further onto a few quiet residential blocks to ensure his return would be undetected. Once there he scrambled for his room key, shot right on past Ian spread-eagled across his bed and snoring at the top of his lungs, TV remote in hand. Chris grabbed his cellphone and barricaded himself in the washroom. He would have to stay quiet and calm he told himself... even though the reception at the other end, he was pretty certain, would not be likewise. As he dialed, he inched the door open slightly, just to get a peek at the clock radio beside his bandmate's head. 12:45 a.m. Barely two hours since they had finished their show. It did not seem possible.

*–Hello?*
"Mmmm? Yeah ... hello?"
*–Who's this?*
"Easy, friend. You will be looking for Bronwyn, are you?

... Hello ... are you still there?"

*–Please tell her that her father needs to speak with her.*

(rustling)

"Dad, what the hell?"

*–Bronny, listen really carefully.*

"Dad, it's bloody 6 in the morning."

*–Who's that with you?*

"None of your goddamn business."

*–Just tell me if it's someone you know.*

"What the hell?"

*–Someone you really trust.*

"Christ, Dad, you of all people?"

*–Bronwyn ... please listen, something bad has happened. We just finished a show in Saskatchewan ... in Swift Current.*

"Not my problem–"

*–Bronwyn, please–*

*(click)*

He told himself there was no possible way he would be getting any sleep that night. Actually whispered it out loud, as he caught sight of his haggard and battered self in the mirror, just before he blacked out, sliding down the wall and landing on the tile floor like a corpse in a field, his feet stretched out against the shower stall.

~

*He's in a restaurant. Or is it a bakery? A café maybe? The tables and the sides of the counter have been done in a common colour .... kind of blue-teal paint over wood. The counter-top looks like it's out of the fifties ... speckled black and white ... some sort of acrylic. On it are clear glass-covered pedestal plates housing cakes and muffins. He's sitting at a table for two beside a window. It has white curtains with an embroidered flower pattern, the sheer kind that you can see through. The road outside is quaintly close. Just the windowsill, a narrow sidewalk and the curb. Leaning further he notices white clapboard houses lining the other side of the street. There is an easy hum of occasional traffic going by. In between is the sound of a gentle breeze rustling through tree branches that seem to arch and meet like a golden-yellow canopy over the road. It must be autumn, he decides, just before his thoughts take him elsewhere ...*

*"The attitude of man is twofold in accordance with the two basic word pairs ... I-It and I-You ..." no wait ... that's not right ... I put in 'You' ... no I put in B-A. Yes that's it. I put in B-A and up pops BABIES? BAMBI? BARBIE DOLLS? I punch in I-it ... and up comes TIME BOMBS, TILLEY HATS, TITTIES ... something like that. But there was more wasn't there? Something about Pennsylvania ... about a fan getting his emails by mistake ... she ran a café too!*

*A shrill squeaky voice interrupts him.*

*"Daddy, I want a coffee."*

*"When you turn sixteen, kiddo," he hears himself say, and turns back across to face a little girl with a purple sweatshirt and faded blue jeans. She sports two long blonde pigtails that bounce when she slaps her sides and pouts.*

*"I want a donut then."*

*"You have one right in front of you—"*

*"No fair. This one's jam. I want chocolate!"*

*He always loved those pigtails, he hears himself say.*

# FIVE

The show the next night in Medicine Hat was a complete
fog. Likewise the following two in Calgary, and the one after
that in Edmonton. With Roy's execution, the threat of danger
was now a dreaded potential around every bend in the road;
behind every set of eyes that stared back at him from the audience; in every face that approached him after a concert. He
was sure it was only a matter of time, and quite correctly – for
that time, as it turned out, came once the tour headed into
British Columbia, along the Yellowhead Highway, on the outskirts of Prince George.

They had pulled into a gas station to fuel up. Ian had headed
into an adjacent truck stop to get a few snacks for himself and
his ever-more-subdued travelling partner. A man in coveralls
and a ball cap came over and grabbed the squeegee from its
reservoir.

"Thanks ... much appreciated–" Chris began.

"First rest stop south of here ... in an hour," the man said
quietly over his shoulder as he briefly feigned wiping down
the windshield. It was a voice he knew – the voice from the
pharmacy back in Minnesota. "You're gonna need a piss. Make

sure Junior there stays in the car." He jabbed the handle of the
squeegee back into Chris's hand, folded up his collar and strolled
off, hands in pockets, across the road and into a diner.

Fortunately Ian had gladly given up the wheel after gassing
up. More fortunate still was that by the time Chris pulled into
the assigned rest stop the piano player – as was often the case
on long driving days – was already head-back, mouth-wide-
open fast asleep with no signs of coming to any time soon.
Chris pulled into the car park in front of the washrooms, down
a few spots from the only other vehicle he could see: a black
sedan with dark tinted windows. The same model he had seen
in Swift Current? Maybe ... he couldn't be sure.

Very cautiously he got out and sneaked a glance into the
darkened windshield. Finding it was unoccupied, he started up
the walk towards the restrooms, pausing a moment for one last
look around the vacant grounds before pushing open the door
and disappearing inside. Like the car, the room appeared empty,
but since the presence of the former implied otherwise, he re-
solved to stay. Soon, whether through nerves or from internal-
izing his instructions to the letter, he found himself subject to
the call of nature and sidled up to the first in a row of a half-
dozen urinals. But it was only nerves, he decided, when after
several moments only a few lonely drops trickled forth ...

The door from the last stall flung open.

"Too bad about Roy, don't you think?" He knew this voice
as well. It was the man from the diner in Rainy River. He
grabbed Chris's coat collar and jammed him forward, his ribs
striking the top edge of the porcelain, his head narrowly missing
a chrome pipe above.

"Did you know he was gonna try that?"

Not wanting to divulge he had witnessed the killing, Chris

sputtered some sort of indecipherable plea of innocence. "Did you?" the diner-man screamed, seemingly with impunity. Chris imagined his partner keeping watch outside the door. Imagined how effectively he could dissuade anyone who happened by from being too curious about any shouting inside. The man's hand thrust up under Chris's jaw, lifted and spun him around, slamming his tailbone back against the top lip of the urinal.

"Answer me you little fucker! Did you know Roy called the cops?" He spewed through a clenched jaw, saliva spackling Chris's glasses and forehead. He was nothing like he had been back in Ontario. There his violence had been calculated and deliberate. Composed even. This was different. He was enraged, his face contorted and crimson as if he himself was enduring the pain of the constricting grip he had around Chris's neck.

"I didn't know ... I didn't know," Chris stammered finally. "His wife told me to meet them for a coffee." With this bit of news, the man's tension eased at least fractionally, and he extracted the songwriter from his perch and tossed him to the floor. He began pacing back and forth.

"Well, thanks to him we've had quite the motherfuckin' detour!" he said after a couple of trips across the room which actually only served to rekindle his anger. "Cost us too much time and a fuckin' shitload of money!"

He reached down and grabbed Chris again, this time sending him sprawling backwards against one of the stall doors, which gave way, leaving the musician more or less inverted with his back arched across the toilet. "Thanks to fucking Roy trying to play hero, Polly couldn't deliver the drop to you, like she was supposed to. So ... new plan, bitch! You're gonna be our little go-between all by your little fuckin' self. Expect to hear from us when you get to Vancouver."

Chris had assumed the sound of the stall door slamming had signalled the end of the encounter. But as he slowly rolled off the toilet seat onto all fours he came face to face with the barrel of a handgun aimed squarely between his nostrils. "And one more thing," the man seethed. "Stop trying to phone your daughter. I consider that tryin' to be a hero too."

*Then* he was gone, but not before one last kick to Chris's shin. Just for effect. Like a little flourish at the end of a good fiddle solo.

~

Quesnel, BC was a new low. Chris locked himself in a washroom down the hall from the dressing room the whole intermission. Pushed the hand dryer on, ran the water full, flushed the toilet over and over ... any sound to mask the screams of agony he was sure he would soon no longer be able to resist. He knew he had butchered the first half, botched all of the harmony on *Schooner* ... completely missed his entry on *Hitch Me to Your Plough*.

He had been trying to bolster himself all day ... through sound check, in his dressing room, in the wings waiting to be introduced... telling himself he had almost made it through the tour. He only had to get through a few more shows ... but now, doubled over on the bathroom vanity, he wasn't sure he could survive one more set. Hell, one more song even. And shit of all shits, if Myles hadn't finally put his managerial foot down and insisted they come back from the interval slow and powerful with *The Monument*. More high harmonies. Great. From his hunched position, he reached up to the shelf above the sink, feeling for his toiletry bag, digging inside for the now-familiar smooth cylinder. Shook out three ... swallowed ... then pulled himself upright to inspect the dull finish of his face.

"LADIES AND GENTLEMEN. PLEASE WELCOME BACK TO THE STAGE – MILL RUN!"

Christ, he was late.

He struggled out the door and back up the hall as best he could, fetched his fiddle – which he had neglected to retune – from the dressing room along the way. Hobbled up the back-stage steps. Too fast. His back began seizing again, so he grabbed a chair from behind the stage manager, and avoiding the incredulous looks from his bandmates, dragged it out onto the stage. He could feel their eyes burning into him but could not, for the life of him, summon the energy to care. He would come up with some rationale later on, he told himself. That he was going for a homey, sit-down kitchen-party feel ... something like that. But even as he tried to sort it out, his focus waned ... his mind wandered.

Dan leaned into the microphone. "We're gonna start out with an old favourite of ours ..."

*So strange. It feels like he's back in the station wagon. Back there, but still sitting on stage too. Like he's both places. Or is it neither? He's knows he's not asleep, but feels himself dreaming. Dreaming about that old car. And just like all those early-years drives, he's at the wheel with Dan passenger-side, plucking away at a guitar, singing ... laughing ...*

"...this is called *The Monument*." There is a ripple of antici-patorial applause as Myles begins strumming the opening chords.

*"See?" Dan smiles over. "Just a bit more focus. That's all you need." Chris looks out his side window ... toward the*

*wings. It's the Lunenburg road again, now all framed by straight black stage curtains, lit up like a summer's day by the racks of stagelights overhead. They shimmer so strongly he has to squint; has to put his hands up over his eyes. "No, I still can't see," he tries to cry out, but can't find the words. Something has distracted him ...*

Shit! He came in too early. Looked down across the bridge of his instrument, watching the bow seemingly play of its own accord. Again he could feel his bandmates' wrath – Myles having actually spun right around to aim the neck of his guitar directly at him, all but conducting the chord changes to get him back in time with Dan's vocal. As the first chorus approached he laboured to stand and lean towards the mic, hoping that some sort of muscle memory in his throat and his lungs might kick in and offer something acceptable.

*(...'til the cold and the pain are gone ...)*

Even Ian was looking over now, studying him.

*(... and there's warmth once again in the dawn ...)*

*"No, you're OK," Dan says again from his side of the car. "You're just fine!" And for a moment he feels comforted by the smile on his friend's face ... Dan's not mad at me, he tells himself. He's not mad at me at all.*

*(...'til you hold what's left of my soul in*
*the glow of the prairie sun)*

# Six

Their room phone rang a mere half-hour after they checked into a mom-and-pop motel out to the east of the downtown Vancouver skyline. Chris answered and the voice on the other end instructed him to head for the harbour at midnight. McGill Street to Commissioner Street. Follow it all the way down to the furthest set of rail tracks until coming to a line of four railway freight containers beside the nearest set of tracks. Each would have a fluorescent X spray-painted on the top right corner that faced away from the road. He was to wait there, out of sight behind the furthest of the four.

Chris went ahead and ordered in Chinese takeout for the both of them, then pointedly shuffled through the room's movie channels to find something that would have Ian fully engrossed; something in either the fantasy or medieval realm, or a combination of the two ... stone castles with long torch-lit hallways, swordplay, warrior-damsels, (boobs and beheadings, Chris used to tease), so often the stuff of the piano player's cinematic taste on so many a down night on the road; so often too the catalyst for his frequent bouts of quasi-narcolepsy. (*Hey Ian, seen the first ten minutes of any good movies lately?*)

Two hours later it was mission accomplished. Chris grabbed his jacket, consulted the Vancouver inset of the BC road map, and headed out the door.

It was dark where the containers sat; almost too dark to make out the bright paint markings that confirmed he was in the right place. Moreover, once his eyes adjusted, he quickly realized that these boxes were but four of dozens, if not hundreds, of such containers all sitting idly in what seemed to be a defunct section of the dockyard. Some up on flat beds, others lined up in rows further down the rails. Countless more still, stacked and waiting much further away, down where the docks seemed more active; closer to the vague but formidable grey outlines of the monstrous transport cranes and moored tankers – both ready to pluck them up, swallow them whole and cart them off to parts unknown.

Suddenly he felt very cold. He stooped down to kneel out of the wind but, with his shaky health, momentarily lost his balance and fell back against the first of the four marked containers. His elbow caused its hollow cavity to echo like a kettledrum. But there was something else. As the reverberation settled, he could have sworn he heard voices ... distant from somewhere down past him, like momentary whispers, there and then gone, eaten up by the passing traffic and gusts of harbour breeze. He stood again and edged his way in what he thought had been their direction. Edged down around the corner of the last container. He found nothing. He was contemplating whether to creep further and inspect around the opposite side, when another metallic boom rumbled briefly, this one not of his doing. This version was more muffled. Quick and less resonant. He stepped out of the shadows and jumped around the corner. But once again there was nothing.

For a moment he wondered if it was all merely the work of nerves and imagination, but then ... yes definitely more drumming sounds. This time an undeniable tapping – dull and deadened – almost right next to his ear. Then, very faintly, a voice. And another ... coming from inside the container. Instinctively he put out the palms of his hands, and spread them across the outer wall.

"You're in the wrong spot, Mr. Lucan."

He wheeled around and his jaw fell open. "You're–"

"I'm Mrs. Polly Turgeon as far as yer concerned." Half a dozen men appeared from the shadows behind her, each dressed in a hard hat and coveralls. There was a faint squeak of brakes up at the road, and for a moment they all stopped to observe a delivery truck creep to a gentle stop, lights off.

"OK," one of the men called out quietly and half of them disappeared into the night. Polly started out too, albeit at a much slower, deliberate pace. "Actually," she called back, "poor old Roy'd been widowed for ten years or more ... ain't that right?" she added, a little bit louder, slapping at the last container on her way by. "Do your thing, Nick. But remember, same rules ... we're gonna need him goin' forward."

Before he could turn around Chris was grabbed by the scruff of his parka and thrown to the ground. A boot landed squarely between his shoulder blades and he squeezed his eyes shut to await whatever blow was to follow. Nick leaned forward and pressed his knee into the songwriter's spine.

"Got another package for you. The one you were supposed to get in Swift Current." A plain brown package wrapped tightly with an overabundance of tape landed on the ground in front of Chris's face. "You don't fuckin' open it. You don't fuckin' show it to nobody. You just hang on to it 'til we find you and tell you what to do with it. You fuckin' got that?"

He tried his best to nod.

"Might be a week. Might be a goddamn motherfuckin' month. You don't fucking know. You just keep the fucking thing safe, 'cause if anything happens to it ... you, me, that daughter of yours, your band. All fucking dead!'"

Was it strange that such a pivotal moment could spring from such a vulnerable position? Strange that the face of ultimate desperation needed to put in an appearance before a turning point could take place? These were questions that in the coming days and weeks Chris would ponder, once he determined that the impetus for his solution had indeed first arrived in the seconds he lay flat on his stomach pinned to the ground with his very life – and the lives of all whom he cared about – being threatened. And it was not just because Nick had curiously confessed that his own fate was somehow wrapped up in the success of whatever task the songwriter was being forced to complete. No, upon reflection, Chris would come to realize it had been something far more simple and subtle that had startled him into action. Something, in fact, right in front of his nose ... just past the dropped parcel and out beyond the heel of his assailant's boot.

He had begun to take in the activity at the truck, trailer doors swinging open ... flashlight beams dancing about ... and voices ... some slow and angry, others quick and pleading. Women's voices? ... No more like girls'. High-pitched, frightened. His imagination flashed with wide-eyed stares, hands and arms clinging to one another in fear. Then his eyes took over, making out the undersized frames stumbling and trotting to keep pace with the men who shoved them forward and ignored their cries.

Then from behind him, much closer – the sound of the compartment door creaking open. Into his view came another line of women, also slight and thin, just as terrified. Their pleas more distinct ... some in English, though with a particular cadence ... First Nations he wondered? Others begged in a foreign tongue. Something eastern European. Russian or Ukrainian? The man in charge shoved at their midst, telling one to shut up, grabbing another by the hair, pulling her back against him, his free hand thrust under her shirt then between her legs. She winced but dared not make a sound. After holding her there and whispering something in her ear, he pushed her back with the rest of the line.

"Get moving," he hissed at the group as a whole. "Beats the hell outa the Motherland eh? ... you and yer filthy whore mothers lettin' some smelly old uncle fuck you for free? ... well, except you – right, sweetheart?" He reached up and pulled back the last in line.

Why was she different Chris wondered? Was it just that she was dressed differently? The others all in wool sweaters, dresses, long boots. She with a faded team jacket ... softball maybe? There was a crest on the shoulder and a team sponsor's name across the back but it was too dark to read.

"I said right?" the man repeated and kicked her back towards the others.

"Right ..." she mumbled, and for a split second her eyes found Chris there on the ground. Instantly – with one lifeless glimpse – the scripted details of her coat ceased to matter. Because suddenly it was undeniably clear. And even had Nick in an unprecedented fit of benevolence released his foothold and allowed Chris to rise and examine the girl's clothing, even let him ask her questions about her life, her family, her past – it would have only served to confirm what had just been revealed to a degree beyond doubt. About her ... about her and her quiet little hometown in northern Ontario, with its river and bridge, its arena-slash-community centre; its quiet little store-fronts and everyday folk, the unassuming little motel just down a block from an unassuming little restaurant, where a man who ran a nearby hunt camp – a family man – used to go for his morning coffee when he was in town running errands. The same man whom Chris had once accused – in that same restaurant – of sacrificing a stranger's health and safety merely for the sake of that hunt camp; a man whose dead-eyed stare Chris should have seen as a sign of a price far more severe. The same man whose rash attempt to end the pain and suffering had cost him his own life in a cold dark prairie field; the man whose last words in that restaurant Chris only now recalled ... words mumbled weakly as the songwriter had bolted from the table, scattering plates and cutlery ... and a pile of photos in his wake.

*They got mine too.*

# SEVEN

*Yes ... this is a message for Bronwyn Lucan from her father, Christopher Lucan. I will be sending some emails through this office for Bronwyn over the next month or two. For reasons of privacy I ask that you please forward these to my daughter unread. It is also of utmost importance for my daughter's safety that you do not inform anyone other than Bronwyn of this upcoming correspondence.*

*Chris Lucan*

# EIGHT

It would be the next day before he would start in on all the contingencies ... googling *London By the Month*; finding the website, the staff directory, the number of one Claire Baker-Young, assistant to (among others) Ms Bronwyn Lucan; borrowing some random tourist's cellphone ... someone who would be OK with him making an overseas call (he would reimburse, he promised). At some point he would *make a point* of calling a band meeting for the way home and make the necessary announcements. And he would need to come up with excuses for Ian to complete the necessary stops along the way home ... a meal here ... a coffee there ...

But really these were all just details after the fact; the means of getting done what he now knew he had to get done even then, as he had lain there with gravel digging into his cheek. As he limped back up Commissioner Street and tiptoed back into his motel room, carefully hiding the brown-paper package in the bottom compartment of his suitcase, before easing his weary body down to sit on the side of the bed.

Finally he had found it. He had discovered a way to get out in front of the pain. He had found his plan.

He would make use of the only true weapon he really possessed. The one thing to which his tormentors would surely have neglected to give any credence whatsoever. With a grimace he reached into his coat pocket and pulled out a small coil-ring notepad.

~

Hours later when sleep finally came, for the first night since Rainy River he dreamed not out of delirium, but from resolve. Not scattered flashes of memories past, but a vibrant intriguing panorama; congruently rich in both empowerment and fatalism.

*The band is set up on a beach facing the lapping water. The sun, setting in front of them, is threatened by a massive cloud line that looms on the horizon. The four of them have formed a line across the front of the stage peering out at the crowd that has gathered to hear them play.*

*Suddenly there's a blinding flash and a crack of thunder. The sky blackens. The water below begins to churn and froth, but not from the pending storm. Six gigantic smoke stacks have risen from the depths like a legion of metallic kraken to tower over the shoreline. The audience is in terror. Parents grab for their children. Loved ones wrap themselves in one another, lest only one of them be spared. 'Where did that come from?' he hears someone cry. 'How have we not seen them before?' from someone else.*

*The rest of the band jumps from the stage, imploring Chris to do likewise. Bolts of lightning shoot to and from the tops of the reactors and then to the ground, as if aiming at specific targets. As if feeding off the mayhem. Sound and light crews abandon their equipment and scramble to save themselves, jumping from rigs and scaffolding. They too scream for Chris to take cover, plead with him to recognize the scale of the danger. 'It's all going to blow,' he hears one of them shout as he races vainly for some dunes. 'IT'S TOO CLOSE.'*

*Chris takes a deep breath. Reaches down and plugs in his fiddle, then walks to his effects board and dials in maximum signal. He points his bow towards the stacks, then strikes down on his strings, just as the thunderous explosion hits and a ball of light blinds the sky.*

# THE BRIDGE

*Though strictly speaking not part of the traditional folk ballad, more and more the inclusion of a third element, complete with its own separate musical and lyrical cadence, has become commonplace in contemporary acoustic songwriting. This is due, in no small measure, to the influences of popular music on the folk genre. And although the purists, to whom I must maintain at least some degree of allegiance, would argue the bridge (sometimes referred to as the 'middle eight') does not belong in a discussion of orthodox folk song architecture, this scholar – begrudgingly– must not be so foolish as to ignore the march of time.*

**~Chetwynd C. Lovett**
*The Orthodoxy of Folk Song*

# ONE

She was already running late when her laptop chimed the announcement of incoming email. She quickly pulled it from her satchel, flipped it open and hit the message browser, even though– checked her watch – shit, it was later than she thought. And her keys. Where the hell were her keys? Hadn't she just had them in her hand? Fished them out from between the microwave and the toaster?

Clearly she would have to stop this, she told herself yet again. Quit thinking she and Keegan could close *The Spoke* and still make it out the door in time for work the next day – even in her current incarnation, nursing soda water and limes all night long. But when your best friend rings you up and needs you ... well, there was an obligation there, wasn't there? Always would be where Keegan was concerned. Because really ... hadn't she been the one who had been there in the darkest hours? Out of the blue, her one and only true friend. The one person outside of therapy who knew the entire unadulterated (and adulterated) story, warts and all. So if she needed to knock back a few pints and vent about how Ivan was resorting to the same controlling jealous bullshit that her ex, Jack, had pulled

154 — A Song With No Words

on her last year ... and Martin before him ... well, even if it was not an evening Bronwyn ever looked forward to, she would be there.

Dr. Emma was intrigued whenever Keegan's name came up in session.

"Perhaps emotionally you aren't the heterosexual you think you are, Bronwyn," she had suggested one day, surprising her patient by assigning her orientation to something less than hardwiring.

"No, let me be clear. All I mean is perhaps your previous life path has taken you places where intimacy simply had to be severed from all other aspects of sex."

Perhaps. Theirs had always been a bit of a vague association, she and Keegan. They could fall asleep spooning in front of the telly with limbs entangled, probably far more comfortably than with any bloke. And sure, she had been on the receiving end of a couple of alcohol-aided public displays of affection at the pub – but that had just been a lark, hadn't it? And if the good doctor thought the relationship needed any deeper defining, it would begin and end with the fact that Keegan was the closest thing to a pure confidant Bronwyn had ever known; that her friend's view of her life was seen, and still accepted, through the widest possible lens.

Yes, her mom had been instrumental in recovery once the ball was rolling with the promise of finishing school, and the hint of possible journalism work just over the horizon. She had been the be-all of encouragement in those areas in fact, with her resumé edits, her ideas for business cards, pep talks and office-fashion advice. But early on, when darkest delving was the order of the day ... well, all of that involved details no daughter needed paraded in front of a parent, right? A year and a half on the street. Eight months of that fully in the trade. The drugs. Yes, Mom and Dr. Emma would eventually be there to work through it all, but it was Keegan who had found her that lowest of nights, passed out in her own vomit, bleeding from the nose, eyes swollen shut from the force of some unknown's blows. This modern-day Samaritan, happening by. She who had not only called for help, but had followed up, visiting Bronwyn every day in the hospital in the weeks to come. Investing in her welfare. She who had made it a complete priority to care in a way and to a degree that no one else had ever managed, and for no other reason than the feeling she had from the start that they both could use a good mate. So Bronwyn had vowed she would always make time for her unsolicited friend. That she would always try her absolute damnedest to care just as hard right back.

And really, Bronwyn had to admit, the night had been quite lovely. Or started out that way at least – until Keegan decided she was being completely stupid about Ivan. That she was guilty of inferring the sins of boyfriends past on her current situation ... that she was worrying over *fuckin' nothing*. By her second pint, she had called him to let him know where they were ... if he wanted to come around and meet up for a drink ... no pressure ... and sorry about the shitty email the night before ... she didn't really mean it, so everything was OK between them with her, if it was with him. Sure enough, Ivan was there in twenty minutes, his mate Peter in tow.

Peter.

Christ, it had seemed like a good idea at the time. What was it? Two months ago now since he had first tagged along? Two months since she had first relented and given in to him like the compulsion to answer the chime of a text message as soon as it rings ... given in to the power of possibility associated with the sound. Of something kinetically more exciting than the silence that had preceded it ... the go-ahead for a new story ... a promotion ... the unknown. (Yes, therapy had not been without its insights.)

In all honesty, he *had* persevered admirably in making small talk and dodging Bronwyn's sardonic jabs. Her curt, *"that's fascinating, but I don't remember asking"*, delivered with eyes opened mockingly wide, peering over the rim of her pint glass, all in response to his *"You will probably be hearing my accent. My mother and father came from Poland, but we moved here in England when I was a boy ... to Boston, in Lincolnshire."* It was a perseverance – assisted, of course, by a set of muscular shoulders and piercing blue eyes – that soon carried the evening. In short order despite her frosty barbs she had found her free hand resting flat on his chest as she let him talk; let him say the things he thought he had to say for the evening to proceed. (*"I am living with a friend and his family now, but if your place is close ...?"*) Bronwyn had all but dragged him out by the hair that very first night. A bit of eye candy, severed-from-intimacy company, thank you very much. A good sturdy shag and nothing else. But then – shit of all shits – of all the blokes in all the pubs in Greater London that night, she goes and picks up the one who actually couldn't see the appeal of the arrangement. Phone calls. Texts and emails at work. He can't stop thinking about her. How about tonight? What about next weekend? ... Bloody shoulders.

Her coat!

She suddenly remembered she had already dropped the keys in her coat pocket ... if she could *now* just pinpoint where the hell she put *that*? Checked her watch. Shit, she should be in a cab right now ... so a coat would be nice. And not just any coat

... the one she and her mom had picked out at the little shop in Notting Hill her last time over. The one that always came through on story pitch days. The one she had, just one goddamn moment ago, dropped her keys into. Shit!

Not in the living room-slash-kitchen – all fourteen-by-fourteen feet of it. (Enough for a futon and chair, a TV and a table for one.) Not in the bedroom either. (Converted closet would be more accurate. Still, so much better than the days of bunking on the chesterfields of friends – and friends of friends – as she freelanced her way around the UK, chasing down contract jobs; certainly better than her four-to-a-room digs back in rehab.)

For a moment her thoughts bounced between memories of that austere accommodation and her current bedroom, her mind's eye lingering more on the latter, watching disembodied as she pulsated beneath his shoulders, her hands all over his face and his hair. It wasn't the first time such a juxtaposition had infiltrated her thoughts. Nor the first time she found herself wondering what, if anything, one setting had to do with the other. She shook her head and resumed the search, cursing and swearing in equal measure, the gods of punctuality and the City of London's untenable level of bustle. Behind the sofa ... no. Under the table ... no. Her eye fell on the pile of instrument cases, stacked as unimposing as possible against the wall between the front entrance and the door to the loo. She'd need to get those sorted sometime soon. Get in contact with someone. Dan probably. Get an address and arrange for their shipment. She had held on to them as per his request. Quite the dramatic little keepsakes; thanks for that, Dad, she thought, and for a moment was lost again.

Her father had passed away and it had barely hit her, even after three weeks of dodging his band's luggage. In fact, if anything the freight was in danger of merely becoming part of

158 — A Song With No Words

the accepted clutter of the place. No more an imposition than the burned-out bulb over the kitchen sink, the missing tiles in her shower stall. She shuffled the cases around, checking behind and between. Again an uninvited image flashed, just as she was lifting her father's violin. She and Peter dozing in her bed, her phone ringing ...

Finally it came to her. In the bathroom. Hurdling the instruments and bending around the door frame, she grabbed her coat from the top of the vanity, instinctively using the moment to check herself one more time in the mirror, even as her feet began to pedal for the door, her toe stubbing on Dan's guitar case, which in turn felled a mandolin, and a banjo. "Fuck!" She kicked the cases back against the wall, donned the coat, grabbed her laptop and flew out the door.

Much of the cab ride was spent subconsciously tapping her foot and playing with her watchband, especially when traffic slowed to its inevitable crawl. At one point she wondered if she had – after all that time wasted looking for her keys – actually remembered to lock her door. This, for some reason, reminded her that she had also forgotten to check the email that had come in just as she was getting ready to leave. Then just a few blocks from the office, just as she was confident she had successfully gathered her thoughts – had put her *game face* on – the image returned once more. Two sweaty bodies strewn together ... one fast asleep, the other reaching for the phone to take her father's call. *"Damn it, Bronwyn, focus."*

# Two

It was possibly the dullest morning he had ever laid eyes on. A pounding rain had turned the gentle slope of the street outside into a steady river, its current picking up speed as it flowed toward the culvert just outside the café window where he had sat for the past three days. He stared at his computer screen, through the hot steam floating from the rim of an oversized mug of coffee. Stared at the message telling him another email had arrived from the Innes Bakery of Ridgway, Pennsylvania. This one – like the one that had arrived the day of Chris's funeral – was marked *urgent* in the subject line. This, paradoxically, had given Ian pause. He took a moment to peer around the room, past the vacant tables to the only other patrons, a little old couple silently sipping their ... (was that stew? In the middle of the morning? A porridge maybe?) He assumed they were local by the way they paid him absolutely no acknowledgement. Surely residents would find nothing novel about a foreigner in their midst – a Canadian especially – what with the Monument that shared their village's name right down the road; the steady stream of proud pilgrimages over the years ... soldiers, then veterans, then the offspring of veterans. The sight of one more *Canuck*, with his feeble tenth-grade powers of Core French, would be business as usual – just another day in Vimy. And yet, unlike all his compatriots who had preceded him, he had so far – despite its proximity – failed to actually make the trip out to the site itself. Tomorrow maybe, he had told himself when he had got up that morning and gazed out into the downpour.

He peered around the room again. Of course nothing had changed in the trio of mornings he had sat there alone. The polished wood of the unoccupied chairs, the drape of the table-cloths gently creased at the corners of the tables under which those chairs kept a home. The singsong staff working away to prepare food for a public he had yet to see. Was it the weather? Did Vimy have an off-season? He grabbed a newspaper left on a neighbouring table, leafed through its pages with pointless haste, a few French phrases here and there sticking, mainly in the sports section – football scores, and golfing results requiring relatively little command of the language – until at length he could resist no more and clicked open the email. There was a brief explanation from the bakery. It explained that Chris had sent them this note along with the first, but asked them to forward it only if they hadn't heard from anyone else in the band after a few weeks. Then Chris's own brief words ...

*... Please don't forget our last chat.*
*About a story inside a story ...*
*... and Bronwyn too. Please make sure she's OK.*

Had Ian still been at home – as had been the case with the dozens of rereadings of Chris's first 'posthumous' message – it would have occasioned an extreme restlessness, followed by a series of menial tasks undertaken in the hope they might subdue said restlessness. A check through other emails. Then Face-book. The previous night's sports scores (in English!). Maybe a walk to the corner store. Maybe the coffee shop. Then back home. A load of laundry. Sweeping. Dusting ... (when had he otherwise ever cared about dusting?) ... recycling ... dishes ... until inevitably, with all possible distractions exhausted, he would be forced either to return to his computer to stare down the note head-on, or else simply pace the apartment, unable to sleep or eat; to play the piano, or look for work. Unable to do what his mother and father, a cousin, and that cousin's husband had all lately, and with varying degrees of tact, suggested – *just get on with things.*

~

The idea for the trip had struck him out of nowhere, but with an overwhelming degree of conviction. Perhaps because so many of his memories of Chris involved their time spent on the road, the idea of stuffing a change of clothes in a backpack and getting out of town carried some sense of homage. Because, in the end, it was actually the manner in which the two of them had gone to their gigs, more than the gigs themselves, that Ian found himself missing most.

~

*"... so there's this Christian mystic out in New Mexico. Diego Delgado. He runs this commune-slash-farmers' market and hosts a lecture series in his yurt. Anyway, he wrote a piece last month for a journal I get, that was all about the failure of religion."*

*Ian's behind the wheel. They're heading west across the up-*

*per peninsula of Michigan. It's morning. There is blue sky and lots of time. All day to get across the top of Wisconsin and over to Duluth for their evening show.*

*"Which religion?"*

*"Well, he cites his own Christian tradition primarily, but he does reference others. Islam, Judaism. Anything with a canon of written text considered sacred and essential to its particular faith."*

*"I am guessing that's where the failure comes in?"*

*"Yes, full points, Mr. Station. In his view, the failure is a result of a means-and-ends mix-up."*

*"I'll need more."*

*"Well, according to Señor Delgado, the Divine Word-of-God claim has continually been put at the wrong end of the stick, and it's a mistake that is inevitable because religions insist on basing their orthodoxy on a closed canon."*

*There is a mile or two of silence, then, "OK once again—"*

*"You'll need more, right. OK it's like this. Religions set their particular scriptures to be absolute. Therefore all that is sacred has to answer to those texts, no matter how ancient and removed they might be from an adherent's current setting."*

*Ian squints from the morning sun reflecting in his rear view. "Well, Grandma Station always said, just read your Bible and let it speak to you."*

*"And what a wise soul Grandma Station was—"*

*"Please don't mock my Gam-gams."*

*"No I mean it. Delgado would say she has it exactly. Except ... according to him ... the sacred part doesn't lie in the words of some ancient text itself, as much as it does in the act of reading them and the act of searching for that personal meaning. So if that's the case, confining yourself to only a small group of scriptures actually denies you of the chance to evolve spiritually."*

*"Well, this is fantastic news! Do you want to call Myles or should I"*

*"Now who's mocking who?"*

*"No, seriously, he'll be pissed if you keep this from him."*

*A half-hour later, they pull into a small diner.*

*"So I've been trying it," Chris states, picking up the conversation as they sit down at the counter.*

*"Trying what?"*

*"Reading with the intent of sacred direction," he replies and flips over his coffee mug for the waitress passing by. She stops, pours, and, not quite stifling a look of suspicion, drops a couple of menus in front of them.*

*"I am one hundred percent serious. I spent the last few weeks reading–"*

*"You're always reading–"*

*"No, let me finish. Every morning I've gone down to the library and just wandered through the stacks. Not even concerning myself with what section I was in or anything. Just running a hand along the spines, trying to tap into the force of spiritual serendipity, if you will. Just letting it more or less guide me ... oh, I'll have the chowder."*

*The waitress aims an eye at Ian.*

*"Ham and cheese on rye with a bit of mustard."*

*"I'm telling you there was something to it. I merely waited for a feeling, I guess you could say. More like a calm really. A quiet in the mind. Then I just grabbed whatever book my hand was touching, took it out, opened up to a random page, and tried to absorb whatever it had to say."*

*"And you did this because ..."*

*"I did this because according to Delgado, if I predispose myself to being radically open to enlightenment, then there is*

*no such thing as randomness. There is only the opportunity for meaning ..."*

*"No matter what you are leafing through?"*

*"No matter. From that page's 'there' to my 'now'. Because if the Divine is truly an everywhere, anytime phenomenon it shouldn't just be in so-called Scripture. It should be just as present in a book on gardening, or travel, or–"*

*"Motorcycle repair?"*

*"Very nice, yes ... thank you, that looks delicious."*

*The woman slides the soup bowl straight-armed under Chris's chin. Without taking her eyes off him, she rips his bill from her pad and slaps it alongside.*

*Ian leans towards her. "He's a very strange man," he says with a nod, and she leaves without a word.*

*"Or think of it this way," Chris continues between slurps. "Think of it merely as the possibility of some alternate form of being."*

*"Being?"*

*"No ... not a Capital B existential thing ... not exactly anyway. I mean 'being' as in living, and acting. A way that's separate from the straightforward 'see-problem-fix-problem' way of doing things."*

*Ian shoots a look that in his heart he hopes will mimic that of the waitress.*

*"OK that's not it exactly, but trust me, this stuff doesn't sound so crazy once you acknowledge the possibility of other modes for making sense of the world around you."*

*"Alright ...But you're not just talking 'world around you' ... you're using words like divine and sacred ... and by the way, you've got some chowder in your beard."*

*"Ah that's not just chowder my friend. That's a little piece of heaven."*

~

It had been such a good day. Later that afternoon, halfway between Ashland, Wisconsin and the Minnesota border, Chris had bounced to attention from what Ian had misconstrued was a nap, and with profound shouts of thanksgiving to the writings of one Diego Delgado, and with a passing nod to a collection of Oscar Wilde short stories he had *randomly* perused a week or two before (the importance of which Ian never quite gleaned) announced he had finally figured out the proper angle of a song he had been stuck on for months; a fresh take on the hell that was the battle of Vimy Ridge. And so were sown the seeds for *The Monument*, Mill Run's seminal tribute to a soldier's trench-life experience, and the song that would sponsor what had been planned to be the band's last performance, at the very foot of the Vimy Memorial itself.

So why not go? Why not exercise the muscle of those alternative means of being? Why not put Chris's words into action, and just *be* there? Open to the possibilities that his friend had strived to impart. After all, who was to say this wasn't the answer to his grief? Right there, ready to be *received*.

Perhaps it was like the savants of the world, he told himself – once the sober second thoughts had tried their best to creep in (sneaking up unexpectedly and tapping his shoulder as he cancelled piano lessons, suspended his newspaper delivery, watched his credit card balance start to soar ... airfare, a train, a room booked for a week in the town). The savants with their well-documented powers of mathematics and memory; whose exploits obviously owed to an ability to see the world in patterns that were completely beyond the rest of the supposedly able-minded world ... whose superimposed mental grids plotted and graphed out calculation after calculation so swiftly and effortlessly. Maybe his friend had found a similar kind of grid, this one stretched over the landscape of creative empathy. One that Ian could honour by going to the place Chris's imagination had seen glimmering so clearly all the way from the westbound lane of a Wisconsin highway. Why not? When the alternative was nothing more than a losing battle to try to forget ... when the alternative was *just getting on with things,* why not? Why the fuck not?

~

"So you are still with us?"

"Excuse me ... um *pardon*?"

"No, please, in English is good." The waitress tossed the towel she was holding over her shoulder, pulled out a chair and sat down opposite him. "I am Sophie," she said, and held out her other hand for him.

"Ian."

"Ian ... it is nice to meet you, Ian. This is ... how many? Three days? And finally you can say hello to me?" She leaned forward and dropped her elbow on the table, her chin into the palm of her hand. A wisp of her hair – dirty blonde – fell from her head over her eye.

"Yes. I guess so ... I mean, three days, yes."

"It is a quiet place now, no? I was thinking you Canadians would all come in the spring. You should have seen our little café then. We were full of your country. Always buses and cars to the Monument and back ..."

"I had planned to be here," Ian replied, as he mulled over how the little town might be the only place where a North

American traveller might be presumed Canadian.

"Yes? Oh you should have come. It was so beautiful seeing the old men and the soldiers. Laughing and crying and telling stories. And there was music and concerts." Her hand dropped from her chin and landed on his.

"Actually my band was supposed to play then." (Yes, he had said it ... *my* band.) "We were called *Mill Run* and we performed a song about Vimy that was popular back home ... unfortunately one of our band members–"

"Wait! You say your band is ... is called what?"

"*Mill Run.*"

"*Mill Run ... Mill Run ...*" She stared into space, drumming her fingers across the back of his hand, then suddenly jumped to attention and skipped back behind a counter to rummage through some stacks of paper stubs and receipts. Peered around the till. Below the bar. On the shelves behind her. There was a piece of paper, she explained. A note she thought she had set aside for keeping, left from a group of young men who said they had come over from England to hear their favourite folk group play for the Vimy Anniversary. And they had been so nice, she said, although by their accents they hadn't really sounded *Anglais* ... Russian *peut-être* or Polish?

"*Où est- il ... où est il?*" she mumbled as she searched, then with a snap of her finger: "*Ha, je me souviens. Attendez.* I will be back very, very soon."

There had been a fortuitous timing to the events of that rainy day. Had the paper she sought been at her immediate disposal, Ian would not have had the rest of the morning and even a fair chunk of the afternoon at his disposal to return his attention to the computer screen. As it was, he was able – thanks, perhaps, to a bit of confidence gained from the lingering hand of a young

French woman – to sink himself into the task of making sense of the curious email left for him by his now-deceased friend. Otherwise he would not have been afforded the time to surf the Internet for ... (what was the magazine called again? *London Calling? London Weekly?* Chris had mentioned it only once or twice, but Ian was pretty certain the city's name was in the title). Certainly there would not have been the opportunity to scour the publication's website with its directory of contacts, then search through the considerable list of hits that had come up in response to a general web search for *Bronwyn Lucan: London magazines*, many of which seemed to be opinions and reactions to a recent article she had written on immigration scams in the UK.

*Dear Bronwyn – my name is Ian Station.*
*I was a member of Mill Run and a friend of your father ...*

Because, as it turned out, Sophie would not be the few moments she had initially promised, but actually two hours or more, searching on and off, in and around her regular café duties, periodically checking in with Ian, telling him how sad these men had looked, having come all that way only to find their favourite group not here.

"I know we are not Canadian," one had said to her. "But they sing songs about immigrants and missing home, so we understand."

So of course she said yes when they asked if they could leave the leader of the band a letter, the one who wrote the beautiful songs. Just in case they had made a mistake reading the schedule. Just in case the band called *Mill Run* arrived later in the week ... *plus tard*. And if so, maybe they could leave her a phone number and she could call them and they could speak to the band ... maybe even come back over from England right away and hear them sing.

In the interim not only had the piano player already typed, edited and retyped his introductory email to Chris's daughter, he had also received its short and terse reply, then clicked on another email marked *urgent* that had just arrived from Myles. Apparently Ian's apartment had been broken into and ransacked the day before. When his landlord and the police couldn't track him down, the latter had got in touch with Myles through the Mill Run website, so they could confirm he was safe and hadn't been the victim of any foul play.

In fact, by the time Sophie squealed triumphantly and raced back into the dining room with paper held high, she could find no trace of her Canadian patron at all. He, his computer ... the luggage in his room upstairs, were all gone.

# THREE

Her assistant, Claire, had assumed she was already in the building and had seen the email rescheduling the pitch meeting back to 2 p.m. Bronwyn's profanity-spiced response, however, proved otherwise.

"I'm sorry. I don't mean to jump down your throat." She tossed her belongings onto the desk and fished out the laptop. "Damn it, I even heard that email come in just as I was heading out the door ... I should have–"

Claire was quite familiar with her boss's penchant for half-sentences, and had long since worked out the time frame in which she could reasonably expect a completion. As a rule, if after sixty seconds, give or take, there had been no return to the clause dangling at large, it was safe to assume Ms. Lucan had permanently moved on to some other superseding matter in her mind. In this case, that *matter* was the realization that the email she had neglected to read at home was not actually about her rescheduled meeting. Was not, in fact, about work at all.

*Dear Bronwyn.*

*My name is Ian Station ... I was a member of Mill Run and a friend of your father for the last few years. Your dad left me a note shortly before he died, asking me to keep an eye out for you. His words – not mine. As we have never met, I haven't felt comfortable before now about making contact. But at the same time I wanted to honour his wishes, strange as this must seem from your end of things.*

*You should know your father's songs continue to inspire and soothe folks from all over the world. Right now I am sitting in a café in Vimy, France where we were scheduled to play before his accident. My own attempt at some sort of closure, I guess. And even this morning, so far from home in this little restaurant, the staff told me about a number of men who had come down from England for the Vimy Anniversary just to hear us play. And not even normal folk club regulars. By the sound of it they were actually recent immigrants from eastern Europe who nevertheless had become big fans of Mill Run and were greatly affected by your dad's music. In fact, as I write this, I'm waiting for the waitress to locate their contact info. I think she is hoping I will give them a call ... tell them a bit more about the band and your dad ... apparently they asked about him specifically.*

Claire turned for her desk.

"Since we're not meeting right away ..." Bronwyn finally spoke up just under the wire, glancing up at the clock on the wall. Just a few moments to herself, that's all she needed.

"Ten minutes?" the assistant suggested.

"Make it twenty?"

Claire nodded, and pulled the door closed behind her.

Bronwyn stared back at the email, shook her head and slammed the screen closed. She had no time for this crap. Not now. She leaned back and squeezed her eyes shut. Took a deep breath and tried going over the opening sentences of her article proposal. Then rehearsed the replies to the questions she anticipated would be fired at her. But the script wouldn't come. Some days were still like that. The monsters of the past – usually so effectively compartmentalized and filed away from the business of the day – could rear their ugly heads, given the right trigger. Make her small. Exposed. Make her feel like the impostor. Make her feel the way she had right back on her very first day two and a half years before, when those first bullets of unforgiving editorial blue ink crash-landed on her desk not three hours after she had started. *Sophomoric ... Provincial.* Not *could use a different description here ...* or even *not in the lexicon of our readership.* Just point-blank value judgements attributed seemingly to her country of origin. But that was Higgins, the fucking bane of her probationary existence those first six months. *It's hard to put a finger on it, Ms. Lucan ... your copy just tends to try too hard, that's all.* And yet somehow by the end of those six months she had, for all intents and purposes, passed Mr. Thurman Edward Higgins's bylines on the food chain, moving – in short order – from the society back pages over to features, first as an assistant ... then as assignment writer. One of a half-dozen they kept on staff to vie for three or four spots every edition. (*Take that, you pompous little twat*). Nevertheless there was still residue from those first challenging weeks when she had dutifully fought to wow one and all with the best damn photo-inset copy journalism had ever seen.

Yes, some days were always just going to be hard. Wasn't that therapy's take-away? Two steps, forward, same steps back? But Christ, why did one of those days have to be a pitch day? And not just any pitch. *The Pitch.* The story she wanted more than anything she had ever written before. Her previous exposé on illegal immigration had garnered so much attention. From government, from Scotland Yard. So much feedback on social media, on blogs and radio chat shows. And debate! Right-wing blowhards lauding the piece for cementing their concerns over the influx of Eastern Europeans into the country. Counter-arguments lamenting how only the simplest of minds could take the case of one set of criminal activities and assign it to a whole ethnicity just to legitimize their own bigotry. Surely there was no way she wouldn't get the green light for a follow-up. Not when there was so much more that needed probing. Not while there was such an appetite for it.

She leaned back in her chair. Tried slowing her breathing. Relaxing the grip her eyelids had on her retinas. But the monster was already through ...

> *Your dad left me a note shortly before he died,*
> *asking me to keep an eye out for you.*

What the fucking bloody hell? She had heard from her father exactly once since those bizarre middle-of-the-night phone calls back in the winter, and that had arrived as some clandestine message on Claire's voice mail with some bullshit promise that he'd be in touch soon. Then ... absolutely nothing until the phone call from her mother to let her know that luck had finally caught up with her father – her mom's choice of words a noted gauge for the extent of the woman's sympathy. He had crashed his car north of Toronto, she learned ... and then learned little more, save for the message from Myles, the presumptuous git, expecting her to drop everything and fetch their luggage and instruments from Heathrow. (Because *that's* the first thing you think of when your bandmate dies.)

But now here was an email from a person she'd never heard of, carrying out her father's final wishes – (as if Dad knew he would be dying in a car crash? What the bloody hell?) – which included a request to *watch out for her*? God, no wonder I miss drinking, she told herself and nodded off into a few moments' sleep.

*She's in Toronto. In the backyard of her childhood home, the bungalow on Hillcrest Avenue. She's riding on the swing set. Can hear her dad singing to her as he pushes gently on her back. No, she calls out. Harder, harder ... she wants to go higher. She wants to go high enough to look right overtop their backyard fence. High enough to see the building tops on the other side. He relents and pushes harder, sings louder ... and all the while she is laughing and giggling ... hanging on to the bars as tight as she can ... thick, sinewy bars. Harder ... harder, she hears herself panting, her voice descending ...*

The dream was still a distraction in the meeting that afternoon, causing her to lose her train of thought on more than one occasion. She caught herself staring blankly out the window at the panorama of Central London, the sea of glass and steel, penthouse suites and office towers. Stared as if that were the elusive view from her backyard swing. She fought back with a series of hard blinks, and hopefully an unobtrusive shake of the head, but the images kept replaying, joined now by a new voice, this one not from her dreaming ... well, not quite, anyway

*We moved when I was a boy. To Boston in Lincolnshire.*

The sound of her editor brought her back. "Now I'm just a small bit concerned about safety."

"Pardon? How's that?"

"I'm wondering if what you are proposing mightn't be too risky. Surely from your outline ... and thank you for that by the way, detailed and precise as usual ... you must recognize that this goes far beyond the scope of investigation that made up your first piece. I mean interviewing immigration policy makers and law-enforcement is one thing, but if you really intend to take this in the direction you are suggesting, you're going to need to find people who are directly involved. Gain confidences, possibly ruffle the feathers of some less than scrupulous sorts ..."

*My mother and father came from Poland ...*

"... are you truly prepared to get your hands this dirty?"

~

"Claire?"

The door opened quickly. "How did it go?" her assistant asked.

"What? ... oh, right. Yes, we got it. Look, all the background notes for the last article. Do we still have hard copies handy?"

"Some. Which do you need?"

"*The Times* ran that series on the buildup of tension between locals and immigrants along the east coast."

Claire nodded. "I can check. If not, I can pull them from the web and make copies."

"Excellent ... and maybe ... unrelated, but while I'm thinking about it–"

She waited at the door, commenced her internal stopwatch. After a good ninety seconds – extra time added because her boss appeared to be having a bit of a day – she reached for the handle.

"My dad took me there, I'm sure."

"Excuse me?"

"To Boston. When he first started touring."

"Ours or the Yanks?"

"Yours. It was right before he lost the whole custody thing. Christ ... it seems so bloody long ago. I'd be maybe thirteen?" She squinted and cocked her head. "And you know what? I told him that. I told him I'd been there."

"You told your father–?"

"No ... no ..." she waved Claire off, her mind elsewhere again. Back at *The Spoke* with Peter. Early on. Maybe even the night they met.

"No ... he was wrong," Bronwyn blurted out, and her assistant paused once more, one hand on hip, the other leaning on the doorknob. "I know because I asked him about the weird church tower my dad took me to. It's got a funny name. Do you know it?"

Claire marched over to Bronwyn's desk and leaned over to Google the name in question.

"The Stump?"

"*The Stump*! Yes, that's it. Why didn't he know that?" She snapped her fingers. "And you know what else? He also looked blank when I mentioned *The Mayflower*."

"The Mayflower."

"Yeah. *The Mayflower*. You know, the ship that took the Pilgrims to America. It left from Boston, England. There are plaques and a museum I think. My dad took me there too. I remember it was down near a river, behind a row of shops–"

"If there's nothing else," her assistant interjected.

"I mean eventually he claimed he knew about it, but he wasn't really all that convincing, was he?"

"Bronwyn?"

"And how could someone grow up there and not know any–"

Claire reset her internal clock ... *(Sixty, fifty-nine, fifty-eight ...) She* watched her boss turn the computer back around and scroll through her messages *(forty-one, forty, thirty-nine ...)* then begin to type, mouthing her sentences – as was her habit – as she composed *(twenty-seven, twenty-six ...)* Somewhere around the thirteen-second mark: "Claire, the email my father sent you last winter. I'm pretty sure I deleted it. Can you find it and forward it again?"

Most of what she feverishly composed, she would also end up deleting, choosing instead, in the end, a guarded, flushing-out approach.

*Dear Ian – I don't know what my dad meant,*
*or what else you know.*
*But it you are still in that café, and if the staff is trying to get*
*in touch with those fans, I think you should get out of there*
*right away. Definitely DO NOT make contact with them.*

Then as an afterthought ... a hunch really:

*In the future please only reply to the address above.*

She sent the email out to her assistant's desk.

"Claire. Will you–"

"Got it. I'll send it along."

"Through at least a couple of your gmail addresses please. Like we did when we worked on the match-fixing piece."

"Will do."

The hunch would be confirmed late that evening as she sat

cross-legged on the floor of her flat with a mug of tea she so wished was Scotch. Instinctively she had opened her father's instrument case. She wasn't sure why. Perhaps to put something tangible in her hands, given the distance of her childhood ... the cloudy images of him holding out the fiddle in front of her; she, no more than four or five, grabbing the bow with both hands and scratching it across the strings. She found the letter tightly rolled and wedged behind the bridge, addressed specifically to *her*.

Her initial fleeting thought was that it was a preposterously haphazard way to send something; stuffed in the innards of his belongings ... and for what? The hope that she might just happen upon it? What if the instrument had been lost? What if it had found its way into someone else's hands before she had time to locate the airport's claims department? Or before she had a chance to identify herself to the agent as the one charged with the safeguard of all these unaccounted-for possessions? Had any of that even crossed his mind?

But then in the next instant, realization hit – full on with a chill reverberating up her back and neck, icing then numbing her skin from her waist to her skull. His instrument case was never *supposed* to land at her doorstep. *"So how could he have even expected me to find this? How could he have known?"*

Quickly she unscrolled and read the letter. Read it several times. Especially the parts about Alzheimer's ... and the passage about sending her a longer more detailed account – yet another promise unfulfilled. On the third pass she began to well up. On the fourth, she began to yell and swear and curse him by name, combining as much filth against God and Man and Sex as she could conjure, dedicating their amalgamation first to him, before she recalibrated and – as was her way – aimed the exact same barrage directly at herself. She threw books. She slammed cupboard doors. Kicked over the other instrument cases. She screamed. And then, only after having exhausted all of these reactive urges, did she roll up the letter and return it to her estranged father's violin case, this time opting for the safety of a zippered compartment inside the lid ... where she would find the last of the day's troublesome epiphanies. It was a burned CD of what appeared to be rough mixes for the final Mill Run album, its title *Swan Song* traced across the homemade cardboard cover in big playful block letters. Block letters she had forgotten she had once known and cherished. Block letters that once upon a time had been the currency of mutual story-concoctions and make-believe afternoons. And for a flash of a moment it left her wondering just when and how she had grown to despise this man so much.

Inside the CD case, in hurried, far less intelligible cursive, she found a folded piece of paper. A set of instructions. It too, like the rolled note, was addressed to her.

She went over them slowly. Then checked the clock. 9:55 p.m. She grabbed her laptop. Grabbed her phone and called the office to see if Claire was still there, working late ... if she wouldn't mind forwarding another email.

# FOUR

Ian settled back, propped up against the headboard. He had pulled down a loose shelf just inside the motel room door and laid it across his lap for a makeshift desk – the same shelf from which he had pulled down the extra pillows and rolled-up blanket that now helped bolster him on the bed. A pad of paper lay open and blank in front of him should a thought worthy of recording suddenly strike. In the interim, his fingers worked the particleboard, subconsciously miming a would-be piano part, the right hand rolling out triad chords and crossovers in a six-eight pattern ... the left locked in a steady tick-tocking fifth interval. His eyes, every four bars or so, glanced from the open laptop on his one side to the open cellphone screen on the other.

It was the same room he and Chris had stayed in on that last tour – the only time the band had ever played in Rainy River, he was fairly sure.

But he grabbed his phone and texted Myles, just to double-check.

~

The idea to go there had come to him in the departures lounge at Heathrow, thanks to another email from Bronwyn, just as brief and terse as her first which – in tandem with the news of his vandalized home – had sent him scurrying from Vimy in the first place.

*Ian. You need to tell me what you know.*

What he knew?  This was simple enough.  He knew absolutely nothing.

*Hi Bronwyn – I was actually hoping you could enlighten me. I'm completely in the dark other than what I've told you already. Chris's message had this request to watch out because he was worried about you. He didn't say why and, really, it was more or less an add-on ... most of the note was just asking me to kind of carry on, I guess you could say. To continue playing music, looking for stories ...*

*Looking for stories.*  His typing had stalled on the phrase. Was that right?  Looking for stories?  He flipped back to revisit the message in question once again.  No, *keep looking for the story inside a story.* That's what Chris had said.  He got up and paced, mouthing the phrase over and over until it played a loop inside his head.  He sat down again.  Slurped the remnants of his fourth, possibly fifth coffee and continued ...

*I had a thought, though. It's a bit crazy I know, but your dad often had some pretty out-there ideas, so at the risk of sounding completely delusional ... what if he had a different reason for making one more CD?  What if he wrote those songs as some sort of puzzle for me to solve? As absolutely bizarre as that sounds, I know.*


   And before allowing any time to talk himself out of suggesting such a notion, he had slammed his forefinger down on the
*send* button. Immediately his mind raced with a myriad of ways
he could have better contextualized the tenuous thought.  He
could have provided a thumbnail sketch, perhaps, about the
kinds of discussions he and her father had shared over thousands
of miles of touring; the endless chats about the power of songwriting, of storytelling; her father's belief that inspiration and
creativity were borne out of being *radically* open to most any
possibility; that her dad had spent a good deal of time exploring
alternative consciousnesses as a means to attaining this level
of open-ness.  Had she ever read any of the Jewish mystic
Martin Buber's work? Any Carlos Castaneda?
   Or perhaps he could have shared something about her father's
keen interest in dream-life interpretation ...
   *(You've probably experienced it yourself, Ian. You wake up
with either a full or maybe even a partial recollection of some
wild and entertaining story your subconscious just whipped
up. The whole thing with its own unique existence. Maybe you
are at home, getting ready to go for a hike. Maybe you open
your front door and, instead of your driveway, you cross over a
mote and into a forest. Now in so-called real life neither of
those things exist outside your front door, but nevertheless,
magically within the world of that subconscious tale, a mote
and a forest is exactly what Dream-Ian expected to see, because
Dream-Ian comes complete with his own backstory. His own
built-in history. So maybe Dream-Ian goes out the door and
over his mote and a woman with long silky hair and a fantastic
smile wanders up and says something like, "I'll meet you in*

*the forest as soon as I call Gillian and cancel her painting lesson. Now ... only after Not-Dreaming-Ian wakes up and begins his day does it occur to him that he actually doesn't know any such person. Because in the dream, you did. You do. You 'recognize' her. You have a memory of her. She is someone Dream-Ian has met many times before. But ... the reality of this whole separate Dream-universe is puzzling, isn't it?*

*Say you have another dream. This time, it's a vivid nightmare. Your dog is about to be hit by a truck. Now maybe you own a dog, maybe you don't ... but here's the thing: Should you be waking up from such a nightmare saying 'Phew, I am so glad that was just a dream'? Or should you be trying to figure out how the hell to get back to that universe so you can save the poor thing?)*

He had wandered the entire departure lounge, visited the loo, then the coffee kiosk once more. Had sat back down and spit-washed his computer screen. Taken a moment to exercise improved posture, having caught a glimpse of the apologetically-stooped figure reflected in a window across the way. Wiped up the crumbs on two nearby tables. Opened his browser and clicked on the website for *London by the Month*, then in turn, on Bronwyn's bio page and the photo that accompanied it. Noted that with her open-collared crisp white blouse, stylish leather coat and probing look of keen intent aimed right back at the camera, she appeared extremely capable and businesslike. Definitely stronger and more poised than the mental image that he had fashioned from what scant few stories Chris had shared over the years. An appearance, the musician could not help noting, that was completely at odds with someone requiring *watching over.*

*Ian –*

*You may be right. I found a note from my father in his violin case. How he could be certain it would find its way to me, I have no idea. Anyway, his note requested I send you song titles from your last album in a specific order. He starts off with two of them. Track #5, then Track #1 (sorry I don't have the titles listed here). Send me a reply if anything comes of this. Again, to this email address only.*

*PS – And for now you should lay low. Definitely DO NOT tell anyone ANYTHING about any of this.*

~

He pulled back the covers on the bed and reached for the bedside lamp, then leafed through the CD liner booklet once more.

Track #5, *An Instrumental*. Perhaps the rest of the band's least favourite of the set of ten songs, first and foremost because, despite the name, it came complete with a chorus and three verses (the sum of which contained, in Myles's opinion, as much lyrical value as if the track had actually *been* what the title professed it to be).

> *This song is an instrumental*
> *I wrote it for myself*
> *But if this song won't grab your ear*
> *Perhaps it's something else*
>
> *So if this song won't ease your mind*
> *Won't let you live and breathe*
> *Look for the tunes instrumental*
> *To the answers that you need*

The very first morning in studio, he had been sitting in the sound booth, arms folded on the console, poring over those very stanzas, shaking his head.

"He said he wanted something ironic," Ian had offered weakly. He wasn't sure why. Maybe because Chris hadn't been there himself to argue his case. Because he had been late for the recording session ... again.

*"But if this song won't grab your ear, perhaps it's something else ...* Really?"

"Well, you know, I guess it's just kind of a simple sentiment."

"Try utter shit," Myles replied, pushing himself up from the console and sending his rolling chair flying back into Ian's knees. "Not to mention a fucking embarrassment."

The other track was the CD's opening song and was, conversely, one of the few pieces – one of two to be precise – with which the others had little quarrel, largely because the chord progression and structure had been lifted from a rollicking reel that all of them had been working on over the past couple of years. Lyrically, however, it too had struck Myles and Dan as unfortunately lacking.

### Night Storm

*Johnny watched the homestead when the clouds began to gather*
*Johnny guarded all he had against the wicked weather*
*But Johnny farmed out on the plain – the plain and clear horizon*
*So Johnny could feel safe from the storm*

*Riley was a hunter, kept his home deep in the woodland*
*Trees and rock make shade, but in a gale can look like*
*weapons*
*And either way by prairie farm or a well-known hunter's*
*lodge*
*If a storm comes in the night, it is unknown*

*And even when the Rain subsides*
*The River she still rises*
*And even when the sun returns*
*Her deadly Current still surprises*

It was thirty thousand feet over the Atlantic – give or take – and somewhere around his second or third drink of the flight (also give or take), with the lyrics to both songs laid side by side on his seat tray, jotted out as accurately as memory could serve, when Ian first noticed something.

*Look for the tunes instrumental*
*To the answers that you need*

Was that not confirmation? Yes, he would double-check against the actual printed text in the CD booklet when he landed, but was it not validation that Chris was posthumously inviting them to read and absorb his lyrics with the expectation that somewhere beneath, around or within them, he had ... well, planted *something*. Something separate and more important than their mere literal flow.

Then, with the second song ... his eyes fell on the words in the chorus. Rain and River, conjuring up the name of the northern Ontario town where the piano player first noticed something amiss; where, the morning after a show he'd found Chris wrapped in the bedsheets, rocking back and forth. And there was the other phrase as well ... *well-known hunter's lodge.* Ian was fairly certain Chris had been talking to a lodge owner after that concert; possibly the person involved with organizing the concert in the first place. The sponsor? An underwriter?

~

He checked his email and phone once more for the night. No messages. Checked that his door was locked, the room key safe inside. Lay back down. Reached for the lamp again ...

*They're both standing on the front stoop of a tavern, peering in through the front window. Both recognize the interior immediately with its dark smoky walls, its tired decor, its barn-staple coat hooks.*

*"Absolutely No Credit for Ian Station," Chris says, and throws himself backwards off the step, but instead of the thud of concrete there is the sound of a splash.*

*"Come on!"*

*Ian turns around to find his friend effortlessly floating around a small harbour. He looks down and discovers he too is no longer on the tavern step but now stands on a narrow wooden dock. It's nighttime but the sky glows from the beam of a full moon bathing the scene with shimmering light, illuminating Chris's suddenly streamlined body as it knifes through the water at breakneck speed, side to side, out and back, pausing intermittently to catch some breath and, seemingly more urgently, to laugh. Ian stoops to sit on the edge of the pier and watch him. Soon he realizes that he too is giggling, as he marvels at his friend's newly-discovered aquatic skill.*

*"What are you doing?" he calls out, just as Chris dives beneath the surface, only to pop up not more than one second later, all the way over near the harbour's opposite shore. Ian notices a vast open lawn just beyond the water's edge. On it sits a huge tent canopy illuminated by patio lights and lawn torches; a huge crowd is there, mingling, with a band ... their band? ... set up at one end, playing away ...*

*"What are you doing?" Ian calls again.*

*"I'm swimming."*

*"Why?"*

*"Because I'm in water."*

*He slips under again, then pops up right beside Ian's dangling legs. "But you have to know ... I haven't forgotten our chat," he says, and instantly his skin falls cold grey, his eyes roll back in his head and, like an anchor, he sinks from view.*

*Ian screams. Jumps up and races up and down the dock, yelling out his friend's name over and over ...*

*"Pipe down, would ya!"*

*He spins around and he's in the kitchen of his childhood home. His dad sits at the table in a crisp pale blue collared shirt with a monogrammed pocket. He is buttering a slice of toast. Steam from his coffee mug snakes up into the morning sunlight that pours into the room thanks to a bank of windows overlooking the meadow. It's a brisk autumn day outside and the morning fire is crackling in the wood stove against the opposite wall.*

*Dad is in fine form, regaling him with yet another story from the school where he is the head custodian. Another story that is, as usual, prefaced with his conviction that teachers and staff alike simply don't seem to see a janitor as anything more than part of the furniture.*

*The account in process is about the school's principal, Mr.*

*Stoddard. How Mr. Stoddard, that old fox, has hired a new
secretary to cover for Mrs. Cutler's maternity leave; a twenty-
two-year-old from the city, with long wavy hair, longer tanned
legs, and a black skirt he was pretty sure was a couple of inches
too short for "these parts". Much the same way, he points out,
Mrs. Cutler herself had got the job two years before. Miss Van-
derheyden before her. And Laura Felder, the first grade teacher.
Moira McDougall down in Special Ed.*

*He had seen the looks exchanged between Stoddard and Mr.
Iverson, the Vice Principal, he says. Seen how their eyes had
spent some less-than-professional moments lingering on the
new hire as she left the office ... how the two remaining candi-
dates, both looking in their forties, with wider girths and more
sensible shoes, stood no chance.*

*"And you should have seen old Stackhouse all over Mrs.
Reynolds in the staff room last Friday. Cuddled up by the coffee
machine, whispering in her ear. And I'm right there emptying
the trash!"*

*"Oh Stan, that's enough ... finish your breakfast," Ian hears
his mother's voice coming from some unseen location behind
him. "And in front of the boy no less."*

*Stan shakes his head. Reaches for the marmalade. "I tell
you, the things you learn when nobody sees you–"*

There was a loud bang on the door.
"Housekeeping!"
Another bang ... a series of them, rapid-fire.
    "Housekeeping!"
 No. He needed to stay there ... to stay back in the warmth
of that massive kitchen with the wood stove and the sunlight
and the windows overlooking the meadow.
"You want me to come back later?"

Wait ... *was* there a meadow outside the window? Or was he adding that now? The outer screen door slammed back shut, just as his cellphone began ringing from somewhere beneath the pillows. He climbed to his knees, fumbled for the light switch, then dug through the bedding to find it.

*-Hey Ian, it's Myles.*

"Myles. Thanks for getting back to me."

*-You wanted some info?*

"Yeah. The Rainy River show we did on the last tour. Can you remember who booked it?"

*-Why, you touring with somebody else?*

"Um ... thinking about it ... maybe. It's for a friend looking for a gig on his way out west."

*-Did he try Gary Krieburg's series in Thunder Bay?*

"... um not sure."

*-Or the folks at Lakehead Music Society?*

"Maybe ... anyway I said I'd look around at other places up there."

*-Well, the Rainy River gig was a complete one-off. Just a fundraiser through the town I think. I can call up the gig sheet here, but I have to say, it didn't strike me as anything they did on a regular basis. Would it just be you and your friend?*

"What? Oh, yeah ... I guess."

*-Here we go. The town organized it but a lot of funds came through the chief sponsor ... somebody named ... Roy Turgeon.*

"Do you know if he ran a hunting lodge maybe?"

*-Hunting lodge? How the hell would I know?*

"Sorry, just thought I remembered somebody like that. And one more question, just 'cause somebody was asking. How did our instruments all end up at Chris's daughter's place after he died?"

*-What? Um ... I guess I made that arrangement. I remem-*

*bered Chris had said something about crashing at his daughter's
if he had to ... when he was scrambling last-minute to arrange
transportation to Vimy. Must have got the idea that way. Hey
listen ... what's the deal with your apartment? Last I heard
your landlord was still trying to get a hold of you. They need a
list of missing items for the insurance ... oh, hang on. Got another call. Later.*

~

Laying low was what Bronwyn had advised, so 'laying low'
he had incorporated into his plans. There would be no mention
of Mill Run or Chris Lucan in any of his sniffing about the
town. He would offer no information about his own identity
either. Would even allow the three weeks of unattended facial
hair to continue unabated, on the chance some local might otherwise recognize him from their show back in the winter. This,
despite the nagging voice in his head that wondered what real
chance there was of that. He, the sideman; the added *bit of
sheen* ... just a pinch is all we need, then back you go, far stage
left. We'll call you if we need any more.

And hadn't this always been the case? The very first tour in
the UK at that folk club in Shropshire ... had he not just left the
stage following sound check, only to be denied access to the
dressing rooms by the club manager, standing there blocking
his path and tapping the 'performers only' sign? The very
same man who had led them *all* into the venue not an hour earlier. Or the following year at the Bowling Green Roots Music
Series in Kentucky when the otherwise lovely artistic director
had brought in pizza, then all but slapped Ian's hand when he
reached for a slice, lecturing him on how non-profit organizations must count their pennies and that it was more than a little

presumptuous for friends and hangers-on of the band to take advantage of her generosity. (Really quite lovely otherwise, Dan would insist.) A minority amidst the hundreds and hundreds of Mill Run shows he was part of, yes, but still frequent enough to net a cumulative effect. Take the half dozen or so occasions when organizers had booked accommodation for only three band members (Charlotte, Fredericton, Cardiff); or the handful that had left Ian's name off of the posters and advertising (South Bend, Syracuse, Medicine Hat).

*"Thanks for not making a fuss, Ian. No idea why she went off like that. It was a slice of pizza for Christ's sake. I don't think you should read anything into it."*

*"I'll get something after the show."*

*"Because I have to say, I don't think this band would function if there wasn't your element of level-headedness. I mean the way you take the high road as a matter of instinct, it's like nothing can get to you."*

*"We'll probably need to get a cot in one of the rooms—"*

*"I mean if that were Dan, or worse yet, Chris? ... whole different outcome."*

A minority, yes ... but still, so it went. Muzzled with faint praise. *Thanks for being so dreadfully innocuous, Ian. We couldn't feel nearly so good about ourselves without you.*

Maybe this was the very reason Chris had tasked him with these strange song puzzles, if that's what they actually were. He, instead of a long-time friend like Dan, or anyone else for that matter. Not because of any perceived powers of perception on the piano player's part, and not from any sense of friendship or camaraderie, but strictly because what was called for was someone completely and acutely *unmemorable*.

He sat in his underwear on the side of the bed patiently waiting for the motel's advertised wi-fi to kick in, then scrolled through the results to his Internet search for 'Roy Turgeon, Hunting Lodge'. The first was a link to a webpage for the man's business that proved obsolete. The next, an article from the local paper that outlined Mr. Turgeon's untimely passing, fatally shot during an attempted armed robbery of his motorhome on the outskirts of Swift Current, Saskatchewan. Predeceased by his wife Dorothy. Survived by one daughter, Christina, of *Parts Unknown*, and by his many friends and business associates of the town and district of Rainy River.

An image suddenly popped into Ian's head: Chris coming out of the washroom of a hotel room, looking tired, maybe even stooped over a bit, clutching a number of towels firmly around his torso. Coming out because the radio was reporting the shocking details of a once-in-a-blue-moon homicide in their *quiet Prairie town* ... hadn't that been Swift Current?

He lunged for the lyrics, frantically leafing to the passage in question.

> *... And even when the sun returns*
> *Her deadly Current can still surprise*

Ian checked his watch and did some math. Nine-thirty in the morning where he was. But the middle of the afternoon ahead in the UK. He would wait 'til the end of the workday. Give it three hours then get in touch with her. In the meantime he could hear the chamber maid, several rooms away now, her call of 'housekeeping' just audible over the rumble of the cleaning trolley on the sidewalk, and the voice still echoing from his interrupted dream .... *"the things you learn when nobody sees you ..."*

He threw on a pair of track pants and a T-shirt, as he quickly tried to stifle yet another voice – this one trying to point out that his parents actually never had a wood stove in their kitchen. That his dad was not – nor had he ever actually been – a custodian.

He grabbed his room key and raced out the door.

~

"Excuse me. I'm in Room 4."

"I'll have to come back to you, sir."

She was wrestling a vacuum into one of the other rooms. She appeared to be a teenager, sixteen or seventeen, maybe. Slight with stooped shoulders. Native. He lingered a moment and immediately felt awkward because of it. She glanced at him again. Was that a hint of a sneer? Did he look old to her eyes, he wondered. Old and what? ... White? Suspicious by default?

She sighed. "Here, you can take back some towels if you need 'em now."

"No. I mean, sure. That'd be fine. Listen, are you from around here in Rainy River?"

Only then did his peripheral vision take in a second housekeeping cart further down the line of doors. A head popped out from the last room. A second woman – much older and even more suspicious – her eyes locked on him, as she flipped a dusting cloth over her shoulder and pulled a cigarette from the pocket of her scrubs.

"How can we help you?" she called out.

"I'm looking for some information about someone I met the last time I was here. Back in the winter. Although it turns out he's passed away since then."

"Your friend got a name?"

"Roy Turgeon. I think he might have run a hunting lodge around here."

The young maid's eyes widened and her gaze dropped to her feet.

"Back to work, Jocelyn," the older woman said and the young girl backed into the next room and closed the door.

"You a part of that lodge?"

"No ma'am."

"Cop?"

"No."

"Reporter then."

She stepped closer, pulled out a matchbook and nodded towards the motel room door. "Because that girl in there is my granddaughter. She's my responsibility."

"Sorry, I didn't mean–"

"So you can stop doin' yer damnedest to scare her."

She thrust a bony finger up to his face and Ian threw up his palms. "No. Listen, I wasn't trying to scare anyone. It was actually a friend of mine who knew him ... well, met him anyway."

"So why don't you go bother your friend?"

It was Ian's turn to stare, suddenly and unpredictably silenced by a moment of grief. It was a look the woman needed some time to take in, dropping her finger and moving in closer to study his face. "Unless," she continued, " your friend met the same goddamn fate."

"He died in a car accident down near Toronto."

"An accident, you say. Is that right?"

It wasn't that sympathy was absent from her reply, for there was also no real ring of contempt either. If anything, it was her note of skepticism. The ease of her doubt. Chills played a glissando down Ian's spine. A series of them. He felt vulnerable. Endangered. He scanned the parking lot, glancing up and down the row of motel doors looking for ... looking for what? Any that were slightly ajar? Any set of menacing eyes?

"Look, I only just found out that Roy was killed," he said in a lower voice. "But it could be my friend knew something about it, so maybe if I could talk to someone from around here who–"

"Nobody 'round here's gonna talk to you about Roy Turgeon, Junior. Nobody that knows anything anyhow."

He raised another defensive hand. Scanned his surroundings once more.

"Well, how about his daughter, then?" he said. "The obituary said he had a daughter. Christine, or Christina?"

"Are you for shitting real?" She grabbed the cigarette from her mouth and fired it at his feet. Turned and marched back towards her cart, stopping halfway there to grab the cloth from her shoulder, and throw it down as well. "You *are* a reporter, aren't you? You know, they said you types would come sniffin' around soon enough, once you had a pretty little white face and some long wavy hair to chase after!"

Ian shook his head. "No, I swear, I'm not. Like I said. I'm trying to figure out how, or even *if* Roy knew something about my friend."

"And you thought me and Jocelyn would just start spillin' our guts to some stranger out of the blue? Sure ... why not? To somebody like you, we probably look like the kind that's got nothing to lose, eh? Out here cleaning up after you ... wipin' away yer shit and piss for a few smokes and groceries. Yeah, they said you'd all show up soon enough. Joshie's mom even predicted it and she's usually hopped up on drugs and liquor and ... God knows whatever else that girl puts in herself."

He watched her pause to pull out another cigarette, light it and draw a long slow drag.

"But as for this one," she continued, her finger now stabbing in the direction of the motel door behind them. "Nobody's gettin' at her, got it? Nobody! So you can just go back to yer room there and leave her the fuck alone."

"OK, OK," Ian nodded. "Got it."

"Do ya, Junior? Really? 'Cause from that look on your face I don't think so. And I've lived this shit-show my whole life, so I don't need to go on about it with some poor pup from down south, do I? Not after my cousin up in Kenora with her daughter ... my stepbrother Malcolm out in Edmonton ... his girl all of 12 years old when she started." Her voice dropped. "And Jocelyn in there?" she hissed. "Both her sisters. Both of 'em! Yeah I know ... neither of 'em were saints ... most of this goddamn town'd tell you they brought it on themselves. Partying away with anybody and everybody. They'd be only too happy to tell you all that and more, and go on their goddamn merry way without a second thought. But put one pretty little white girl's face into the picture and, well holy shit and a hockey stick, we got company, don't we?"

She stooped down, snatched her cleaning rag and banged out the dust on the windowsill. Glanced up to see Ian's open-mouthed stare. For the second time guessed correctly what was on his mind.

"Yes, Junior, this kinda shit happens way up here in pretty little Rainy River ... and Atikokan and Dryden. And Kenora. And Thunder Bay. And Winnipeg. And Regina ... pimps and girls and drugs and trafficking ..." She began to beat harder. "Blow jobs in parking lots for truckers and hunters and off-duty cops. Sex for rich horny middle-aged men who like 'em nice and young when they're booked into a room all alone away from the missus ..." She nodded over Ian's shoulder toward his open door. "Or the richer ones who can afford to fly into certain hunting lodges for a week of so-called huntin' and fishin'. Hey, what happens in the middle of fucking nowhere, stays in the middle of fucking nowhere, right?"

She tossed the rag back towards her trolley and closed in on him yet again. "What's the matter, son, you never heard a grandma talk like me before? Rather I was wearin' a fucking apron and baking you a pie?"

It was too much. He had to get away. He needed time to process; needed to filter the anger out of her words and distill what he was learning. Needed to, first and foremost, answer the sudden urge to get out of the bright light of day. Out of the open. He bolted for his room and she called after him.

"Aw, did I ruin your image of a nice little grandma? Or maybe that image of beautiful northern Ontario? All them pretty lakes and trees ... hell, as long as you watch out for the moose and bears, it's all good, right? Except for girls like Joshie in there ... her and her sisters ... they got a lot more to watch out for than a fuckin' moose, don't they? Or are we just part of the wildlife too? Sure, one of us might go missin', but what the hell, eh ... there'll be another one 'round the next bend in the road. Tell ya what, Junior. You stop by the office later and I'll buy you an official Rainy River postcard to take back home. On me. Just lakes and trees ... who knows ... maybe even a goddamn *hunting lodge*."

He shut his door. Heard her footsteps fade back down the row of rooms, likewise her voice. "Jocelyn, get a move on. We still got the whole other end to get through."

~

He would spend the rest of the day back on the motel bed, tapping out arpeggios and composing drafts of his next email, taking particular care to be clear and orderly with the message. He would first go back over how the song *An Instrumental* seemed to serve as an introductory confirmation that Chris had indeed imbedded clues into his lyrics;  how the second, *Night Storm,* had confirmed Rainy River, Ontario and a man named Roy Turgeon who had lived there were the proper starting points for their search; how Roy had been involved in bringing Mill Run in for a concert the previous winter, how he had been found murdered a week later in Swift Current, Saskatchewan, on the same night Mill Run had performed in that town.

He would show his work.

He would make sure to cite the specific lyrics that pointed to both these conclusions.  Then and only then would he attempt a link between Roy's tragic end and Bronwyn's father; recounting the information received from his conversation with the motel's cleaning staff ... the grandmother's venom ... her granddaughter's wary eyes.

*... so all I can figure at this point is that something bad happened to Roy and your Dad must have witnessed it.  Or maybe Roy confided something incriminating to Chris, and whoever it implicated caught wind of it.  Like I said, from what this cleaning lady was saying, it could have something to do with prostitution or drugs.  Maybe Roy was pleading for Chris to help him in some way.  Deliver some message?  Help find his daughter maybe?  Anyway, if any of this makes any sense from your end, please let me know.  Ian.*

This time he would linger quite some time before finally sending the note; would drum through the chords for the better part of an entire Mill Run concert as he reconsidered, but then upheld his decision regarding not only what he had included, but, more importantly, what he had left out. Namely any seed of speculation the housekeeper had planted about Chris's death being something other than accidental. Surely that would be too much for her. Too much, as it already seemed to be, for him.

Her response was back in fifteen minutes.

*Good. OK, next are tracks nine and three.*

# FIVE

Bronwyn spent a good deal of time with her father's letter over the next week, rereading and reinterpreting his words – in the evening, alone in her flat with the lights dimmed low, the phone turned off, knocks on the door left unanswered. She went over particularly all the references to the onset of his supposed illness, now noting how carefully he had selected his phrases, how deeply he had buried clues which only now vaguely illuminated the disease as the ruse it was intended to be.

*Rest assured, I have researched my fate quite well … I have been 'putting myself' around the second or maybe third stage of the disease.*

Why? Why all of this?

Why the push and pull of hidden messages instead of reaching out directly? Or had that been what those phone calls had been about? Either way, yes or no, she was a journalist for Christ's sake … not the helpless little victim-in-waiting that his bullshit latent paternalism had obviously conjured up. Besides, of what *actual* use were the measures he had taken? Under the threat of organized crime – and it was certainly starting to appear this was what he had been dealing with – exactly what physical protection did he expect a piano player to provide? Ragtime them into submission? Screw that. She was the one with the skills and contacts and resources. She was taking charge.

After all, had she not – with her follow-up article now green-lighted – in fact been gearing up to do just that anyway? To dive headlong into the depths of this very underworld? Reveal it. Expose it. Portray it as the bottomless pit of misery that it was. And not just the lives of the predatory assholes who used and abused the loopholes and flaws of existing immigration practices, but the women who suffered so greatly under that use and abuse. *Her* women. The dead-eyed souls working the streets and the brothels, whose makeup and bruises so often meshed together, like the palette of a painter who saw the world in only black and purple and blood-dried rust. Those were the interviews she would be careful with. The ones she would conduct under the promise of anonymity. No names. No mention of where they lived or worked. Not even a description of their appearance or wardrobe if they so wished. She would work to gain their trust slowly ... even admit to her own tainted past if need be ...

"You do have a bit of compulsion to creep back towards to your previous life," Dr. Emma had noted during a session a few weeks before. "I feel there is still a push and pull deep down inside."

Push and pull. Well, she came by it honestly.

"Think about it. First the organized crime piece dealing with sports wagering. Then your immigration scamming story. Now you're telling me you want to delve further with a follow-up article. Please don't be offended when I wonder whether you are really finished trying to profit from this industry yourself."

It had been a harsh assessment, denied vehemently by Bronwyn for the duration of that appointment, and a good portion of the next. But in the shadows of her barely-lit apartment, with each passing night, she could not help wondering if it rang true. And perhaps Dr. Emma wasn't even the only one who had seen it. Even as far back as the match-fixing exposé, did she herself not wonder what some of her superiors were thinking? Did she not suspect a few skeptical glances on the part of her boss, Natasha, amongst all the other congratulatory handshakes and hugs for such a provocative piece. The unasked question of how a Plain Jane Canadian girl had managed to make so many effective contacts with society's underbelly. What life experiences had facilitated such an ability? Had she not suspected the young journalist's past, if not in specifics, then at least by some faint echo of skeleton bones clinking away in her imagination just beyond provable sight or sound?

"I guess what I'm saying is, sometimes you come across as simultaneously reformed and restless," Emma had said. "As if you see danger up ahead on the side of the road, but instead of crossing safely to the other side, you choose to just barely step off the curb. Like you're making sure to appear sensible, but also making sure you don't miss anything exciting."

Perhaps. But then again, even if the good doctor was right, who better to muddy the lines from arms-length journalist to active player? Who better to cross them if need be? To be drawn in and dig in the dirt with these pricks? And even if the observation was not valid with regard to the magazine piece, it surely was now. Yes, she was drawn in. How could she not be? Because, estranged or not, somewhere along the way it looked like one of these low-lifes had figured out some useful association between her, an annoying investigative but ulti-mately harmless journalist, and her estranged folksinging father. And somewhere along the line, as his cryptic warnings to his bandmate regarding her safety would suggest ... Daddy Dearest had caught on to it.

And yet for a good while – the first five nights of her apartment-floor vigil in fact – the scenario had no logical trail. She had not been contacted by anyone untoward. Had not been leveraged to cease and desist with her investigations. Had not been subject to any threats or blackmail of any kind, which in the world of human trafficking, she well knew, was the fuel on which the industry was propelled ... with threats not only against the exploited, but against their loved ones. Against mothers and daughters and children ...

Then on night six she began, as her journalism had taught her, to work on the roadblock by starting at the opposite end and looking backwards.

*Your dad left me a note shortly before he died,
asking me to keep an eye out for you.*

That's when it struck her. What if it wasn't her they wanted, but him? What if her father was the one who had been threatened ...

From that evening on, deadbolt be damned, she would slide her sofa in front of the apartment door. Would stay well from away from the windows. In the morning she would stay in the flat until she saw the taxi pull up to the curb. Would ask the driver kindly to get out and wait for her on the street outside her door until she was safely back at the end of the workday. And under the shelter of these precautions she would let the swirl of all of the available information – the letter, Ian's emails – also work its way backwards from this conclusion, so that she might come up with the answer to *why*. Why would a singer/songwriter be of any use to human traffickers? She would let it all clatter in her mind, hour after hour, day after day, aligning each possibility with the next to see if, like a row of dominoes, one might give way to another and then another until ... *for the love of shit, why had she not seen it?* Right in front of her face. How could she have so completely segmented her life? *Even* after learning about those possibly unscrupulous sorts looking for her dad in Vimy. After all, it had never really ever been just some serendipitous hookup, had it? Not really. What had Keegan said when she rang up that first night? That she had met a couple of quality boys down at the pub on her birthday. That they had suggested she call up a friend and make it a proper party.

Not that she had any truck with all the right-wing media mouthpieces and their anti-everybody-with-an-accent crusades, but, for Christ's sake, eastern Europe was a fucking hotbed of trafficking ... she herself had already *researched* at least a half-dozen cases for the article thanks to contacts from her past life. (The 18-year-old Romanian girl – or so she claimed – whom Bronwyn tracked down working at a private *spa* out in Chippenham. The Slovak up in Norwich ... two others in Charlton who had come over from Russia.) Given her investigative enthusiasm, one would think that once – just once – she might have asked her new Polish hook-up what he thought about any of it.

She began retracing, as best she could, the paths of their conversations. What, if anything, had she shared with Peter about her father? They would have talked about him after the-middle-of-the-night phone call. However she was fairly sure he had asked about family before that. She could remember him being interested that her father was a musician; that he had asked where Mill Run toured and how much they travelled. But with all those intoxicated, horny nights spent fondling each

other at the bar, then sprawled across her bed (always *her* bed)
God only knows what else she might have volunteered. At
some point she must have said *something* about her childhood;
about her parents' divorce and not seeing her dad much after
that. She could recall him leaning in, saying, "But he would
still love you, yes? A father would always be there for his
daughter, yes?"

But no, this was still the wrong end of the stick, wasn't it?
How could she have even inadvertently given Peter the idea to
use her father as some sort of pawn? No, if anything these recollections she was struggling with could only smack of a plan
already in motion. A plan that had seen *both* her father and her
targeted.

It was the final domino to fall and, as the last in a line of
possibilities, it landed the hardest; more forcibly than all the
rest combined, for it revealed her father's fate without any
shadow of doubt. The danger of which his letter spoke had *undoubtedly* been real. *Undoubtedly* painful and for him ... *undoubtedly* fatal. Had she made it happen? Had she somehow
unwittingly led the assholes right to him? She and her relentless
journalism exposing the world-wide failures of immigration
systems upon which so much of their business empire was
built. After all, it was right there for anyone to see, right in the
byline bio of her first *London by the Month* piece ... written
that way despite a decade or more of non-contact ...

*Born and raised in Toronto, Canada, Bronwyn Lucan's writ-
ing style, so lean and yet provocative, no doubt borrows from
both her mother, Jane – a practising corporate lawyer – and
her esteemed folksinger father, Christopher.*

# Six

Like *Night Storm*, the ninth track of the *Swan Song* CD was a reworking of an existing idea born out of a collaboration between Chris and a fan from the town of Haileybury, Ontario. Lorne MacIssac was a God-knows-how-many-generation northerner who for years had been sending materials for song topics, the overwhelming bulk of which the band had filed away as uninspiring.

In one particular case, however, an envelope of clippings about the 1930s gold rush in and around the then fly-in-only town of Red Lake had managed to pique the songwriter's interest. This had thrilled Mr. MacIssac no end, since he himself was a descendant of one of the two brothers credited with finding the original vein of treasure in that neck of the woods – fortuitously sparkling out of the Canadian Shield from under an uprooted tree ... or so the story went.

But while it was, no doubt, that particular tale that Mr. MacIssac had been most interested in hearing Chris immortalize in song, a corollary reference to a much more recent event from the 1970s was what actually ended up igniting the songwriter's creative impulse. It was a brief account of a Manitoba man named Ken Leishman who had organized the broad-daylight robbery of a shipment of Red Lake gold as it was being transported into the Winnipeg Airport. It seems Mr. Leishman and some associates had forged requisition papers, commandeered official porters' uniforms and talked their way into diverting the cargo off of its intended connecting flight and into a waiting truck. But even as dramatic a caper as that seemed, the intriguing part of the story for Chris was found in *its* postscript, long after Mr. Leishman's arrest and years of incarceration. Because the ex-con emerged from jail a most curiously reformed man. On one hand he had renounced his past misdeeds, but on the other had taken up residence in the very town of Red Lake from where his once-absconded Pot of Gold had been mined. He became a pillar of the community and was even elected deputy mayor for a term. For Chris it begged the question. What was his motivation? Was it to make genuine recompense to the town he had once indirectly robbed? Or did the man have other unfinished nefarious business there? It proved tantalizing fodder for a bit of playful fake-lore, and over the next few years had been a work-in-progress quite familiar to the rest of the band. And having seen its inclusion on Chris's song list for the final CD, they had all assumed it was one that would not need fretting over, once recording began.

"What the living crap?"

"Myles, just hear me out."

"It's nothing like before. *Paint the Lake Red*? What happened to *Rush For Gold*?"

"It needed a new title to reflect where I took the lyric."

"Yeah. Where the hell is that exactly?"

"It's a musical collage ... a tribute to the phenomenon that was the Gold Rush town."

Myles threw his clipboard to the floor, sending lyric sheets and chord charts flying like oversized confetti. His mind strained to summon the effort and words for yet one more battle of artistic differences – but, worn down from three weeks of studio warfare, he could conjure up nothing of substance.

"It's my last kick at the can, Myles. I don't want to go out slagging some town's name just so I can indulge myself with speculation about a chapter in its history."

"So you're gonna do a laundry list of historical dates and events for the town of Red Lake instead?"

"No, like I said, I've switched to a montage about the overall culture of the town. And look, I still make reference to the Leishman affair. There – in the third verse."

"And you truly believe this is an improvement? Really?" He sifted through the papers at his feet, snatched up those for the song in question. Grabbed his guitar and tuner; headed for his spot in the studio, all the while mumbling undiplomatic obscenities just above his breath. "Reads like a fucking tourist brochure."

"It will work."

"Yeah, yeah ... let's get this bloody thing over with."

~

Ian saw it immediately. The parallel between the song's hunt for gold and whatever sort of greed had sponsored Roy's downfall was completely transparent. Moreover the lyric now struck him as an obvious directive for him to begin a search.

> *Read the lay of the land, my friend*
> *Read the tales that lie beneath*
> *All the long soulful lines of an old poet's verse*

*Behind the brush lines of the painter's designs*
*Of the clear blue waters, the blue skies above*
*A miner for gold dares to reach*
*A miner for more should search further beneath*

As for *where* he should start this search ... well, that would become clear a moment later, upon consideration of the subsequent song, the third track on the *Swan Song* CD.

*Still Life*

*You were slim and sagged and dressed threadbare*
*Still life was there*
*You were dust-worn weary at the top of the stairs*
*Still life was there*
*There we could laugh to the small hours of night*
*Take what was offered – though dim was the light*
*Watched the world go by in black and in white*
*And still ... life was there*

It had originally seemed like just a quiet little ballad – unfinished, to Myles's ear – with only Chris's solo voice and a bit of gentle mandolin for accompaniment. But for Ian, now fully acclimated to the idea of the song within a song, the deeper message now struck him as completely evident. And so the next morning he rose before dawn and as quietly as possible drove out of the parking lot with the intention of heading for Manitoba. First, however, he would head east, towards the larger centre of Fort Frances, where he would leave his car in the rear parking lot of a local shopping mall ... then rent another for the trip back.

The reason for the added precautions? A visitor from the night before. Because of the panicked, terrorized look on that visitor's face.

~

It had been well after midnight when she banged on his door, panting; out of breath ... glancing over her shoulder up and down the street before barging past him into the room, slamming the door shut ... falling back against it, still gulping for air.

"You gotta get outa here," she said, swallowing hard.

"What? Why?"

"Christina Turgeon was my sisters' best friend. Mine too, even though I was way younger. She always treated me good. She and my sisters were all in the same class at school. They all played ball together too. Cops said she woulda probably been there when my sisters went missin' ... said it was probably somebody passin' through, but my cousin Billy told me it was that friggin' asshole Darryl Donavan over in Emo. He says he's a landscaper, but he's more likely to be feedin' underagers drugs and beers and shit. Get 'em to jump in his pickup ... go party at that lodge with a bunch of old white men ... "

"Wait, slow down – Josie, is it?

"Jocelyn."

"Right. Does your grandmother know you're here, Jocelyn?"

"No." She was waving him off. "Just shut up and listen. I checked with Billy and he says the guys that he thinks got to Roy have been back through town a few times since and they're still real pissed off about whatever he did. Probably ratted them out to the cops. I told him 'bout you askin' questions and having a friend who died too. Billy told me to tell you to get the hell out of here. He said they could come back any time. Said they could be watchin' you already. So go ... OK? Just go."

And with that she took her own advice, slipped out the door and was gone, her light footfall tapping on the sidewalk, then the parking lot, picking up speed as it faded away.

~

Once in the rental car he would return, quickly and quietly, through Rainy River and cross into northern Minnesota, over to Warroad, then north and back into Manitoba. He would tell customs he was just taking a bit of a trip. They would ask him if he was carrying any alcohol or firearms. They would make a cursory inspection of the back seat before they let him through. He would drive on to the first community inside the border, to the village of Sprague and its one lonely tavern. He would ask the waitress if he could have a look in one of the rooms; the one right at the top of the stairs which he and a friend had stayed in a while ago (he would not say just how long) because he thought he may have left an electric razor behind. She would agree to the bizarre request, mostly out of curiosity (having never seen the room rented out even once in her eight months working there). She would find the key and let him in. Once she had vacated the premises, he would search all around and under the saggy cot mattress, through the dresser drawers, behind the curtains and finally, upon going over the lyric one more time – *the world go by in black and in white* – would look behind the small television still adorned with the same clothes-hanger antenna he and Chris had twisted on years before. There he would find a brown envelope with his name on it, written unmistakably in the familiar block-letter font his friend used for the band's set lists. Inside, with no accompanying explanation: a bundle of work permits for housecleaners and nannies, some describing singing and acting work; all folded around a half-dozen passports with women's faces ... young women's faces. Younger in appearance, Ian would note, than the ages the documents attested.

His hands would start to shake. His palms moisten. He would race down the stairs, out the door and jump back into the rental car. He would not stop until late that afternoon in Winnipeg. There he would change cars once more, then find a string of motels out towards the airport. He would park in the lot of the first, but walk all the way to the last in line and check in at that one. Once inside, he would send his next email ...

*Bronwyn – In Manitoba now.*
*Used the song about Red Lake to locate some items Chris left for me to find.*
*Pretty scary stuff.*

Towards morning he would dream he was back in the café in Vimy, chatting with the blonde server ... he would dream that she took him by the hand and led him up the stairs to a room with one saggy cot and a black-and-white TV perched atop a dust-coated dresser. On the cot would be his best friend, Chris Lucan, arms folded across his chest, the sides of the mattress gathered in around him. He would scream and awaken; would shoot upright and, instinctively, reach for his laptop.

# SEVEN

Her mind had been racing all morning. Who to talk to at her end?   Smithson at the Constabulary?   Carmichael in Vice? There was that assistant communications officer at Scotland Yard who years before – she had come to learn – had a predilection for tall, dirty blondes. Would he be of any use?  She made a note of it, all the while waiting on hold to talk to her contact at Immigration, her free hand typing 'current criminal investigations: northern Ontario' into her search engine. She clicked on the first hit, dated that very same day.

## THREE MEN HELD FOR QUESTIONING AT RED LAKE MINE

(CP) - Three men with possible connections to organized crime, human trafficking and drug smuggling were arrested on charges of trespassing and mischief in the small mining town of Red Lake, Ontario late last night. Police are not releasing the names of the accused but did tell reporters they are interested in 'following the crime trail' to see if there are connections between the accused and strong rumours of gangs and crime organizations infiltrating northern Ontario reserves and businesses. The three detainees were apprehended following a tip to police from a mine worker at the Oak Roots Site who reported a group of men loitering near the fences with some tools just before midnight. Sources say the three men had also been spotted an hour earlier, walking the perimeter of the mine located just north of the town. Asked if there was any connection to the ongoing investigations of smuggling and trafficking in the Rainy River District, Police Spokesperson Const. Gail Mulvaney chose not to get into specifics but would confirm that all investigations are top priority and that any possibilities of common links would be investigated fully.

Bronwyn hung up the phone and focused instead on revisiting the email she had awakened to that morning. He said he was in Manitoba. Safe for now, hopefully, though she realized it was probably just a slight breeze of good news in what was otherwise a hurricane of bad. Because if the detainees in her news feed were indeed part of the group that had gotten to her father, she could come up with only two ways they might have reason to be searching a mine in Red Lake.

The first was the possibility that these people were not fooled one bit and were also using her dad's lyrics to find whatever it was he wanted Ian to get to first – most likely forged work papers, possibly passports ... the same items she'd bet Ian had just come across. She sifted through the papers and notes covering her desk, searching for the CD booklet. (Not that a copy of it had been easy to procure ... not a lot of folk music shops in Central London, it turned out. Thank God for Claire hunting one down in the Canadian Consulate Gift Shop.) Track Nine, *Paint the Town Red*. *"An ode to the culture surrounding the rise of Gold Rush Towns, such as that of beautiful Red Lake, Ontario, the inspiration for this song."* Could that description have been enough, in and of itself, to lead them there?

If not, the only other explanation – the far more likely one – was that they were hacking into her correspondence. She read Ian's note once more. *Used the song about Red Lake to locate some items Chris left for us to find.* She glanced at the time-stamp. 5:47 PM Central Time. Could these men really have had enough time to intercept that message and get from, well, wherever the hell they were operating out of, up to Red Lake? Highly unlikely, was her first thought as she called up a map of Ontario's north. Not unless they had a float plane or a chopper at their immediate disposal. *And not unless they were completely desperate,* she heard herself say, and instantly a particular queasiness she hadn't felt since her days in the trade overwhelmed her. Quickly she scrolled through a myriad of online ads for private air charters in the area. *Same-day service. No reservations! Satisfaction guaranteed.*

It was clear what had to be done even as she felt the muscles in her stomach involuntarily asking to heave. She swallowed hard. Began typing her reply, giving him the next two songs from her father's instruction: 7 then 6. "So in over his head," she mumbled, shaking her head, grabbing at her abdomen. She would have to meet with Natasha to request protection and a leave of absence for both herself and Claire. Especially Claire. It was her computer that had been fielding Ian's notes, after all. And Keegan. Shit, she would have to warn Keegan! But Christ, hadn't the last two or three messages she left for her gone without a reply?

Her intestines were churning now. She was tying up in knots. She grabbed for the wastebasket, slamming her desk drawer to mask the sound of the wretching, and motioned for Claire, who had already come running, to close and guard her office door. Bronwyn grabbed at a box of tissues hand-over-hand to wipe her chin and her desk, then grabbed her leather coat and bolted for the outer office, stopping only to ask her assistant – amid terse reassurances she was just fine – for directions to the nearest internet café.

*"Like it even matters at this point,"* said the voice in her head.

Once there, from what she hoped against hope was an anonymous terminal, she sent Ian her last note.

*Ian, I think I can guess what you found, but won't mention it here.*
*Hang onto everything for now. Show no one.*
*Next are tracks 7 and 6 ...*

Then after a moment's more grave consideration:

*And just in case I can't be reached ...*
*after that it's 2, then 5 again, then 4, then 8.*

## THE LEAD BREAK

*At best, what one can say for the lead break – or solo, as it is also known – is its potential to invoke an element of emotion into the mood of a song, should lyrics fail. From the balladeer's perspective, however, it could be argued that such an occasion should never really need come to pass within a properly-written folk song.*

**~Chetwynd C. Lovett**
*The Orthodoxy of Folk Song*

# ONE

*He grabs her by the shirt and tears it down over her shoulders. Drops his pants and boxers. Lies back on the bed, directing her into his crotch, his grip firm on the back of her head. After several minutes he shoves her over onto her back, crawls on top of her and stuffs himself inside. She closes her eyes. Squeezes them shut as tight as she can. Focuses entirely on the muscles in her eyelids. If she does not let in any light, then she isn't there.*

*This had been her way right from the start, the very first times ... except for Darryl. Darryl had been different. Darryl had told her she wasn't ugly, wasn't too big. Told her she was more than just a good softball player, that her ass wasn't like some friggin' first baseman. It was hot. Darryl – who had bought her the tattoo she had once been so proud of, when he used to stroke it and stare at it – his family's initials scrolled out in a swoop, he said, because that's how much she meant to him. Darryl – who had convinced her to come with him and his friends. Told her that some of the regulars up at the camp had asked him and his buddies to party with them; to bring any friends they wanted to. Told her he had never bothered because he had never really been into anyone else ... but if she wanted to, well, that'd be different. Darryl – who'd been gone for months now. Maybe a year even. But he'd be back for her pretty soon, the others always told her. Pretty soon, they'd say, and then laugh. Laugh hard and often enough that, after a while, she stopped asking.*

*He starts to pant, and all his weight – every pound of his furry pale weight, moist with the stench of himself – lands down on top of her as he ruts away. For a moment he falls out, swears and rises to his elbows to fumble with himself and get back inside. He sounds angry ... like he might start slapping her, as some did when they couldn't keep it up. Slap her like it was her fault, or out of embarrassment ... or because that's just what they did.*

*The breathing quickens again, mixed this time with the grunting and swearing that lets her know he's almost finished. When he finally ejaculates she waits the requisite ten seconds, then carefully extricates him from her body, slithers beneath the sweat of his armpit, and out from under his mass. Only then does she reopen her eyes. Opens them to see how angry he still is. So she smiles and tells him how much she loved it. How bad she needed it. Tells him he was good ... really, really good.*

~

*Thirty minutes later she hears the key in the hotel door. She turns off the TV and stands up to present herself again. Pulls the short pink skirt tight to her hips, her top down around her shoulders ...*

# Two

The confines of the garden shed were dark and blurred.  He was aware of a shovel and a push broom, and the riding mower behind which he was huddled.  Strictly by feel he had found a pair of coveralls and thrown them over his head and shoulders; a contingency which had no doubt saved him when the door had swung open with frantic clouds of breath and the threatening spray of a flashlight's beam strobing back and forth overtop his hiding place.  In the eternity of the instant he had held onto his own breathing, straining to calm every fibre; eyes squinted closed, face pinched in dreaded anticipation.  His body was soaked with sweat, his face with tears.  Part of him wanted to jump up and scream and get it over with.  But then, just as suddenly as the threat's arrival, amidst urgent, seething whispers, the door slammed shut again and the footsteps retreated, as did the calls to check the car once more, to look across the road, behind the store ...

~

He had been on such a roll.  In complete lockstep with the

directions of his best friend's lyrics. Completely focused and energized by the task at hand: the single-minded purpose of collecting the forged work permits that Chris had left for him to find.

The next two songs had yielded instant results. *Riverbank Dance*, with its spare Metis fiddle-tune motif ...

> *Could you stand in the shadow of Riel's Long gaze*
> *Stand where he keeps his long mourning gaze*

There they had been, wrapped and hidden, adhered to the underside of a bench directly in line with the *morning* shadow cast by the patriot's statue on the grounds of the St. Boniface Museum; the same grounds where Mill Run had once played the city's Winter Festival and just down the street from where he and Chris had stopped for the night on their last trip home.

The second was in a train station-turned-art-gallery in Virden, Manitoba behind an oil painting of a fishing village leaning against the wall ... thanks to Chris's ballad *Prairie Choir*.

> *Took a call out in a Prairie Town –*
> *there's an old train station there*
> *Kinda reminded me of my hometown,*
> *so I stopped to let the distance come to bear*
> *From the shores and the boat lines –*
> *To this platform all alone*
> *Against the furthest edge of midnight ...*
> *and me, a thousand miles from home*

Ian had remembered having stopped there too; grabbing a sandwich in the café next door, the day before St. Boniface.

He had emailed news of his findings to Bronwyn. Brief

notes without detail, as she had insisted. Two days later he would repeat the process, following his retrieval of two more now-telltale brown envelopes, the first from behind the ice machine on the upper floor of the motel where they had stayed in Swift Current, thanks to another line from *Night Storm*

> *... blow your ice two storeys high*
> *I surely fear the night*

("I have absolutely no fucking clue," he remembered Myles moaning.)

The next, as hinted at from stanzas in *How Does Your Garden Grow?*, was located another four hundred kilometres west ... taped under the slide in a village playground on a Blackfoot Reserve, just off a secondary highway south of the Trans-Canada that Chris had picked out of nowhere on their last drive home ... *just for a change*.

But as fruitful as those latest finds were, they also yielded the first pangs of despair, for in both instances Ian's emails chronicling the discoveries had gone unanswered. He was left to wonder whether Bronwyn was safe. Whether she had she been forced into hiding. Fled from her home ... her office. Or worse yet, God forbid, had she actually been tracked down? Had she been harmed? *Keep an eye on Bronwyn, I think she may be in danger* ...

That night he would revisit her magazine's webpage. Would surf through the contact directory, only to find her name no longer there. Her assistant – Claire ... Claire Something-or-other ...her listing too was missing.

The discovery would reawaken the same dread that had afflicted him in Rainy River; the feeling of eyes on his every move, of unseen adversaries watching to see what he knew, where he was going. He fought the notions repeatedly for the next four days ... the first two spent driving, as the next song lyric decreed, all the way back to northern Ontario, just east of Thunder Bay, to the monument that paid tribute to Terry Fox and his Marathon of Hope. Or at least to the gift shop next to it inside the interpretative centre – the title itself, *Where Can We Dance The Foxtrot?* having all but given the location away. Once inside, he located a shelf of local and regional histories and looked for any book that might correspond to the reference from the first stanza of the song ... *I am a simple lumberjack chopping up the North.* He would soon spot the familiar corner of manila brown peeking out from the back panel of the bookcase, hidden behind several copies of a coffee-table book about the history of sawmills in the Kenora District. Confidently he would extricate the envelope from where it had been taped in place, panic only setting in with the discovery that the flap, though clearly once sealed, had already been forced open with the expected contents nowhere to be found. Desperately he would grab at other books, yank them down to the floor and feel around and beneath the shelves themselves, dropping to his knees to peer underneath the unit, groping blindly at the casters and footings. In so doing he would draw the shop's staff over to protest. Immediately he would apologize and begin gathering the mess and piling the fallen texts, all the while trying to take some deep breaths to deal with the spasms of dreaded questions bombarding his head.

*How could they have been onto me?*

But wait ... anyone could have found them, he reasoned. Anyone could have merely opened the package out of curiosity. Customers ... staff. It was a public place after all.

*But if so, why was the envelope still there?*

Why *was* the envelope still there? And not just *still there* but taped to the back of the bookshelf ... taped like all the other packages Chris had found.

*Maybe because they wanted you to know you're being watched, Einstein.*

But he had changed cars, He had kept hidden.

*Yeah, yeah ...'It's like they don't even see us'. How long were you really planning to hang your hat on that one?*

"But I was never front-and-centre," he blurted aloud.

*You were in a car with Chris all the way from Rainy River to BC and back again, dumb-ass. If somebody was watching him then, don't you think they got a pretty good look at you too?*

He would kick over the stack of just-piled books, would run into and knock down the bookshelf itself, then sprint from the shop amid louder and angrier shouts from the clerks. He would speed back to Thunder Bay, changing rental cars again, before continuing west. Once out on the prairies, he would keep to regional roads, driving as long as possible each day ... stopping to park and rest in only the sleepiest of towns, preferably in the shadows of dark vacant buildings. He would lock his doors, recline the driver's seat and drift off almost immediately but unlike previous nights, he would dream very little.

This would be the routine for the next three days until he found himself closing in on Chris's last hiding spot, heading down Highway 22 alongside the foothills of the Rockies ... well south of Calgary, just past the town of Longview, the very town that shared its name with the song sheltering the final clue (though Chris had insisted on adopting a more generic two-word title, *A Long View*). For Ian, and for Myles and Dan as well, it had been the most curious inclusion on the CD – and a telling sign that something was amiss with their prolific band-mate, because the track was not one of Chris's songs at all. It was a cover, a tune he had heard another band playing at a festival in southern Ontario the previous summer. Never before had Chris Lucan, songwriter-extraordinaire, ever contemplated recording someone else's work. But he claimed this was a song that *had been haunting his creative energy relentlessly* all throughout their last trip west – and that the idea of its inclusion simply could not be denied.

~

He had pulled into the roadside campsite next to a bridge that crossed the Oldman River where Ian remembered the two had stopped for a brief walkabout on their last drive home.

*There in the morning light ... I won't forget the sight.*
*Something was left behind that day*

It was an otherwise breathtakingly beautiful and peaceful-looking place: ribbons of frothy water bubbling gently over a rocky riverbed; a handful of camping sites with picnic tables and firepits, nestled beneath the stark green-brown of the rising foothills and the jagged polished silver rock face of the mountains just beyond. But on the afternoon of his arrival the sight that greeted him was anything but serene. Traffic was stopped and lined up along the road on either side of the park's entrance. Five squad cars in a circle in the parking lot inside the grounds. A labyrinth of police tape everywhere.

Ian got out of his car and walked toward the crowd of onlookers, edging near a woman who was listening intently to a couple of RCMP officers, their heads bent toward their notepads as they compared points and jotted down details. Two paramedics emerged from over the riverbank and dropped the wheels of their stretcher to roll a motionless figure back to a waiting ambulance. Blood was seeping from bandages bound around the crown of the man's head, its trail the only discernible sign of life.

"What happened?" he whispered involuntarily.

"Not sure ... sounds like that poor fella got attacked down by the river."

Ian swallowed hard. "Was it wildlife?"

The bystander shook her head and appeared to make a sign of the cross. "No, not wildlife ... well, at least not of the natural sort. I heard one guy telling the police he saw a black car come racin' out of here just as he was coming in to do some fishing. Said he didn't think anything of it 'til he headed down to the river and could hear somebody moanin' away. The guy was worked over pretty bad."

Ian scanned the crime scene. He noted a small pup tent, mostly pulled down, camping equipment strewn all around a picnic table, all next to a burgundy Ford Taurus – the same make and colour he had rented before his last switch back in Thunder Bay. Its doors were wide open, its upholstery ripped and shredded apart.

He grabbed at the lining of his pockets to stop his hands from shaking. "Is he going to–" But the question caught in his throat.

The woman shrugged. Made another cross. "Just some poor fella," she shook her head and mumbled. "Some poor fella out to do some fishin'. Lord Almighty, what kind of a world are we livin' in?"

How he had wished he could have answered her. Wished he could stride right out into the middle of the emergency crews, interrupt the investigating officers and tell them that he knew *exactly* why this senseless beating had taken place, and why it had occurred in this beautiful pristine location. That he had illegal documents which a friend of his had been forced into keeping by very, very dangerous men. That his friend had attempted to double-cross these men by hiding the documents in locations around the country and leaving clues to their whereabouts; clues that these dangerous men might not pick up on. Then confess to them that his friend's plan had failed. That the men *had* caught on, and they were callous and desperate enough to do absolutely anything to regain possession of said documents, including attacking an innocent man out doing a little fishing if that innocent man's car happened to look like the one they had been searching for ... then tell them – *confess* to them – that despite the ransacked campsite, and despite this poor soul's life-threatening beating, these men ... these traffickers, these dangerous animals ... were still roaming the countryside at large. Because they would not have found what they were looking for.

It was that last detail of his imagined confession that sent Ian back to his car instead, without a single further word to anyone. He headed north towards Calgary with the longing to lose himself in the anonymity of the city, to cower under the cover of crowded streets; the blanket of thousands of passersby. And then paradoxically, as go the tides of fear and their inevitable ebb and flow, it would be that same detail which would lure him back a few hours later, with a yearning just as fervent for isolation. To be in the middle of a vast and endless vista without any constructs or foliage or impediments of any kind to obscure approaching danger. By early evening he would be once again at the little park by the bridge, slowly approaching the now-deserted grounds, collar up, backpack slung over his shoulder and, even though the sun was well behind the mountains to the west, sunglasses on.

He would find the package under the fourth picnic table he inspected, at the opposite end of the park from where the camper had been attacked. And he would find it just as a set of headlights appeared on the horizon from the south. Coming fast. Very fast. It could be anybody, he assured the cacophony of voices gathering in his head. Nevertheless he worked faster to extricate the envelope from its hiding place, pulling and hacking at the duct tape with the teeth of his car keys, sneaking glances back over the tabletop toward the highway. Once it was free he raced for the car, throwing the packet into his backpack, the backpack through the open window. He fumbled with the ignition as he glanced again. The other car was only seconds from the bridge and slowing to turn into the camp. There were two men in the front seat, possibly another in the back. There would be no time to beat them out the laneway, so he pushed his sunglasses up hard against his nose, leaned his elbow over the open window, feigned a yawn and lowered his face. He let the car come past him, then as calmly and casually as possible put his vehicle in gear and drove off, once again heading north.

Only when he had safely made it over the first hill and out of sight of the campground did he dare accelerate. 110 km/h ... 115 km/h ... urging, swearing, pleading the car forward ... imploring it to eat the distance away as quickly as possible. 120 km/h ... 125 km/h. A set of headlights blinked into view in the rear mirror. 130 ... 135 ... He thought of Chris, thought of what must have been horrific last moments for his life, careening down a highway out of control ... 140, 145 ... Still the headlights grew closer and brighter, until finally, mercifully, the distant illumination of a small town blinked on the horizon ahead. Longview.

Soon he could make out the outline of a gas station and variety store. It would be his only hope. Moments later he was screeching to a halt, grabbing his backpack and abandoning the vehicle on the shoulder of the road. Desperate for nightfall to swallow him up, he sprinted away from the road toward the shadows behind the store ... his eyes darting frantically for somewhere ... anywhere ... to hide.

# THREE

*Her arms are pinned out wide against the mattress. She cannot move her legs. She throws her head from side to side to make a blur of the heavy form straddled tight against her groin. She moans to drown out the angry, wordless panting in her ear; and to thwart the thick dank smell of saliva across her cheek. Shuts her eyes and longs for the days when these measures actually had even the slightest effect. Like the drugs had once afforded. The booze and the pills.*

*He pumps faster; rougher ...finally speaks ... "Come on you fuckin' little whore ... come on" ...*

*Dutifully she moans a bit louder ...*

... the office phone rang. Instinctively she screamed. Pumped her arms in a violent bench press and sprang to her feet from the makeshift bed done up with blankets and cushions tossed against a wall of filing cabinets. Threw her eyes around the room, then dropped her face into her hands. A second ring ... a third. For a moment she needed to pace. To reorient to the here-and-now. The call went to message ... and she heard Keegan's voice.

*Bronny, it's me. I think I'm in trouble. Ivan and Peter are getting super weird. It's fuckin' freaking me out. And it has to do with you. They keep stopping by the flat, even came to work yesterday saying they were looking for you ... where have you been anyway? They think I know and I'm just not telling. I'm really scared, Brons ... I think they're actually into some really bad shit. Ivan got rough last night. Had me pinned up against the wall outside the pub. I told him I don't want any part of whatever's goin' on, but he was just like, "I'm afraid it's too late for that."*

*I'm going north to hide out at Mum's for a bit. You should think about doing the same. Shit, somebody's at the fuckin' door ... Shit–*

# Four

The shuffling of feet on gravel and the hissing of instructions returned several times over, each visit sounding more enraged than the last. In each instance Ian dropped his head, re-clenched his jaw and worked as hard as he ever had to be completely still – at first for preservation's sake, but then, as the night deteriorated, as an exercise in resignation. Making peace with the fact that this once seemingly epic and grand enterprise with days spent circumnavigating a never-ending open prairie had now been reduced to the finite singularity of one little blackened spot in the corner of a shed. A spot where – surely it was just a matter of time – he would soon meet his end.

The fear of it all, that was his enemy now. The *real* enemy. The only task remaining was to battle *it*, wage his own private war against it in the silent moments between the frantic noises outside. And war against this darkness was of a different order. One borne of a lifelong despair that he had always suspected would accompany him to his dying day; a black cloak of the unknown history and severed lineage that was his life. Everything borrowed and second-hand. Nothing of his own. No tales of fearless ancestors; no anecdotes of courage or struggle or heroics. No fodder for a folk song. He was a tune with no tale. A costume with no character inside. An echo from no sound.

And this was why – despite all the recent examination of Chris's songwriting, all of the parsing of verse and chorus – he now realized that he had never really *heard* the wealth of his friend's words for himself. The turns of phrase, the evocative style, the use of allegory and irony. It was all lost on him.

Yes, there had been endless irrefutable evidence all around him ... every time Mill Run released a CD, received a concert review, or even took to the stage. Chris's genius had always been the topic at the fore for critics, and fans, and fellow musicians alike. But in the brutal honesty of his mortality, Ian found himself forced to confess that he had never really come by those riches naturally. Never directly. The closest he had ever come ... *would ever come* ... was as a third party, just off to the side, stage right, observing the effect of Chris's genius in the wide and eager eyes of a *Mill Run* audience, the collective attention hanging on each word sung, heads bobbing, sometimes smiling, sometimes in tears, sometimes with sudden spontaneous eruptions of pleasure and enthusiasm.

~

*"You're not really a master-plan kind of guy, are you?"*

*They're having breakfast in the front nook of their hotel. The early sun beams in across their table. It's the morning after the first show in a run of a half-dozen out around the Great Lakes, just a few months into Ian's tenure.*

*"You sound like my ex."*

*"Recent ex?"*

*"Walked out a week before I joined you guys."*

*"Good thing we came along when we did then."*

*Ian sits back, rips a bite of toast and chews a moment. A smile crosses his face.*

*"The day I dropped the last of her things back at her parents' place, I came home ... saw the answering machine blinking. I said to myself, 'If this is somebody who knows a guy who runs a studio who knows a folk-roots band specializing in storytelling songs and Canadiana, looking to hire a keyboard player, well shit, I'm all in!' ... Why do you ask?"*

*"About the ex?"*

*"Mmm ... the other. The master plan thing."*

*Chris waves his hand and swallows a mouthful of coffee. "Oh no reason really. I was just thinking about back in the car yesterday. You were telling me how you've been trying your hand at writing. You mentioned a few half-finished manuscripts–"*

*"Half-started would be more like it."*

*Chris sucks some jam from his thumb and thinks a moment. "Now when you say half-started, would that be because you can't translate your ideas into something tangible, or is it a case that you've got so many ideas all competing with one another, that it kind of paralyzes them all, if that makes any sense."*

*Ian nods, closes his eyes a moment to try to crystallize a reply. "That's ... sort of it," he says. "But I wouldn't say it's because of any huge volume ... more like whatever ideas I do get never quite feel like I really belong to them."*

*Chris stops chewing. "That* you *belong to* them? *Interesting."*

*"Yeah ... well, sort of ...OK, think of it like this ... by way of analogy. I, Ian Station, was fostered into this family of very definite people."*

*"I would hope so."*

*"No, what I mean is, it's this clan where lineage is very im-*

*portant.*"

"*So strong family ties then.*"

"*That's putting it lightly. Take my own dear foster mother, Arlene Millicent Henley-Station, for example.*"

"*Henley-Station?*"

"*What the hell is so funny?*"

"*Nothing ... just thought of a joke about your conception ... I mean, if she had been your birth mom, that is.*"

"*How's that?*"

"*You know ... pulling into Henley-Station—*"

"*ANYWAY, Mother dearest can trace both the Henley and the Station family trees back about five generations ... and I mean every single bloody branch. And since we grew up in this big old farmhouse with lots of wall space, she took it upon herself to immortalize as many of those branches as possible. Photos of grandparents and great grandparents, great uncles and great aunts, second cousins, second cousins once removed ... But here's the thing, I couldn't put a name to half of them. Maybe even two-thirds. Couldn't tell you how one was related to another. Yet there they all are, staring back at me from these old shots, a good number of them taken out in front of the very same farmhouse I grew up in, staring back like—*"

"*Like they can't place you either?*"

*Ian snaps his fingers and points back at Chris.* "*Exactly. A stranger in my own house. And you know what else?*"

"*What?*"

"*For the life of me, I can't remember what the hell any of this has to do with whatever we were talking about.*"

*Chris reaches for his notebook, puts it at the ready next to his elbow, but doesn't open it.* "*Well, it sounds like you are saying you're not comfortable self-identifying as part of that clan.*"

"*Right. That's it ... but, wait ... how does that relate to ...?*

*Oh yeah, I remember now. So, here's my point. Because I've lived with this kind of orphaned interloper, don't-quite-belong vibe, maybe it's the same when I try to attach myself to any one specific idea for a story. Before there's a chance of getting really immersed, it starts to feel too restrictive and I get this restless notion that maybe I'm missing out on writing something else. Something more important, or truer to who I am ... whoever the hell that is."*

*Chris drops his head, and taps the cover of his notebook, a mischievous grin creeps to the corner of his mouth.*

*"So what you're saying is, you have commitment issues."*

*"Well, when you put it like that—"*

*"Sound like your ex again, do I?" he says and they both let out a laugh. "Why, I bet you're just putting in time with us. Just biding your time until The Tragically Hip come a-calling. Finally decide they need a piano player."*

*"Hey, when I get home, if that answering machine is blinking again ..."*

*Chris lifts his mug in a toast and, still chuckling, says, "Well, here's hoping Mill Run can buck the trend."*

*He leans his elbows on the table and folds his hands. "And in all honesty, it's great to have you on board. At this point, it might still feel like you're just a sideman. Trust me, I know how Dan and Myles garner a lot of the glory up on stage ... and before you think it, yes, I am well aware they would say the same about me."*

*Ian nods. "I'm thinking maybe Myles more than Dan."*

*"The point is we all truly want you here, plain and simple. You weren't hired by accident. And while I can't sit here and promise you this band will turn out to be the answer to all your creative goals, if it can give you even some bit of belonging, well maybe that's at least something. As for worrying about*

*finding the perfect idea for a story, I wouldn't sweat it too much."* He taps his notebook again. *"I mean, it's not like every page in here turns into a song ..."*

~

He woke with a start, his elbow striking the inner wall of the shed's shell with echoing force; his foot against what sounded like the hollow thud of a plastic gas can. There were voices calling out in instant response, back and forth amidst the sound of running feet ... first distant, then closer.

"Back here behind the store," he heard someone call out and suddenly in that instant, with his position compromised, with the end near, he missed his life. Every single part of it. The music. The travelling. His bandmates ... each and every song of each and every show they had all ever played together. He longed to stretch out his arms, and hands. His fingers. Longed for the weight of a chord beneath the wail of Chris's fiddle strings. For the stretch of an octave or a run up the keyboard, like those nights when his wrists had felt locked in and light as air; floating straight over the piano, fingers brushing the notes below; a ground left-hand drone under some Celtic-flavoured progression; the loft of a chord rooted over its third or its fifth. How he so wished he could once more set the musical bed from which all those magical, mystical story-songs took flight. Wished he could once more help them soar that inch or two higher ... add that extra bit of colour ... that sheen.

And yet despite the danger – for the *life* of him – he could not hold his head one moment longer. Could only surrender to the hopeless inevitability, as he slumped to his side and let the crash of the steel wall reverberate anew.

*They're back onstage. Chris has his fiddle up under his chin.*

*He steps back to lean over the keyboard, stomping his foot in time with Ian's left-hand piano line. They are in the groove, playing as one. Ian looks up just as his friend lets out a whoop and dances back across the stage ...*

"Check that shed!"

*No! He's not ready. Not yet. But the voices inside implore him to summon all his remaining energy and burst from his hiding place. To run as long and as hard as he can, screaming the bloody murder that surely awaits him; the soundtrack of his demise and his nothingness; the music of being mere seconds from no longer knowing, or hearing or feeling anything ever again ...*

The door of the garden shed crashed open and the dawn's low sunlight exploded inside. He raised his hands to block the glare; squeezed shut his eyes. He could smell the stale stench of fear on his body; could feel his bowels fighting to release.

"Sarge, over here!" came a voice cutting through the light and he was aware of more footsteps running at him.

"Are you Ian Station?" the officer panted. Ian squinted up around his fingertips. It looked to be an older man. White-haired, but strong and confident. The officer reached down and pulled the piano player to his feet.

"We've been looking for you, son."

# THE FINAL REFRAIN

*Given the strains that modern music has put on the folk song with its ever-increasing reliance on bridges, instrumental solos and other gimmicky interruptions, the need for a return to the familiar – that is to say, a strong final verse and a rallying refrain – has never been more acute. Simply put, the musical foundation upon which the initial narrative was established must return in full force for the song to be a success.*

**~Chetwynd C. Lovett**
*The Orthodoxy of Folk Song*

# ONE

*You're listening to Angie Cavano and the Sunday Night Folk Show on CBZT, Community Radio. Tonight we are pleased to be joined in studio by former Mill Run front men Myles Thomas and Dan LaForge. Gentlemen, welcome and thanks for doing this, especially given the fact we're coming up on the two-year anniversary of the death of founding member Chris Lucan. Myles, can you let our listeners in on what the past couple of years have been like?*

"Well, obviously we were gutted for quite a while. But I think the last few years have given us the time to put *Mill Run's* legacy in the right perspective. I think Dan and I, in our own ways, have made our peace with the hand we were dealt."

*How so?*

"Well, I think it's fairly common knowledge that Chris had been suffering through the early stages of some form of dementia that last year. I mean, give him credit. Knowing his fate, he was still out there, trying his damnedest to get out one more round of songs ... leave one more chapter in the *Mill Run* catalogue. Unfortunately, as both Dan and I have mentioned in other interviews ... certainly the *Roots Cellar* articles focused on it ... we were frustrated."

*Frustrated how?*

"At working with material that was inferior to everything that had preceded it. I mean, I don't want to come off sounding cold, but those songs simply weren't Chris. Then add to that the frustration later on when we actually first learned of the illness and realized he had kept it from us intentionally."

*So you didn't know about the Alzheimer's?*

"All we knew is Chris wanted that last CD recorded fast. And after that he wanted to call it a day. Otherwise we were scratching our heads just like everyone else."

*And then came the car crash.*

"And then came the car crash."

*Was there any thought that his diminished capacity was at fault there too?*

"There was some speculation, sure. But anybody who knew Chris knew he wasn't exactly the most attentive driver to begin with, so at the end of the day, who's to say?"

*Fair enough. How about a track from more favourable times then. As many Mill Run fans will remember, Chris Lucan was heading to the airport en route to one final gig when he lost control of his vehicle north of Toronto. As a tribute to the show he never got to play, here is the Mill Run classic,* The Monument, *on The Sunday Night Folk Show.*

~

When those investigating were satisfied that his statements were the extent of information they could extract, Ian was released from the bowels of the RCMP offices with the reassurance that anyone who might have posed a threat to him had now been identified and arrested. This was – as the anti-trafficking task force manager assigned to his debriefing explained – thanks in no small measure to the actions of one Bronwyn Lucan, who had prompted contacts at Scotland Yard to reach out and coordinate with the RCMP, the FBI, US and Canadian Immigration offices and a half-dozen other foreign agencies. *The tenacity of a bulldog* was the phrase quoted from the notes describing her efforts.

It was explained that what Ian and his friend had become entangled in was actually something of a hybrid criminal organization dealing mostly in human trafficking and forced prostitution, not only in cities across Canada but also in the US, the UK, Europe and Asia. Buying, selling, moving girls about here and there, from one country and crime ring to another whenever law enforcement got too close.

"We think the people who were after you were local traffickers ... the equivalent to street gang levels of crime. But we're also pretty sure they had pitched themselves to much larger operations out of the US and Eastern Europe. Probably offering to do transit work for them ... promising delivery of so many girls in and out of the country, not to mention the means to forge documents to get them here and there. That's what those passports and work permits you found were all about. Earmarked to get women through Britain from the continent ... via France or Belgium most likely. You said your friend who hid them was a travelling musician. Our guess is if any of that touring included Europe, he would have eventually been forced to smuggle them over there."

The officer described how they had been tracking the ring for quite a while and were fairly sure they were using a combination of reserves along the US border and at least one fly-in hunting lodge to move both girls and documents. When provincial police started putting the squeeze on, they most likely got very desperate, given how ruthless most of the big international syndicates are. They would not have taken kindly to one of their subcontractors failing to deliver on promises, and the locals would have been well aware of that. That's when the idea of "recruiting" Chris would have come about, she had explained. With the help of operatives from the syndicates over in England tracking down his daughter for leverage.

"But thanks to you and her, we have them all rounded up."

The officer glanced up from the paperwork she had been working on throughout her exposition – ticking boxes, flipping and stapling pages, signing here, initialling there. "But that said, the reality is, given our resources and the courts, at the end of the day, even something as big as this is still only a drop in the bucket."

She flicked a nod toward the wall of filing cabinets behind her. "Affects maybe two or three out of a hundred trafficking rings we have on file there. Everything from organized operations down to some individual prick who'll keep a girl or two locked up in a motel room on a regular basis. What's that expression? Power hates a vacuum? Well it's pretty much the case with this kind of power. Truth is, there is a good chance that taking down this outfit will actually prove to be a great business opportunity for other trafficking operations to step in. Because, at the end of the day, we may have gotten some pathetic slugs off the street, but we haven't done a thing about the market that exists for these girls. It'll still be there tomorrow, and the next day. Just as popular as ever."

~

Later that afternoon he would visit a bank to extract the last thousand dollars available from his swollen line of credit, the bulk of which he would use to make his way home – first by way of Northern Ontario to retrieve his own vehicle, then south through Minnesota, Illinois, Indiana and Michigan ... this time at a far slower, deliberate pace, stopping often for long breaks at coffee shops and roadside diners to linger with the world he had been racing past for the previous three weeks.

Those weeks had taken their toll. Frequently he would catch himself; in larger cities, scanning the sidewalks and intersections, watching for any sign of women working a street; in the smaller towns, for girls whose posture or demeanor, suggested a similar future somewhere down the line. Teenagers ... high school students walking to or from a school. Groups of girls in a mall or outside a plaza, all of them ... observed as either precarious or safe. Self-assured or manipulable. Then he would catch himself again and try to just shake it off – this reductionism that had smeared itself all over his world view. Try to scrape it from the soles of his shoes ... on the side of a curb, or the cracked and crumbling sidewalk of some poorly-lit street. Wipe it from the restaurant benches where he ate his lunch, from the doorknobs of the motel rooms he rented.

Eventually he would take some of his money – three hundred dollars – and fold it into a clipping from one of the first newspaper articles about the arrests; one he had chosen because it dealt with the issue on its broadest terms, linking the RCMP manhunt through western Canada to the investigations in Ontario and the US, to England and Europe. He would underline and highlight the paragraph that chronicled how many arrests had been made in all of these jurisdictions. Then in the margin, in thin black felt, he would write: *"Thanks to a granddaughter's courage."*

He would think about signing his name, but decide against

it. Would put the clipping and the money in an envelope, find the address of the Rainy River Motel online, and label the letter: *To the maids who clean up after us.*

He would do it because he hated the world in its current appearance ... reduced to hunter versus prey ... attacker versus victim. He would do it because he somehow felt complicit. But mostly he would do it because he had no idea what else to do.

# Two

*So Dan ... can we address what might be a bit of an elephant in the room, thanks to some social media speculation that has popped up here and there in the past few months? And from the look on your face you know what I'm going to ask, don't you?*

"Pretty good idea, Angie, yes."

*For those listeners who might not be aware, there have been, well I don't want to say 'reports' ... there have been theories? ... allegations maybe, that your bandmate Chris Lucan had somehow got involved in some criminal activities towards the end. I know, I shake my head, every time I read this stuff too, but it would seem conspiracy buffs and folkies are not mutually exclusive groups, because these stories just won't go away, will they? Suggested links between the dates of Mill Run concerts and the movements of certain trafficking rings in Northern Ontario and in Saskatchewan. Now I know you and Myles have addressed this previously ...*

"Oh yes–"

*...but I wanted to give you the chance to clear the air on that score with our listening audience. Because you should*

*know, despite the years away, you still have a very fervent core of 'Mill-Runners' out there, requesting your songs each and every week.*

"Which is always nice to hear. Thanks, Angie. But this idea that Chris was involved in something nefarious ... I guess if I have to speak to it, I would just remind your listeners that Chris and I formed this band over twenty years ago and you simply don't spend that much time with someone and not know what he is or isn't capable of. So it took me approximately a nano-second to conclude the idea of Chris being part of this, in any manner, was pure fantasy."

*'In any manner', yes ... I should clarify for those that haven't been following these threads on social media. In fact, while a good number of these 'speculations' suggest Chris was in league with criminal enterprises, many others hold that he was actually working either on his own, or with the authorities, to fight them.*

"It is an epic notion. Heroic even. But I'm afraid my previous answer still applies. That just wasn't Chris. At his essence, Chris was an artist who lived his life inside his head, honing his creativity. And for this, we all should feel eternally grateful. Feel blessed even. I know I do. Because I was the beneficiary. Myles too."

*So where do you think these notions come from?*

"I suppose a good portion of the population entertains them-selves with theories like these, don't they? And usually it's something negative, to level out the successes of anyone whose status they deem to be soaring a bit too high. But in rarer in-stances, maybe when an inspired soul like a Christopher Lucan has met an untimely end, there is a need to mythologize. To lift up and exalt. So the genius that he truly was can still grow in the face of grief. A folk hero, if you will."

*It brings the dearly departed Stan Rogers to mind.*

"Perfect example. The number of theories I've heard at festivals and folk clubs about Stan's passing–"

*I should just cut in again for any listeners late to the dance ... the great Canadian folk legend Stan Rogers died in a fire onboard an Air Canada flight after an emergency landing in Cincinnati back in ... 1983 was it?*

"'83, yes. And since then I've heard everything from him dying because he insisted on staying on board to help get the other passengers out, to the theory that the fire started in the first place because he had snuck into the washroom for a smoke."

*And which side do you come down on?*

"I come down on neither. Because when it comes to mythology, who's right and who's wrong doesn't matter, does it? What matters is that all those versions, for better or worse, have served to help fans keep Stan's memory alive within them. It's the same with Chris. Yes, there were some weird coincidences. We did play a show in Rainy River that was organized by a man who ended up robbed and killed a week later in Saskatchewan. And yes, it was in a town where we had also played that tour ... but like I said, if you knew Chris Lucan as well as I did ..."

~

Ridgway, Pennsylvania. Ian couldn't remember much about the place other than the fact that, like most of the towns in the region, it sat at the bottom of a rather steep and wooded valley. That, and the fact the summer festival they had headlined a number of years before had been held in a park next to a shallow stone-bottomed river that meandered through said valley. Nevertheless there was something vaguely familiar about the cafe with its spindle-back chairs and checkered tablecloths. The chrome-edged counter lined with glass-covered displays for baking. The tree-branch-filtered view of the sleepy little side street outside. Like he had read about it, or had it described to him at some point or another.

The owner was a round but spry woman in her sixties, who came bounding out from behind the counter upon first sight of him.

"Oh no need to introduce yourself, dear," she said as she pulled off her apron, grabbed him by his cheeks and with locked-on eyes voiced her condolences over the death of his Mill Run partner. Her absolute favorite musician in the whole world, whose music had helped get her through some difficult times over the years, what with her own husband passing away from Alzheimer's just a year before Chris had confided in her his own illness – her of all people! –and had asked her to send on all those private emails, but only after he too was gone, which she thought wouldn't be for years, although when news of the car accident reached her, she decided to send them on anyway, heartbroken though she was.

"We were such big fans," she told him before finally taking a breath. "Both me and my Tommy. Why, we drove all the way to State College one time just to hear you boys. Erie too. Twice."

"One thing I was wondering," Ian asked, his face still compacted between her palms. "We didn't see much of Chris in those last weeks. By any chance was he down here?"

The woman smiled, released his head and reached out for his hands. Her head bobbed in an enthusiastic nod, her eyes welling up.

"This is why I so hoped you would come one day," she said.

"I mean I suppose I would have just sent it on eventually ... like the rest ..."

"Sent what on?"

"But then I'd say to myself, no, Marjorie. Chris left this with very specific instructions. I was to forward the last email only once you were safe. Except I don't actually think he meant just safe. I think he meant when you were *OK* ... which I took to be more than just your physical safety ... more like making sure you had gotten through the whole ordeal without too much unbearable trauma ... both of you."

"Both of us?"

The woman nodded some more.

"So you ..."

"Marjorie."

"Marjorie ... so you knew about everything Chris was doing?"

"Oh yes, dear."

"And everything I was doing?"

A tear tracked down the woman's cheek but her head kept bobbing. "My brother Ted is retired from Philadelphia Vice. And let me tell you, he fought more than his share of trafficking operations in his twenty-seven years on the force. Chris remembered meeting and chatting with him when you played the festival."

Ian collapsed onto the nearest chair and slung his computer up onto a side table. He stared into space, his mouth moving noiselessly as he worked over the woman's information. "So ... it wasn't just because of the email coincidences?"

"Well, I'm sure that's where the idea started. At least, that's what I always assumed anyway. But one of those mix-ups probably tweaked his memory of talking to Ted. It happens sometimes, doesn't it? One thing suddenly suggests a solution

for something else. If you're paying attention, that is. The trouble is, people today miss so much all around them. Either because they're too busy, or because it's just not what they're expecting to find. Take my Tommy ... if he hadn't happened to turn on NPR one night, and hear the end of *Barn Dance Romance* ... I mean he never listened to public radio ... Never. But there you were, singing away–"

"So Chris asked your brother to help him?" Ian cut in.

Marjorie nodded. "He asked me to get in touch with Ted for him. And I was only too willing. I mean the poor man. On top of already being sick ... getting blackmailed by those roughnecks up there in Ontario ... and seeing that poor fellow get murdered. But you know ... in spite of it all, Ted was never sure how much actual help Chris was looking for. He was so gosh darn scared they would find out and harm his daughter. I mean it was all my brother could do to persuade the man to let him contact the RCMP and Canadian Immigration. And it sure as heck was no picnic getting him to agree to police protection."

"Chris was under police protection?"

"Stowed away on some island in the Great Lakes, according to Ted."

"Did he say where?"

The woman shrugged. "I'm sorry dear, not to me." She pulled over another chair and sat down to face him once more, her hands reaching out to rest on his kneecaps. "Please know my brother tried his best to help," she said. "It's just he always suspected Chris's fear for his daughter was going to be too much for him to put his trust in anybody. Well, besides you and me, I guess. Anyway, when Ted learned that Chris had left the safe house the very day he died–"

"He was on his way to meet up with us in France."

"Well, that may well be true, but according to Ted, the OPP

... that is what you call them, right, OPP? ... they figured it was a case of Chris getting so frightened he felt had to take matters into his own hands and make a run for it. My brother, on the other hand, was of the opinion that Chris had planned to bolt all along ... agreeing to let the authorities step in had always been just a bit of insurance, in case things went wrong."

"*In case* things went wrong?" Ian slumped back against the chair-back, his arms falling limp to his sides. She bent down in front of him.

"How be I set up that email now?" she said, and gathered up his dangling limbs to lead him to a back room with a small wooden desk and a computer console iced in a thin film of flour. "We haven't quite progressed to something as portable as that laptop of yours," she said, dusting off the keyboard and reaching beneath the tabletop to fire up the tower. She clicked on a file labelled simply *Mill*, then wheeled over a rolling chair, patted the seat, and backed out of the room.

*Dear Ian,*

*If you are indeed still with me ... I need to thank you.*

*With all of my heart, my friend.*

*And if you are still with me, I need to apologize now for every degree of deception I have put you through, starting with the sudden decision to retire from the band. Then the need to record the songs as hastily as we did. And, of course, if not outright feigning a disease, at least my allowing the rumours of it to go unfettered.*

*There are a couple of details, however, that I want you to be fully aware of, just in case they are still in doubt. The concert in Vimy was of my own concocting; a favour called in to Veteran's Affairs from my ex-wife who represented them in some legal actions back in the day. The passports and work papers that I hid (and can now only hope you have found) were forgeries. They were made by the most vile of men, who hit on the idea of using a harmless-looking folk musician to hold onto them and deliver them to a place of their choosing. That call came a month ago, as I write this now. I had four weeks to get them to their people in Europe or else they told me they would rape and then kill my daughter. I needed an excuse to go, and, as you may have already suspected, another to never arrive.*

*This is the last day of my life.*

*Tomorrow I will make a hasty plea to Myles to join you all for one more performance. Myles will be livid, but Dan will overcome those frustrations with his hope for one final show all together. I will race for the airport, most likely with members of this crime ring in close pursuit. Even with the safeguards we have taken, I know they are watching my every move. I will not take the highway through Orangeville and Brampton, but will instead lead them east through the Hockley Valley. At the bottom of the second steep downhill, I will take my hands from the steering wheel. And with my last breath will know that the power these pathetic excuses for human beings have held over me will finally be over. My daughter and my friends will all be safe. This is, at once, my fuel and my solace.*

*Always be well, my friend.*

*Chris*

~

There was more hugging upon his return to the storefront. More gentle inquiries about his mental state, if he was *still OK*. He concluded quickly, ahead of the fast-approaching wave of numbness, that Marjorie could not have been privy to the note herself, not given the series of offers for baked goods, her need to list her favourite *Mill Run* songs and describe how she played them in the car constantly ... especially for the grandchildren when she babysat on the days her daughter Audrey worked a shift down at the grocery store. Audrey would have been on the stage crew when they played the street festival, she said. Used to be full-time at the library but after the baby, what with husband Mike's hours at the dealership in town, part-time work was the best she could manage ...

Finally ... mercifully ... as a growing queue at the till bade her retreat, Ian sat back down in his previous chair, this time straight upright against the spindles, eyes glazed forward staring into space. He felt the stiffness of his own posture; decided it was perhaps from the shock of Chris's bluntness; or maybe, he then thought, possibly the result of months of shock wearing off ... the grave finality of his friend's fate only now fully sinking in.

*Was he still OK*? Really?

Without thinking he grabbed for his laptop and flipped it open. There at long last, cruelly coinciding with the message he had just read, lay a response from Bronwyn.

*Ian.*

*I have been on indefinite leave from work, so I have only now received all of your emails from my assistant. She is just now returning to her job having been put in police protection for the past two weeks thanks to me involving her computer and her desk with our little foray into the world of organized crime. My best friend Keegan did not fare as well. Suffice it to say the most genuine and generous person I have ever known is dead – because of me. Those bastards tried to get to me through our friendship, but because she was completely innocent in the whole matter, and because she actually knew nothing of the shitstorm that you and Daddy dearest put me through, she could offer no information no matter how many times they beat her and violated her (the details of which I will not share). So in answer to the question about my well-being that seems to permeate your many, many email inquiries, please know that I am, and will always be, eternally fucked up. However I am alive and breathing, as my father so charged you to ensure, so on that score ... mission accomplished. You are hereafter absolved of his wishes. Goodbye.*

It was truly a horrible misstep to attempt a response. Truly idiotic to ignore the brutal honesty of the note and give in to the temptation to remedy her rage. *Fix* it. Temper it. Frame it in consolation and would-be empathy. (Give it that bit of sheen.) Certainly the bit about understanding how all of this turmoil, on the heels of losing her father, was more than anyone should have to cope with ... yes, that had been a mistake.

The next email arrived in less than fifteen minutes.

*Let me be clear. I despise my father. I disown, disavow, reject and condemn the very things that all of his adoring fans ever grabbed hold of and celebrated. The so-called creativity, sup- posed capacity for empathy? I wrap all of it up in one blanket judgement and proclaim it to be nothing more than a festering pile of bullshit.*

*Chris Lucan had absolutely no time for me. Chris Lucan was far too busy basking in the sunshine of praise and acclaim. It was his crack. And trust me, a ten-year-old cannot compete with that level of addiction. But just in case you are thinking of writing all of this off as the latent petulance of some whiny schoolgirl, please let me also say this.*

*For better or worse, I have made my way in the world on my own. All that I have accomplished has been in spite of my father, not – save for one initial shot of sperm – because of him. Furthermore while you may have seen Christopher Lucan as some sage visionary, a man of the people who invoked music and metre to their otherwise mundane lives, I only saw a beggar and a thief, living off the avails of those peoples' stories. Yes, I've read the reviews and the articles. How my dad could find the hidden gem of the profound amidst the everyday ... the divine within the ordinary ... again I say, bullshit. Utter fucking bullshit.*

*But I guess my father rather enjoyed his own press, didn't he? How else could someone actually believe he could take down the bloody mob by planting clues inside song lyrics, instead of just calling the goddamn cops in the first place. And for the life of me, I don't know why you're not pissed off too. Leading you around the country playing fetch like some hapless hound dog ... the fifth song, the first song, the ninth song ...five, one, nine, five again, almost getting killed in the process. Fooling absolutely no one!*

*For Christ's sake why aren't you angry about that...*

Even though it was correspondence by email, it was – if not also another outright mistake – at the very least, less than good form to abandon Bronwyn's diatribe when there were clearly several more paragraphs detailing the depths of her rage. But in his defence, it was not done out of insensitivity, but rather as a function of how quickly a notion had hit him. What was it Marjorie had said? Sometimes one thing suggests a solution for something else?

It was in the way she had written out the track numbers, or at least the way he had read them. He scrolled back through all of Bronwyn's old emails that had instructed him which songs to study when. Scribbled down the sequence and studied it, mouthing the numbers over and over until the cadence that had first suggested itself became clear again. He inserted the breaks he now could infer ... 519-376-2548.

~

*-Johnston's Island Cottage Rentals*
"Hi ... yes, I was wondering if you could help me."
*-Certainly, we have several weekly and monthly rental packages.*
"Oh, sorry, no. I wasn't calling to ... excuse me but could you tell me where I'm calling exactly?"
*-You've reached our Owen Sound number. Our units are all*

*on the islands adjacent to the village of Oliphant, Ontario on Lake Huron. So what can I do for you?*

"I was wondering if your business has ever had any dealings with a man named Chris Lucan."

(There was a pause at the other end of the line.)

*-The fella that died in the car accident?*

"Yes."

*-Friend of yours?*

"Bandmate, yes."

The man informed Ian that Chris had been staying in one of their cottages right up until the day of the crash. Had asked to be checked on just once a week or so, for supplies, which was just as well since he had picked a cabin out on one of the furthest islands, out past the channel and around to the south. Really just an over-glorified shoal of rocks, he said. Even though the mapmakers had given her a name.

Vimy Island.

# THREE

*Gentlemen, since it's now been over two years since your last show, I was wondering if I could get you to share just a bit about what you miss, and maybe even what you don't miss about life on the road. How about we get the 'don't miss' part out of the way first. Dan, let's start with you.*

"What I don't miss? Geez, that's an interesting one ... let's see, what don't I miss about Mill Run?"

*Sounds like not much.*

"True. I mean I was and will always remain completely and wholeheartedly in love with that band. That band was my saving grace. Waking up on the day of a show, knowing we were going to be in front of an audience that had collectively shaped its day around our music ... bought tickets, often drove great distances, made a night of it ... how does that not put a huge bounce in your step? But ... if I have to come up with something, I guess it would be that last tour out west, and then recording the last album. Seeing Chris trying to soldier on. And then, like we were saying before, learning that he hadn't felt he could share his illness with us. That he didn't let us in. Those are things I could have done without."

*For sure ... Myles, how about you?*

"What I don't miss?"

*For starters.*

"Well ... I guess I would have to say it's the business side of folk music."

*Now that's an interesting answer. Can you elaborate?*

"Well I'm not sure if your listeners would be aware of it, but in the hierarchy of duties and responsibilities, the job of booking and management fell on my shoulders, and even for a hard-working band that was as successful as Mill Run, there was a sense in which each day was a brand new struggle. Even at the best of times, there was always a hint of desperation to touring life."

*Fair bit of stress on you particularly then?*

"Well, don't get me wrong, I did love it at the time. Getting Chris's songs, getting Dan's voice in front of as many people as I possibly could."

*And yet you used the word desperation.*

"I did. Because after doing that job for a while, even with the best of intentions, the procedure becomes a bit stale ... the same venues booked every year, often the same month as before ... things seem maybe a bit predictable ... a bit stagnant."

*Sorry, not to quarrel, but with so many acts out there struggling to make a go of it, even on a part-time basis, it sounds like what you're describing is more or less a built-in guaranteed tour schedule.*

"So where's the desperate part?"

*I guess that's what I'm asking, yes.*

"It comes in realizing that your band may not actually be progressing. That it's merely holding its own. And if that's the case, well as they say, if you're not moving forward, you're going backwards."

*But was that really the case with you guys?*

266 — A Song With No Words

"Well that 'built-in' audience you mentioned can't sustain itself forever. All the old folk clubs from back in the day rely on the efforts of volunteers and staff that come from a demographic that's rapidly aging and not being replaced. And commercial clubs that still book folk and roots stuff are getting few and far between, so unless you are completely on the very top shelf of touring acts, it's a grind because the mid-size venue is quickly going the way of the dodo. The scene now is smaller coffee clubs ... single and duo acts. If musicians want to be in a band, they might unite for occasional projects, but not for their bread-and-butter gig. Add to that the fact CDs no longer sell, since music is virtually free online ... and I don't know if a four-piece like ours could make a go of it now."

*Really? Just a few years on?*

"Not if we were starting from scratch. I mean, I click on my Facebook just like all my musician friends. And sure there are lots of pictures of smiling faces strumming away on café patios and in restaurants, but I have to say ... I'm not sure if posting a couple of dozen shots of a set in front of twenty-five diners is really making a go of it, do you?"

*So if I am reading you right, would it be safe to assume that what you 'do' miss about the band, is the old days when these worries weren't so front and centre?*

"Well, let's be clear. Keeping four guys gainfully employed out on the road was always a challenge. But we were up for it. That was the thing. We answered that challenge with our shows, themselves. I'd like to think that we even, in some sense, defied the odds and the economics with what we put up on stage each and every night. Where so many others had come and gone, we had maintained this status as a hard-working touring band. So yeah, you could say that's what I miss ... that success. Absolutely."

~

They would finally meet – just once – eight years on, in an arts café in Toronto, at the launch of Ian's third novel. She would surprise him when her spot came up in the line of friends, neighbours and relatives performing a loyal duty to queue for an autographed copy, then surprise him once more by lingering afterwards with an invitation for coffee – if he had the time.

The conversation would begin carefully, she not sure if he would even realize who she was, he replying that he was fairly certain, having seen her interviewed a number of times on the news. She was living in Toronto now, she said. Had been at CBC Radio for the past three years, producing a local weekend show; she had even covered one of Dan's solo concerts down in the Beaches a year or two before as part of a piece on the arts scene there. Things were well with him. He was writing (obviously), teaching some piano, playing in a local group in and around Guelph, the city he now called home. A roadhouse band. Lots of Zeppelin and Eagles and The Stones until one in the morning most weekends. Nothing like touring with her dad, he did slip in. Just age-old songs that had been heard a hundred million times before, and would be heard a hundred million times to come. Musical meat and potatoes. Friday night beer. Safely familiar for all involved.

He would acknowledge he had been keeping up with her career. Had, for instance, caught every night of the five-part feature she had produced on human trafficking in Canada. Had kept an ear out for all the other work she had been doing in that regard: her Safe Harbour Initiative for victims of forced prostitution; various symposia and panel discussions where he had seen her lobbying for stiffer laws and stronger sentencing. He told her how impressed he was by her open and honest manner, including her own backstory as a recovered victim herself, something he confessed he had no clue about eight years before.

"The first few times were scary as hell. I'd be doing interviews with images of my mom or my grandmother bouncing around in my head, scowling away. Once I got past that, though, it was pretty liberating actually. This is me. Like me. Don't like me ..."

"Well, your dedication is admirable. I can still remember that officer who took my statement back in Alberta, talking like she had all but given up any hope of changing anything."

Bronwyn shrugged. "I don't know. I can forgive those guys for feeling like they're drowning. I mean it's still a bit of a joke in this country, given the size of the problem and the lack of dedicated policing. Some victories, for sure. Immigration finally recognizing trafficked women as victims instead of criminals, for example. But it's been like trying to move a glacier. Same with funding for the halfway shelters."

"So how do you do it?"

"What?"

"Not drown. Not just feel like it's a war that can't be won."

"Trust me, Ian, I have my why-the-fuck-bother days. I mean, you do understand these are still just baby steps, right? Christ! This country didn't even have a formal law on the books against human trafficking until 2005. And no specific mandatory prison sentences for trafficking minors until 2010."

She sat back and stared out the window into the passing row of headlights. "Of course it can't be won," she said quietly ... mostly to herself, Ian decided. "Even with proper funding, better enforcement and conviction rates. But that's exactly why you keep going, isn't it? War is life, in the end. And I don't just mean in the far-flung impoverished bits of the world.

I mean right here, right now. Right below our eye-line. Right below the blinders we put on when we proclaim our glowing mythologies about how inclusive and fair we think our country is. Or our city, or town ... neighbourhood. Right out *there* behind any one of those doors and windows ..."

She snapped from her trance and returned to the table, leaned forward on her elbows. "The truth is, I don't rail against all this shit because I think I can eradicate it, or even a thousand of me could eradicate it. I do it because somewhere out there behind one of those doors and windows, a girl is being sold and violated and raped. She needs some place to go. Some place to get nourished and detoxed. Some place to break the psychological bonds her handlers have lorded over her. Where she won't just end up resold on the street in a week or month, or a year. Because I don't know how much you've actually read up on this, but over and above all the physical abuse, it's actually those bonds that imprison them. Take my dad even. It wouldn't have been the outright violence that got to him. And trust me, knowing what I do about some of the syndicates that were involved, I have no doubt he was beaten up pretty severely. No, it was the threat of them coming after me. Maybe you too ... or Myles and Dan?"

For a moment they both went outside the window with their eyes, the floor-to-ceiling pane serving as a movie screen for their thoughts. She, nursing the image of a fetal-teenager, malnourished and unresponsive. He, the vague memory of his bandmate reaching awkwardly for a stacking chair at the back of a stage.

"I don't know," she continued softly. "I just do it in the hope that someday that girl will get to sit in a nice café, in a nice business-casual blazer and sip tea like a grown-up."

Her gaze returned to the cup in front of her and she leaned

further over the table so what heat remained could nestle between her elbows. Ian glanced around the room. It was a place for grown-ups wasn't it? Or at the very least, for playing grown-up. *Successful* grown-up. Sitting atop bright shiny chrome stools next to shiny chrome-edged tables with tempered glass tops. Drinking from trendy irregular-shaped ceramic ware with offset handles and matching creamers and sugar bowls. Crisp and white. The fading daylight wandering through their window-wall, giving way to a subdued atmosphere from the square-box steel lamp fixtures strung overhead.

He had also worn a blazer. Picked out – much against the usual contents of his wardrobe – and purchased specifically for book-launch day. Similarly, the stiff new white dress shirt beneath it. The new pair of jeans and black polished shoes. He had liked the selections when he had put them on that morning, but now – sitting across from her, and amidst the other clientele seemingly playing grown-up so much more effortlessly – he felt out of place. He glanced back across the table to find Bronwyn tugging at the bottom of her jacket, smoothing down the front pockets. She drew a long slow breath, like she was going over something previously rehearsed; like a woman regressing to deliver a grade-school speech.

"Can I confess something?" she asked, only then looking up at Ian. "Throughout the whole ordeal, there were times ... not a lot of times, maybe four or five occasions ..." She shifted her weight, looked about the room again, an awkward almost embarrassed grin flashing across her face. "I mean, he had gone through all that trouble of faking bad health and Alzheimer's and then the hidden messages, and all ..." Another glance out into the glow of the headlights parading past; then right past him, avoiding his gaze, to the coffee counter on the other side of the room. "Did you ever entertain the notion ..." A weight shift. Another ... back and forth ...

"He might have staged his death too?" Ian finished for her, nodding. "Once or twice," he said, joining her in averting his eyes. "Yeah, I thought about it."

"Yes, but did you phone up the OPP and demand information from the accident report? Demand to see the documents that matched his dental records with his remains?" The smile widened then quickly disappeared. She reached for her tea. "The thing is, I was in such a head space back then ... I was so goddamn angry, I think it was actually a relief."

"That he died?"

"I know, I know." She swiped at a tear and blew out a sigh. "You have to understand ... all I could see back then was the manipulation. The orchestrating of things at the expense of others' emotions. That's what my dad was doing when he wrote his songs, and that's what he was doing when he left that bread-crumb trail around the prairies for you to find, and the talk about the onset of Alzheimer's. He planted those seeds. Never mind all the shit that people who actually *have* the disease go through ... or their loved ones. Everything was fair game when it came to the Master-weaver. Take it, grab it, appropriate it for your own needs. And to think that bitch from the *Toronto Sun* article called *me* the retired whore."

"Jesus."

"Hey, the tree has the most say where the apple falls."

Ian stood up. He wasn't sure why. To assuage her words most likely; break their momentum. "You really still feel this strongly? Even after all this–"

"It's not that simple, Ian!" she blurted out, far louder than she had anticipated, then let out another long sigh, waving him back to his chair. "I don't *just* blame him for all of my crap. Really, I don't. But in all honesty, I can't just absolve him either."

"So what's left then?"

Once again she smoothed her garments, then folded her hands in her lap. "I don't know ... carrying on, I guess."

She grabbed the tea bag by its string and plunged it repeatedly in her mug.

"Clearly, as you just witnessed, that means not going back and delving too much."

"Sorry. My fault," Ian offered.

They would visit another half an hour or so, but for the most part it was a conversation in retreat. An anecdote about working in radio here, a story about playing a gig there ... until, with darkness descending and the evening traffic waning, she rose to leave.

"I have another confession," she said, pulling a copy of his book from her handbag. "I actually pre-ordered mine online. It came last week."

It was Ian's turn to squirm. "Have you started it?"

"Finished."

"Really?"

Bronwyn nodded. "Right to the very end, with the letter to the estranged son."

"Yeah, about that. You know I changed the details to keep anything resembling you and your dad–"

"Ian, it's OK," she cut in. Placed a hand on his. "Yes, it did have me remembering your phone call about this alleged letter you found."

"Which you made very clear you wanted no part of. I thought about sending it anyway, but figured you would probably just throw it away, or ... you know, burn *before* reading."

"Most likely," she agreed. "But remember, I already had a letter from him. The one he left in his violin case that started the whole merry-go-round. I could never really imagine there was anything more to say."

She sat halfway back down, one leg straddled on the bar stool, and closed her eyes. "I couldn't trust him then. And I'm sorry, I still don't now, Ian. Not fully. The fact that he died hasn't changed that. You may have looked at my dad and saw a man reaching out from concern for my safety. I couldn't get past the fact he left us such a mess in the first place. For you *and* me."

"But he needed to make sure you were safe."

"Yeah, I needed saving long before then, my friend." She shot up a hand. "I'm sorry, this is just the way it is. I will always be skeptical when it comes to him and me. Or you and me if you insist on defending him. I don't know ... me and men in general? That's what my therapist used to think. It was my fate. My consequence. And it's not like it hasn't borne out. Christ, some days it's all I can do to *not* see a would-be john or child molester in every guy I come across – no matter how upstanding and moral he looks or sounds. Some days *because* of how upstanding and moral he looks or sounds."

She planted her elbow on the table, dropped her chin onto her hand and looked back at him.

"I was in a restaurant in this little town last week, out on assignment. Back-to-back in a booth with a couple of old farmers having this hilarious conversation about wedding dresses."

"Really?"

"Yeah, I think one of them had a granddaughter getting married, because he was going on about how much he liked the style she had picked out. I swear to God. How the material had just the right amount of *beading* on the bodice and the waist was *gathered*. Not the sounds you expect to hear coming out from underneath a John Deere cap, right? And his friend was in there too, asking questions about the train and the neck-line and whether the sleeves were ruffled. I mean these two were talking women's fashion better than I could ever hope to, and I was just about to stand up and tell them how unbelievably refreshing it was to hear, when one of them spotted a woman – a teenager actually, by the looks of her – up at the counter in a tank top and a pair of cut-off shorts. And the same farmer who had been doing his best Ralph Lauren tells his buddy if he was only thirty years younger he'd be bending *that* over his tailgate to see if she screams. Now I know I am psychologically dam-aged goods and I always will be, but you assholes don't make it any easier, do you? You and your unbelievable ability to compartmentalize."

It was Ian's turn to play with his mug, to dance his hands from handle to spoon to creamer, staring down at his lap through the clear-glass grown-up table.

"One last confession?" he heard her ask quietly, and nodded. "I did some research on you, quite a while ago now. Call it a journalist's impulse. You were a foster kid, weren't you?"

"Still am," he replied.

"Any chance this ... well, obsession is probably overstating it – this interest, how about – in *still* trying to reconcile me with my father ... any chance it has something to do with that?"

Ian shrugged. It was a question for another time and place. A journey as of yet without a map. So after a moment, she stood again, slung her handbag over her shoulder and sighed.

"Anyway, if this so-called other letter was really so heartfelt and beautiful, why leave it in some drawer out in the middle of nowhere?"

Ian reached for his last mouthful of coffee, then rose from the table as well. On this point, he had an answer.

"Because that was Chris," he said. "For better or worse, it's what he more or less did with everything he wrote. You were right when you said a good portion of his legacy is bullshit. Maybe it's taken me a while to accept it, but the truth is whatever history will remember of your dad owes just as much to Dan's voice, and Myles's drive to get the band in front of as many people as possible. Without them, all those beautiful songs that folkies still want to hum and strum and quote, they just as easily might have ended up in some drawer too."

He reached out to shake her hand. "But I still do have the letter if you ever want to see it."

She made no discernible sound or gesture by way of a response; instead she opened his book and fanned the pages back to front, stopping only at the dedication inside the cover.

*In memory of Christopher Lucan*
*Who taught me the power of the story inside a song*

"Thank you, Ian," she said, and taking his hand, stretched to her toes to kiss his cheek. She quickly saw herself out.

# FOUR

The lake was a significant distance from the lot where he parked, with a vast field of packed sand stretching for hundreds of metres in between, interrupted only by a narrow reed-lined boat channel dredged back inland to a dock that had obviously been built in an era of higher water levels. Beyond were The Fishing Islands, according to the map on the billboard in front of him – fanned out parallel to the shoreline at a distance of half a mile or so. It was a strangely hot autumn day, more like summer, with barely a breath of wind. Quiet enough that a roofer's hammer and the hum of a motorboat somewhere beyond his sight were the closest sounds to the piano player's ears.

"Are you Ian?"

He turned around.

"Doug Johnston. We spoke on the phone."

"Hello. Thanks for doing this," Ian replied, his eyes turning to scan first the billboard and then the string of islets in the distance. "Which one is Vimy?"

"Oh don't go by that thing. I know it's a map and all but they put that up back in the sixties when the water came right up to the shore road. Levels have gone down a fair bit since then. Some of them islands are attached to shore now. Others you can wade to. Anyways, the one you want, you can't see from here. It's off beyond those near ones. I'll take you out the channel around to the south and then it's another quarter mile or so. But I only got about an hour ... we got a lot of cottages to get closed up while the weather's good."

It was exactly as the man had advertised on the phone. Not much more than a rocky shoal, a few hundred feet of limestone that had managed to creep up over the waterline serving as a bit of breakwater ahead of the open waters of Lake Huron. There was one lonely spindly tree toward the south end that offered absolutely nothing in the way of shelter or shade for the tiny cabin perched on cinder blocks a few metres further on. Doug steered the boat around to a small floating dock on the far end of the island, cut the engine and jumped out to wade the last few feet to their mooring.

"Best keep an eye out for the snakes," he called back over his shoulder. It's late in the season, but they do like to sun on the rocks, and it's been warm."

Inside were spartan but comfortable surroundings. A vinyl couch behind a wood laminate coffee table with fishing magazines and *National Geographics* fanned out on top. Some board games stacked neatly on the shelf underneath. A small kitchenette with a hot plate and a mini fridge tucked under an open counter.

"The generator's out back. Toilet's charcoal filter," Doug explained, from force of habit Ian surmised. There was one bedroom. Two twin beds separated by a table with a reading lamp. A chair in the corner. Back in the main room, he noticed a desk, under the window that faced away from shore. He thought it the obvious place for Chris to sit and scribble down his ideas and thoughts. Although, now months later, there was, of course, no indication that his friend had done so. The desktop was clear. Pens stacked away in a cup. Chair tucked in.

For a moment Ian lingered, tuning out the boatman's continuing barrage of cabin specs – the baseboard heating, the weekly rates, the water pump – and imagined his friend seated there. Maybe in the evening with lights low. A month all by himself, no one to share ideas with, no one to talk to, save for Mr. Johnston when he came to check up.

"Yeah once-a-week is what he wanted ... we usually do twice ... Wednesdays and Saturdays ... especially with the rentals further out. But your friend must not've eaten much 'cause he never talked about coming in to get more food. And he sure as heck didn't arrive with much. After a few weeks the wife got worried and had me be bring out a care package ... some milk and cheese, instant coffee, things like that ... but that turned out to be the morning he met me with his bags all packed, saying he had to get back to the city right away."

A month of biding. Four weeks of knowing that when those days were up he was going to drive himself over the edge of an embankment. Fly off the earth for the sake of his daughter. How did he manage? Did he still try to conjure up new songs to pass the time? Mull over his dream life? Read up on some speculative philosophy?

"Oh yeah, I almost forgot. There was this," Doug said, coming up from behind, holding out an envelope. "The wife found this with his copy of the rental agreement. Pretty sure he didn't mean to put it there, but like I said, he looked to be in a real hurry when he left. It's for his daughter ... sounds like she was quite a handful."

Or had he spent his last weeks doing what he always had? Trying to get a story just right. But this time, for an audience of just one. The one he had yearned to reach more than anyone else. The one he would die for. Because he had to. He needed to. Because he had absolutely no idea what else to do.

~

*Dear Bronwyn,*

*This is for you. You, whom I can still feel cradled on one arm as I rock you and plunk out a lullaby with my free hand on the old upright piano in Grandma Lucan's kitchen. Back when we used to visit there at Christmas ... you, your mother and I, and all the cousins.*

*This is for you, the silent but strong-willed toddler who knew exactly how a game of make-believe, or dress-up had to go. How a hobby horse should be ridden and how a swing should be pushed.*

*For you, whose round motionless eyes have forever haunted me ever since the day I packed my bags and left; the moment my failures as a father exploded into your childhood and ruptured all hope of adding to those memories. The numbed look of confusion on your face I feared*

*even then would be something etched forever.
That the pain you were swallowing up would be
worse to come, like a time-release capsule, and
over months and years it would work deeper
and deeper to try to influence who you were ...
and who you could become. Would influence
whom you could love. How you could love. If
you could love ... or trust ... or forgive ...*

*I have some specific things that I need to say.
And I need to at least try to put them in a manner that you might yet trust and forgive. I will
start with what I know will read like nothing but
a preposterous statement, but here it is nevertheless. I have never forgotten you, Bronwyn.
Abandoned you, yes. That I cannot defend. But
never ... ever forgotten you.*

*I should divulge here that I have been shadow-
ing your own troubles from afar for a number of
years now. I have known all about them thanks
to the efforts of your most amazing friend, Keegan. Shortly after she found you on the street,
she took it upon herself to contact me. (Not
knowing the particulars of our relationship at
the time, she innocently defaulted to me instead
of your mother.) And she kept in touch intermittently with progress updates on your therapy
and recovery. News of your burgeoning writing
career. The condition from me was that she do
so without your knowledge, so much did I fear
any news of it reaching you would shut down*

*her correspondence once and for all. She
agreed and, I'm sure, after a while understood,
once she learned a little more about me from
you. And yet she still called now and then.
Filled me in on your promotions at the magazine. Your accolades and successes. And I was
proud. So proud of the person, the woman you
had become in spite of me.*

*But having said all that, there is no point to this
letter if the whole truth is not at its core, so
while I do avow my unconditional love, I also
confess – here and now – that you, my dear
daughter, have always been my stumbling block.
Your resentment has been a wall I never knew
how to climb, or tear down, or – after a while –
even approach. But, Bronny, please know you
have always been right in the middle of my soul.
In previous failed iterations of this letter, I tried
to describe just what you mean to me. That
your breath was the life of my chord progressions, the bow stroke of my fiddle and the strum
of my guitar. But here again, I doubt that would
read as trustworthy, would it? So here instead
is the heart of the matter for me. The heart of
my failings and my troubles.*

*You, Bronwyn Lucan, are the story I could never
seem to tell. My song with no words. Because
the truth is, the pain that I've caused and that
I've felt reflected from you is a more complex
melody than I know what to do with.*

*So this is my message instead, sadly lacking in impact from someone who's supposed to be able to carve and hew the deepest sentiments out of words. Whatever part I played in seeing you fall to the depths of hell that you alone scratched and clawed your way out of ... had I truly understood then the potency of that capsule I made you swallow ... had I known the extent of your pain ... every bit of music I had ever written, every story and every acquaintance I had put to song, would have been reduced to its proper size. Weak and faint shadows of the real lives I had impacted. Because despite my parental failures, you, my dear Bronwyn ... you are and will always be my, and no doubt your mother's too, finest creation. Our one and only co-write.*

*Our song.*

# FIVE

*And finally you, Dan, what do you miss most about Mill Run?*

"How much time do we have?"

*No doubt. But if there was one thing?*

"Well, when you were asking Myles just now, my mind flashed back to the *Roots Cellar* article that we were asked to do shortly after Chris had passed away ... too shortly probably. And I was thinking back to a paragraph I had included. How my favourite moment on concert nights was sitting in the empty hall a few hours before the show, out in the seats, looking back at the stage ... 'taking in all the trappings that touring life had afforded me', I think is how I put it. And I'd mentioned something about the stage lights shining on the wood of the guitars and the chrome mic stands. The spectacle of the stage and how it put me in this head space that was one part peacefulness and one part anticipation."

*Sounds like a great memory.*

"Well, that's the interesting thing. Now two years on, I just realized I haven't pined for that once since we've been off the road. And I think it's because the moment was only rich because of the promise of the show to come.  So since you're asking me what I miss most *now*, it's not that moment, but the promise itself.  Because there really is no promise anymore, is there?"

*What do you mean by that?  No promise.*

"No promise that anything I do musically will ever generate the excitement I felt back then.  And remember, I'm speaking as someone still quite actively involved in the scene, with solo work, and producing some CDs for other singer-songwriters. Look, you and I both know the preconceptions of folk music that exist out there.  That it's either flowers-in-the-hair navel-gazing or guys in ponchos and tie-dyed shirts singing gentle introspective melodies with wispy voices.  Well Christ, we set all of that on its ear, didn't we?  When we'd stage behind a curtain and be introduced, and the spotlights would fire up ... Myles's arm would rise for that first powerful strum and Chris would take to the air for that first bowstroke.  Each and every time there'd be this little voice in my head telling me, 'Yeah! Here we go!'

"That's what I miss.  That's what I will always miss."

~

The spray from a wave dotted the letter with droplets. Quickly Ian folded up its pages.  From his perch at the tiller Doug was gesturing towards other nearby islands, calling out their names and histories ... Whiskey Island, Deadman Island, something about bootleggers one time smuggling booze across to Michigan during prohibition ... the bulk of it was lost below the buzz of the outboard motor.

The boat began to bounce on the chop, finally striking a wave crest with enough force to send an even bigger splash across Ian's lap.  He returned the letter to its envelope, carefully folded it in thirds and slid it into his back pocket, then sat back to watch the shoreline grow closer. For the first time in a very long while, the idea of trying his hand at writing came over him. Of finally trying to put something compelling to paper. Something with intrigue and misdirection. A bit of mystery even. Maybe with the element of word play and hidden meaning, like the coincidence with the name Vimy that Chris had happened upon; if coincidence it had actually been. Or maybe a story woven around music and someone as prodigious as his friend ... maybe there was something to be found there.

The sun was higher now, the rippled silver-water glint of early morning replaced with the richest of blues. He could see more now. Could see not just the brightness but what the brightness illuminated. He scanned the surface, making sure to take in the full extent of the panorama. The sandy beach, the thick green line of cedars beyond, the hovering seagulls ... the sound of the boat, constant and steady. He stretched back further against the seat rest, crossed his feet up on the bench in front of him, and as beautiful as the vista before him was, closed his eyes for the duration of the ride ...

*"... so there's this mystic out in New Mexico. He runs something of a commune-slash-farmers' market and hosts a lecture series in his yurt ..."*

*Ian is behind the wheel. They're heading west across the upper peninsula of Michigan. It's morning. There is blue sky and lots of time.*

# A NOTE FROM THE AUTHOR

I have spent many years touring with bands that played venues similar to those described in this book. However, it should be noted that *A Song With No Words* is a work of fiction. So while I have borrowed a number of descriptions and remarks from those days out on the road, the plot and situations portrayed in the novel are fabricated constructs composed with the aid of experiences gathered from my life as a touring musician.

The inclusion of issues surrounding human trafficking was possible only after absorbing a number different sources of information on the topic.

First were two books that investigated the subject at both the international and regional level. They were *The Natashas* by Victor Malarek (Arcade Publishing) and *Invisible Chains* by Benjamin Perrin (Penguin Canada). In addition to these were numerous newspaper articles, reports, opinion pieces and news features in response to the Government of Canada's National Inquiry Into Missing and Murdered Indigenous Women and Girls.

I also came across a number of articles and interviews regarding human trafficking as it pertains to the Great Lakes provinces and states along the Canada-U.S. border. Many were reporting on a Minnesota-based study called *Garden of Truth: The Prostitution and Trafficking of Native Women in Minnesota,* by Melissa Farley, Nicole Matthews, Sarah Deer, Guadalupe Lopez, Christine Stark and Eileen Hudon. This was a project of Minnesota Indian Women's Sexual Assault Coalition and Prostitution Research & Education published in October 27, 2011 by William Mitchell College of Law in Saint Paul, Minnesota.

Some depictions of trafficked woman in this book borrow from the 'boyfriend method' of recruitment, which is mentioned in many of the above sources and explained more fully in the Native Women's Association of Canada's 2018 Paper, *Trafficking of Indigenous Women and Girls in Canada*, by Arina Roudometkina and Kim Wakeford

Also in 2018, TV Ontario published an online article by Jon Thompson that investigated the extent of human trafficking in The Lake of the Woods region of northwestern Ontario, near the town of Rainy River where I have set a portion of this fictional work.

## SPECIAL THANKS

I am indebted to the work of my editor, George Down. I have come to rely on his skill and dedication to detail and could not imagine going through the process of publishing a novel without him.

Thanks also to all my other readers, starting with Ande Ritchie. Nothing literary of mine leaves the house before first undergoing her consideration. I am also so grateful for the time and attention given the manuscript from Maggie Roberts VanHaften and Anne Judd, as well as the input and support from Tim Nicholls-Harrison, Mike Ritchie and Brenda Foster.

I would like to acknowledge my mother, Betty Ritchie for her ongoing support. The world of music and song that has been so much of my life surely began with her and my father, Wally. That world grew up to include playing in a number of bands, with some fine musicians and even finer friends. A big shout out to my brother Steve, and to Joe, Al, Terry, Sandra, Beaker, Dave, Bill, Sterling, Ramsey, Brooklyn and Josh. It's been a privilege to share a stage with you all.

Finally, thanks to my wife Ande, and my sons Josh and Toby for their constant support of and participation in a home fuelled by love, friendship and creativity.

9 781554 834624